LOVE AND RUMORS

A Beach Reads Movie Star Billionaire Contemporary Romance

The Summer Sisters Tame the Billionaires Book I

Jean Oram

Oram Productions Alberta, Canada

This is a work of fiction and all characters, organizations, places, events, and incidents appearing in this novel are products of the author's active imagination or are used in a fictitious manner—unless stated in the book's front matter. Any resemblance to actual people, alive or dead, as well as any resemblance to events or locales is coincidental (unless noted) and, truly, a little bit cool.

Love and Rumors: A Beach Reads Movie Star Billionaire Contemporary Romance
Copyright © 2014 by Jean Oram

All rights reserved, including the right to reproduce this book or portions thereof in any form whatsoever, unless written permission has been granted by the author, with the exception of brief quotations for use in a review of this work. For more information contact Jean Oram at JeanOramBooks@gmail.com. www.JeanOram.com

Printed in the United States of America unless otherwise stated on the last page of this book. Published by Oram Productions Alberta, Canada.

LIBRARY OF CONGRESS CATALOGING-IN-PUBLICATION DATA

Oram, Jean.
    Love and Rumors: A Beach Reads Movie Star Billionaire Contemporary Romance / Jean Oram.—2nd. ed.
    p. cm.
    ISBN 978-1-928198-18-5 (paperback)
    Ebook ISBN 978-0-9918602-9-6
1. Romance fiction. 2. Sisters—Fiction. 3. Paparazzi—Fiction. 4. Romance fiction—Small towns. 5. Love stories, Canadian. 6. Small towns—Fiction. 7. Muskoka (Ont.)—Fiction. 8. Motion pictures actors and actresses—Fiction. 9. Interpersonal relations—Fiction. 10. Photographers—Fiction. I. Title.

Summary: Photographer Hailey Summer must decide whether to use her photography skills as a member of the paparazzi on movie star, Finian Alexander, when he comes to visit her hometown in Muskoka, Canada. Things become complicated when he seems a lot more 'boy next door" than the "bad boy of Hollywood" and Hailey finds herself choosing between love and saving the family cottage with yet-to-be-earned paparazzi money.

Second Oram Productions Edition: May 2015

Front cover design by Jean Oram

Dedication

To my grandmothers. For helping me rediscover Muskoka each summer.

A Note on Muskoka

Muskoka is a real place in Ontario, Canada, however, I have taken artistic license with the area. While the issues presented in this book (such as water shed, endangered animals, heritage preservation, shoreline erosion, taxation, etc.) as well as the towns are real, to my knowledge, there is no Baby Horseshoe Island nor is there a Nymph Island, or even a company called Rubicore Developments. The people and businesses are fictional, with the exception of The Kee to Bala and Jenni Walker—you can read about how she ended up visiting Muskoka in the acknowledgements.

Muskoka is a wonderful area where movie stars and other celebrities do vacation. Yet, having spent many summers in the area during my youth and adulthood, I have yet to see a single celebrity—though a man I presume to be Kurt Browning's (a famous Canadian figure skating Olympian) father did offer to help me when the outboard fritzed out on me once. Damn outboard.

You can discover more about Muskoka online at www.discovermuskoka.ca/

Acknowledgements

A very special thank you goes out to Jenni Walker and Clare Cox. Clare Cox of CLIC Sargent organized an amazing fundraiser called Get in Character which raised money for families with children who have cancer in the United Kingdom. The organization provides tremendous support for these families during difficult times. Through an online auction, Jenni Walker won the opportunity to become a character in this book. Thank you Jenni for supporting CLIC Sargent and families with cancer. Any errors in representing this wonderful woman are mine alone.

I would also like to thank my critique partners who do an amazing job of keeping me on track, as well as the rockstar group of authors I nerd out with on Facebook. These five women are amazing authors with mega brains. I love that I can get my business geek on with them and they are there for each and every step of the conversation. As well, on the book end of things, I need to thank my editor, Margaret, who beefed up my sentences when I kept using the same words over and over. You rock, girl! Oops! I mean something less colloquial—You rock, woman! As well, thank you to Emily Kirkpatrick for her eagle eyes proofreading. Any oopsies that remain are due to my stumbling fingers.

And finally, a big thank you to my family. For my husband for believing in me and telling me to go for it with this new series. My kids who put up with me disappearing into my computer. And to my parents and grandmothers who introduced me to Muskoka and its quiet beauty and helped me go there almost every summer as a kid. To my brother—thank for throwing me in the Indian River, repeatedly, and to Sarah and Lindsey for walking to The Store in port with me time and again. I think it's time for ice cream, don't you? And finally, to all of those working to preserve Muskoka, its heritage and beauty, kudos and thank you.

LOVE AND RUMORS

To the Sylvan Lake Library,

Thank you for hosting the 2017 RWA Retreat.

Happy reading.

xc

Jen Cram

Chapter One

"*Finian Alexander, do something* bad," Hailey Summer whispered. The alley was quiet as she kept herself squeezed against a white catering van, waiting for the actor to make a move outside the town's black tie gala.

She pressed her eye against the camera's viewfinder as a streak of sun broke through the clouds, making her LCD impossible to read. The light was incredible and she was the only one there to see Hollywood's bad boy break the rules and mess up once again, but she needed him to move faster. Much faster. The light was going to fail when the clouds opened up, or someone was going to interrupt him and send her home with nothing. Again.

Come on, Finian. Do this for me.

As a sunbeam shone down on his shoulders, he looked more like an angel in the shadowed alley than someone about to go joyriding in a stolen sports car and make her rich in the process. Well, at least tug her out of her life-swallowing hole of debt.

Patiently, she waited, lining up shots. Brick and clapboard. Parked cars. Faded jeans resting low on his hips. She couldn't have asked for a better setting. Better light. She just needed Finian to *do* something. To flub up in that distinctive way of his so she could cover her past mistakes. Then her three younger sisters would never have to know how close she'd cut things and how their legacy, their birthright, was teetering on the brink of being lost.

"Come on, hunky-hunk, open it. That's right." She smiled as the movie star carefully tried another car door, casting his eyes sideways to see if he was being watched. Door locked. On to the next. One of them had to be unlocked. This was Bala, Ontario, a small town known for cranberries, quaint cottages, tourism and bridges, not crime. He'd find an unlocked vehicle and go for a joyride; she'd capture the image of him breaking the law, sell it for big bucks, and kaboom. Her problems would be solved, without impacting his life other than adding another celebrity-life-gone-wrong story to his bulging portfolio.

She fidgeted, her anticipation building.

"Come on, come on…"

She glanced over her shoulder, half expecting Austin Smith, a local photographer who did occasional paparazzi work in L.A., to appear and ruthlessly scoop her. Hailey had wrestled long and hard with her conscience to get to this point, and now that she was here, ready and waiting, Finian was taking his sweet time, giving the angel on her shoulder plenty of time to make arguments on why she should back out.

Hailey wiggled and refocused her camera. Finian hunched over as specks of rain started to fall as he tried another door. His hair was disheveled. He looked tired. Rough. As if he'd been up all night—like her.

Apparently, it was hard work being a party-man celebrity raking in millions.

The Mercedes he tried was locked, and he moved on to an Audi, his strong hands lifting handles with a care she hadn't expected. Maybe he was worried about setting off alarms. She could see that being a problem. A problem for both of them. She shifted slightly. Was there a law against watching someone break and enter?

She could report him later. Right now she needed images. She snapped a few photos of the light bouncing off Finian, then sighed as she lowered her camera. Officer Cranks would seize her photos as evidence. Her late father's poker buddy would give her that unblinking stare that undid her every time. Teary-eyed, she'd be handing over these shots before he felt the urge to blink. Hell, years after getting busted egging houses with Austin, she still felt guilty buying eggs near Halloween. That night had been the beginning of the end for her and Austin, both as friends and as boyfriend-girlfriend. She'd gone back to being safe and reliable as he'd dived into his newfound persona, a hellion who'd laughed at her for crying in the cops' office. Not long after that her father had passed away and Hailey had begun to wear safe and reliable as if it was her own personal shield against the pain.

She cursed Austin under her breath for giving her a taste of fun and freedom before the burden had come. He was still waltzing around, living the life, raking in the dough, and she was barely surviving.

She propped herself against the old building, leaning her supporting arm on the van so she could line up her shots as Finian moved farther down the alley. She'd hand over the evidence after she got paid by the tabloids. But first, she would take care of her family's needs.

Come on, Finian. Do this for both of us. I'll help you if you help me.

"You really think he's going to get into one of those cars?" scoffed a male voice. Hailey jumped, nearly dropping her camera. "You should have set it up ahead of time and led him into it. You're wasting your time." Austin leaned over her shoulder, his cheap aftershave familiar in a way that made her distrust him.

She turned, pinned against the wall, his large build crowding her.

"Make your trap irresistible to a man like Finian." Austin's eyes roved over her and she wondered why on earth she'd pined for the annoying button-pusher after he'd broken up with her. He got under her skin faster than anyone she'd ever met. Although maybe she'd just pined for freedom and a life she could no longer have.

"I knew it wouldn't be long before the worm crawled out from under his rock," Hailey retorted, turning to face Finian again. "Did your mother run out of canned lasagna?"

"This is my arena and this guy hates the paparazzi," Austin said, his mouth turning down. "Go back to your pretty art shots and leave this for the real photographers."

Hailey gritted her teeth so she didn't make an enemy out of Austin and took a few haphazard shots as though Finian was doing something intriguing. This was just like with the high school paper, when she'd wanted to take different pictures than he, the photo editor, had demanded. He'd wanted the publication to be a tabloid. She'd wanted it to be a liberal arts paper that covered anything and everything. An outlet and extension of her own artistic needs.

"I said—" he began.

She ducked as Finian looked their way. "Shut up! You're scaring the subject." She whacked Austin on the chest, just above where it softened into a small beer gut.

"He won't stop because we're here. Movie stars need the paparazzi. Free publicity—and he hasn't had any in almost a week." Austin glanced around the corner of the van. "They're all locked."

"I know," Hailey said darkly.

"He's not the joyriding type, you know."

"Says who?"

Austin hitched his camera bag higher on his shoulder. "I'm going for a beer. Call me when he gets desperate enough to do something interesting."

"Dream on."

"Only if you're in them and naked." He gave her a wink.

Hailey bit back a snort of laughter. "You're the nightmare and he's the dream, honey."

"Mmm. I love it when you call me honey." Austin lightly pecked her cheek, then backed away, his arm outstretched, pointing at her. "I know you still have my number."

"Only because you live with your mother."

He clutched his chest as if shot, and with another wink, disappeared around the corner.

Austin actually made a pretty decent enemy seeing as he helped motivate Hailey to work harder and follow the path she truly wanted. Well, except when he was a complete ass and she wanted to shove him into the turbulent water near the falls in hopes that he'd drown.

Shaking her head, she turned to Finian once again. She'd had such a crush on him ever since his first movie—*Desperate Cowboy*, a low-budget film nobody remembered. But she did. Especially the way his tight little butt had featured in one of the scenes. Mmm. That scene had replayed in many of her fantasies. Add in his black cowboy hat, the swagger and the way his bright blue eyes had blazed out of his dark, tanned skin, and she'd been a goner for life.

She vaguely re-aimed her camera, trying to calm her body's reactions to thoughts about Finian. For several days she'd been casually tracking him, but all she'd seen was a regular man hanging out on vacation. Which was so wrong. He was supposed to mess up, with only her around to capture it in digital, not be a man she could envision living happily ever after with.

She was only supposed to catch him screwing up once, then sell it. That was the deal she'd made with herself to justify violating his privacy. Because even though he was a movie star, he was also a human. And in Muskoka there was an unspoken code—a code Austin regularly broke—stating that celebrities in the area were to be left alone if they weren't obviously seeking attention.

She almost turned away when something caught her eye. Finian had finally opened the door to a 1950s Jaguar Mark I. She barely dared breathe. What had she missed while fuming to herself?

Finian rolled up the car's window. Closed the door. Gave the roof a little pat, then walked away as the clouds submitted to the weight of their load.

What had she missed?

She popped her head above her camera for a 'real world' look. Why hadn't he hot wired the car? Had he found something to take instead?

Whatever had happened, she knew one thing for sure: she'd missed her chance to save herself as well as her sisters.

HAILEY STOOD UNDER a shop awning, keeping an eye on Finian, the Big Letdown, as he ambled up the other side of the street, seemingly unaffected by the pouring rain. Which bar had Austin gone to for his beer? She needed to talk to him about a little thing called ruining another photographer's shot. Preferably while keeping Finian in her sights, but not within Austin's.

Hailey tried to sidestep the person who popped up to block her view.

"Hailey? Hailey?"

She glanced down to see her youngest sister, Daphne, clutching her arm, peering at her with concern.

"You okay? You look kinda pale."

"Yeah, fine." She peered around her sister, who was trying to rein in her bouncing five-year-old daughter, Tigger, who resembled Tigger from Winnie-the-Pooh more than her seldom-used given name, Kimberly. Hailey relaxed as Finian paused under an awning across the street. She looked toward a nearby bar. "I was just thinking about how I'd like to rip Austin Smith a new ass—"

"Hailey!" gasped Daphne.

Tigger looked up with a sparkle in her eyes. "Auntie Hailey said a bad word."

Hailey sighed and gave herself a shake. "Sorry, kiddo." She placed her hands over Tigger's ears and gently rocked the girl's head back and forth. The little girl's long plastic raincoat rustled as she moved, one of her ever-present secondhand party dresses peeking out from under the hem.

"There." Hailey held up her fisted hand. "It fell out." She pretended to throw something on the ground and stomp on it. "It's like you never heard that word."

"Ass," replied Tigger.

"Tigger!" Daphne clutched her daughter's shoulders. "We don't use words like that."

"Auntie Hailey used it."

Hailey winced. "Sorry," she said again.

Daphne gave Tigger a stern look and turned to Hailey. "So, what's up with you and Austin? You've barely talked since high school."

"Professional complications."

Daphne's nose scrunched and her eyes followed Hailey's to where Finian, protected from the rain, was leaning against a building as though he had all the time in the world and not a care to burden him.

The jerk. He wouldn't last a second in the real world.

Daphne laughed. "You still have a crush on Finian Alexander."

Hailey snorted and rolled her eyes as though the idea of her harboring a flaming, scorching torch for the movie star was the most ridiculous thing she'd ever heard.

Her sister giggled and stared across the street. "I can see why. He's *delicious*."

"Very delicious," Tigger agreed.

"*And* I heard he just broke up with Jessica Cartmill," Daphne added. "Hello!"

Hailey squinted at her niece. "Do you know what we're talking about?"

"The ice cream store."

Hailey found her attention drawn to Finian again. Yep, he was standing near the sign advertising twelve different flavors.

"I wouldn't mind licking that," Daphne said in a low voice. Hailey placed an arm across her sister's chest, pretending to hold her back. Daphne let out a sigh of longing. "It's been over five years. I'm dying here."

"Do they have bubble gum ice cream?" Tigger asked.

"No sugar, Tigger," her mother answered. Then she clutched Hailey's arm again. "Tell me you're not following Austin's lead on photography. What he does goes against your principles."

"I know."

"You said the paparazzi are the ambulance chasers of the photography world."

"They are."

"Use your powers of photography for good, not evil."

Hailey laughed and adjusted the heavy bag digging into her shoulder. If only her sister knew how out of options she was. It was either become an ambulance chaser or lose the one place that had always brought the four sisters together. The place where not only their great-grandmother had fallen in love, but their grandmother and mother, as well. It was the very place where little Tigger had been conceived. And as much as the grown sisters teased Tigger for thinking the small family-owned island was enchanted, Hailey knew they all secretly agreed. There was something about Nymph Island and their cottage, Trixie Hollow, that grounded people. The place had kept the family together when they could have easily ended up spread across the country, barely speaking to each other.

"You're up to something," Daphne said.

"Nope."

"You won't meet my eyes."

Hailey stared into her sister's blue eyes, willing her to realize that her own slim tax contributions toward the cottage hadn't been enough. That none of what the four of them—especially Hailey, who held the cottage in trust—had done over the years had been enough, and that by the end of August the whole kit and caboodle would be sold off to cover years of back taxes. And it would be Hailey's fault. For failing their ailing mother, her sisters and niece, and most of all, herself.

The jokingly used nickname Hailey-Failey would finally fit. Big time.

Familiar anxiety swirled within her and she tightened her hold on her camera bag's strap. She needed something lucrative, and fast, or she'd be forced to ask her sisters for help. And she couldn't. Just couldn't.

Not yet.

She glanced across the street to where Finian was still standing. Maybe it was true, what her mother always said—that if the cottage was meant to stay in the family, a solution would present itself. Maybe Finian wasn't in Muskoka by coincidence. It was fate. Destiny. Karma giving Hailey a hand up for her years of taking care of the family.

Tigger whispered to her, "Mom always finds out if someone is up to something."

"Not always," Hailey whispered back.

Especially since she was going to solve this problem. Right now. Before anyone knew the gambles and risks she'd taken, and how she'd messed it all up.

She straightened her spine. If anyone in the family were to be voted most likely to succeed in solving this dilemma, she was. She'd pulled them through their father's death when they were teens and kept the family afloat with after-school jobs. Then five years ago, after their mother's debilitating stroke, Hailey had moved in with her and taken over responsibility for the cottage. When it came to the point where their mother needed more care than Hailey could provide, she'd found the perfect nursing home offering the right balance of support and independence.

Not only that, but Hailey had been there for Daphne when her sister's summer boyfriend went home, never to be heard from again, leaving her heartbroken and pregnant. And she'd been there to help however she could when their two middle sisters, Maya and Melanie, went off to university.

Their mother had placed the cottage in her trust for a reason. Hailey solved problems and made things happen. And yeah, things looked bad right now. Really bad for the 110-year-old cottage. But she'd solve this problem just as she had all the others, and her sisters would never have to learn how close she'd come to losing the place they all loved.

Besides, telling them would just stress them all out, and they'd start running around in a panic, distracting her from getting the job done.

She could do this.

Her solution was waiting for her across the street.

Easy as drooling over apple pie.

"What's wrong?" Daphne repeated. "What did Austin do?"

Hailey waved a hand. "He pissed me off, that's all."

"Auntie Hailey said 'pissed'!"

"You didn't hear that," she replied quickly.

"How did he rub you the wrong way?" Daphne asked, head tilted.

"It doesn't matter."

"I heard he moved home to chill out for a while after that last fight with George Clooney." She leaned closer. "Did Austin ask you out? I don't think he ever got over you, you know."

Hailey scoffed and pushed her away. "Don't you have a protest to organize?"

"Oh, that reminds me. Can you join us for the picnic and protest for the dam?"

"Picnic?"

"It brings out more families."

"Um, I think I have a…" Hailey scrambled for an excuse.

"It's tomorrow and we desperately need a good photographer."

"Please?" Tigger asked, jumping up and down as she yanked on Hailey's hand.

"I think I have to take Grandma to an appointment, hon. Sorry."

"I already asked Maya to take her," Daphne said. "It's just a few shots for a brochure and the website. Please?"

Hailey felt like a poser when she went to rallies. Yes, she usually believed in whatever her sister was protesting, but felt awkward yelling and shouting and making a scene about it. Although maybe if she helped her, Daphne would speak up for Hailey if she lost it all. The cottage. Her business. Her home. She gulped for air and squeezed her hips like a runner after a sprint, knocking her swinging camera bag out of the way. This wasn't good. Not good at all. She was going to default on all the promises she'd made their mother. All her cover-ups were going to be revealed. She was going to fail.

"Relax. Maya will take good care of Mom." Daphne rested a hand on Hailey's shoulder. "She only forgot her that time by accident. She won't forget again. And besides, she didn't even get all the way out of the parking lot." Her sister squeezed her shoulder. "It's okay, Hailey, we can all take turns helping. It doesn't always have to be you."

Hailey sucked in a deep breath, her mind tangled in the complications of allowing Maya to help. "It's faster and easier—"

"On your own. We know. But she's our mother, too, and we've all grown up. The doctor has all her medical info, you don't have to be there to tell him everything. Let us show our love for you, Hailey. Let us help."

Hailey cringed, knowing her sister was about to launch into her sappy, let-love-cure-the-world philosophy which in her current mood would make her say something that would hurt Daphne's feelings.

Across the street, Finian was stretching, looking as though he was preparing to vanish on her. Hailey tried to breathe past the tightness in her chest as the pressure built within her. She squeezed her eyes shut until the burning passed. "I have to go. Now."

Finian was walking away, as the rain let up to a light drizzle. She was going to lose him.

"Hailey, I love you."

She turned to her sister and niece. "I've got to run. I have work to do."

"Oh, I almost forgot," Daphne said. "We're rescheduling the

Canada Day picnic on Nymph Island because of the rain, and because Maya got called into work."

"Okay." Hailey stepped away.

"We're thinking of having it in a day or two."

"Okay."

"When do you need this year's tax money for the cottage?"

She paused and cleared her throat. "Um, before the end of the month." Guilt rose within her as she thought about how Daphne's portion of the annual tax bill and back taxes would not only clear out her savings for taking Tigger to Florida, but would make going to the cottage the only vacation she could afford from now until her daughter grew up and went off to college.

"I heard taxes went up. How bad are they?" Daphne drew Tigger close.

"Not too bad," Hailey lied. "Maybe you can call in some honorariums with your environmental work or something?" Her niece's bright eyes flicked between the two, and Hailey stepped closer to lightly tap Tigger's nose. "Don't worry, we'll get you to Florida little monkey."

Tigger grinned and began bouncing around on the sidewalk, singing about airplanes, Disney World and her mom.

Hailey glanced down the street, her shoulders sagging. Finian was strolling along, hands in his pockets, kicking an empty Tim Horton's coffee cup. He caught her eye over his shoulder, beckoning her to go save her family.

WHAT KIND OF CUT-RATE paparazzo was this girl with the crazy hair, anyway? Finn had seen her following him off and on all week, her massive camera bag always over her shoulder. A few minutes ago, he'd ducked into an alley, hoping she'd follow, and mindlessly tried door handles on fancy cars as though seeking a joyride. Thankfully, none of them had opened. Until the Jag. But by then he'd given up on her helping him into the tabloids and had, instead, walked away.

What did he have to do to get her to take shots of him?

Right now, when she could easily be stalking him, she was across the street chatting with someone, her hair growing frizzy from the rain. He began to stroll away, noting her panic and how she tried to extricate herself from her conversation with the woman and child.

Gotcha.

Maybe she had potential after all. He paused for a little fake window-shopping, allowing her to catch up. In the reflection he watched as she stopped at a food truck to purchase a cup of coffee, chatting with the vendor as though they were friends.

How was she going to aim that big camera at him if she was drinking coffee? What kind of paparazzi did they have in Canada, anyway? He ought to stomp over there and give her a few tips.

He hadn't been mentioned in a single tabloid—other than the odd post-breakup speculative whisper—since coming to Bala. Even after three days of this lady tailing him.

And yeah, sure, he'd selected Canada because he needed downtime to sort out who he was and where he was going with his life. But he hadn't been expecting to slip out of the spotlight in doing so. He'd just broken up with Jessica Cartmill and finished a movie. It shouldn't be easy to lie low.

Either that, or him breaking up with Jessica, a beloved star since the day of her debut, back when she was three years old, wasn't earth-shattering news as he'd assumed. Their breakup had come as a shock to the public, but instead of milking it he'd fled to what turned out to be backwoods Canada, where the paparazzi preferred to drink coffee rather than snap shots of him.

Maybe Jessica had been right. Maybe he *was* nothing without her.

His phone rang and he whipped it out, frowning as the rain started up again. His agent, Derek Penn, probably wondering why Finn hadn't delivered anything fresh for the celebrity news.

As if he needed that kick in the nuts right now.

"Yo! Finnegan!"

"Finian. Finn," he reminded him kindly. Finn cooled his temper, telling himself that he worked with Derek because the man was great at building stars. Derek knew who Finn needed to align himself with. What to do—and when—in order to keep his name out there, build his image, and which rung he should climb to take him up the ladder to A-list notoriety. Then on to the Hot List. No more B or C, or heck, D list for him. He was so close he could smell it. And it smelled like irresistible women hungry for him. Redemption. And cash. Lots of much needed cash.

"You haven't been in the rags in almost a week, man. What's up? I know you're chilling out and mending your broken heart and all that B.S., but you can't leave the planet. People will forget you exist."

Finn's heart thundered at the thought. If fans started wondering what had happened to that guy who was in all those action movies, everything would crumble. Not just his finances, but his promises. He'd be a broken man sent right back to the horrible place he'd struggled to escape.

He spun in a slow circle on the sidewalk. Not a camera in sight.

Goddamn it. He kicked over a trash can and stalked on down the street. When he turned, a family was clustered around the barrel, righting it and placing the refuse inside. Canadians. They were making him feel guilty when he was supposed to be a man with no regrets and certainly no remorse.

Finn paused, spotting his little shadow with her face buried behind her phone as she sipped her coffee. She glanced at him, frowned at her cell, and continued on past him.

Maybe she wasn't a paparazzo. Maybe she was just a fan. A stalker. Though, she seemed much too indifferent for that. Those women did a lot more giggling and bumping into him. He'd be eating a meal, lost in his own world, and suddenly look up to see an excited face shining with the thrill of having locked eyes with him.

That was surreal in a way that made him shudder every time. It was as though they were looking into a pool where their own wishes and dreams were being reflected back at them. They weren't seeing him, they were seeing a man he could never truly be, and they expected so much from him. Things he couldn't give.

"And dude, what the hell's up with your tweets? They're like friggin' cotton candy, they're so sweet," said Derek.

"What do you mean?"

"A puppy? *Really*?"

"What? It was cute."

"Yeah, but a golden retriever? Are you trying to kill me?"

Finn smiled. "I'll have you know that got over seven hundred retweets."

"Finn, man, listen to me. Bad boys don't tweet cute puppy photos. They tweet beer bongs and cleavage, and their hundred-and-forty characters are loaded with swears. Got it?"

"Yeah." Finn stared at the cracked sidewalk. He knew what men from the wrong side of the tracks did. He just couldn't seem to stay in the role. That was probably why he had fallen off the planet. He sucked as an actor.

He let out a jagged sigh and stared up at the rain clouds. Cool drizzle landed on his face, weaving its way through his stubble.

Maybe that was the problem. If he pretended to be a bad boy long enough, he might succeed and become the people back home. The people he'd promised not to become. And tweeting out crap felt like going back on the promises he'd made himself. It was though he'd be taking a step back to the place he'd struggled to leave behind.

"Find someone with a camera and get back in the rags, man," Derek continued. "You can't afford a vacation, not for the next five years. You've got to get high in the rankings or your next paycheck will see a decrease. You gotta keep dry-humping the ladder until you own the Hot List. You want it, right?"

"Of course."

"Then get your ass in gear. Do you need me to leak part five of the plan? Because if you can't handle this and I leak it now—"

"Yeah, yeah, I know, Derek. The fall will come too soon. I won't stick to the top, career is over, et cetera, et cetera."

Finn didn't like Derek's elaborate plan for falling from grace, but it had worked for a ton of his stars when their careers had started to flag. Stars who never quite made the A-list, but nevertheless enjoyed one last hip-hip-hooray joyride on the fame train before drifting off into oblivion where they belonged. Washed-up nobodies living in obscurity. People like him who just missed becoming a household name.

But Finn wasn't ready for that. He wanted to climb to the top and hang in there for as long as he could. He had too many changes he'd vowed to make in the neighborhood where he grew up. Once he fulfilled those promises, then he could fall from grace. Then he could let Derek give him that little bonus bump before vanishing into obscurity, his bank account bursting. His promises and family taken care of.

Finn studied his little shadow with the wild curly hair. She *had* to be more than a nature photographer which was what he'd first suspected since tourists didn't walk around with that kind of equipment slung over their shoulder. And she wasn't taking pictures of the stunning woods and water scenery that surrounded them. No, this girl was a serious photographer. The problem was, he'd yet to see her take a single shot of anything.

He shook his head, phone still clutched to his ear. It didn't matter who she was. It mattered who she would become.

He stepped out from under a green and white striped awning, wishing for some crazy drunken revelry he could crash. It was their Canada Day long weekend, which should mean party time, but he hadn't come across a single party to dig into. They were having cake.

Politicians, who nobody had heard of, were cutting cake and taking complaints about garbage pickup. Kids eating cotton candy, with red maple leaves fake tattooed on their cheeks. No floozies in short skirts. No drugs. No booze. Just beautiful nature and a sleepy town sandwiched between rocks, trees, and water. A bunch of kind, warm-hearted people doing lovely, family-oriented things.

No wonder Derek wanted to hold his hand through all of this. Finn had come to familyland for his vacation, not bad-boy nirvana. His cottage might be crazy expensive, but he was having a hell of a time finding temptation.

He "uh-huhed" into his phone as his agent rambled on about his image. Running a hand through his hair, Finian shook off the light drops of rain. Only a cloud or two remained in the sky. Nothing to spoil the face painting.

"I'll get a flight out of here soon if I can't scare up some stories, but I think I might be onto something," he promised just before he pocketed his cell, the devil on his shoulder drumming up a plan to get him in the tabloids.

If he couldn't get this gal following him to take shots on her own and sell them, then maybe they could collaborate. Stars did it with paparazzi all the time. He could have his quiet vacation and still stay in the tabloids.

He changed course suddenly, heading to the first bar he saw. The woman with the windswept hair noted his movements and followed.

Gotcha again.

He reached the steps to the bar, planning to go inside, have five rye and Cokes in quick succession, and see what Canada had in store for a drunken celebrity early in the afternoon. A throng of people suddenly surrounded him, cameras raised. He flinched, adrenaline surging through his veins. Holy hell. Where had they come from and how had they trapped him so quickly? They'd slipped out of the bush like moose or mice or something.

He shook off the fear and gave the crowd a crooked grin, knowing his two-day stubble was making his blue eyes sparkle in contrast.

Finn waited. Nobody snapped a photo. What the hell? Had he stunned them all with his craggy good looks?

"Uh…" He held open the screen door, making an ushering motion so the crowd could enter the bar. "Going in?"

"Are you Finian Alexander?" asked a teenager.

"Yup."

"Can we take your photo?" asked a breathless granny, a camera clutched to her ample chest.

"Yeah." He nodded slowly. What the heck was up with these people? They appeared out nowhere, pressed in on him, all eerie and silent, and then asked if they could take photos? Didn't they realize his fame had put him in the public domain, and they could take a shot of him taking a crap in the woods and he wouldn't have a case for them invading his privacy?

They lined up like obedient kindergarteners, making room for each other, polite and quiet. His nature-nut shadow wove through the group, her hair still in knots, her face buried behind her phone. She glanced at him with dazzling eyes that took his breath away, then frowned at her phone again as she came up the steps to where he was holding the door. She apologized to someone nearby, although he couldn't figure out why.

Finn gave her a little bow and smile as she met him on the landing, and shot her a wink. She blushed and looked away. So very cute.

He began envisioning ways he could woo her. Have a little affair, wrap her around his finger so he could break up the boredom of this peacefulness. They could collaborate, or if that didn't work, he'd get her to betray him by releasing a story of how he was a jerky badass. Somehow he'd find a way to get her to spin a story of his making, which would hit the rags and thrust him into the limelight. Just in time for his upcoming summer blockbuster release.

He shot her a massive grin as she moved through the doorway, and gave her a playful tap on the butt. Her eyes grew wide and she took a quick, unsteady sidestep before making it into the dimly lit bar.

Easy bait.

Plus she looked like she needed a drink. Even easier.

Finn shook his head and followed her inside. She looked so serious he wanted to pry her open, expose her to fun and make her smile.

Preferably while naked.

Yep. This vacation was about to get a whole lot more promising.

FINN FOLLOWED THE WOMAN through the bar, ignoring the rough floorboards under his sandals as he watched her narrow hips sway. There was something about her beanpole body that did strange things to his mind. He wanted to bend her around him. Feel those long limbs. Skin to skin.

He gave himself a shake. Booty call later. Right now he had to friend her, draw out her photography skills, plant the idea that she could, and should, sell photos of him and get rich. Everyone wanted money.

He paused. This region, Muskoka, was a summer playground for the rich. Did that mean she was wealthy? Was that why she wasn't snapping photos of him? She was an heiress to a multibillion-dollar company, and didn't need to sell photos of the rich and famous because she was one of them?

If so, then he'd take the fame angle. Who wouldn't want the prestige of selling an exclusive photo for thousands of dollars? He took another look at her swaying hips. Her jean shorts were faded white in the butt. They were a tad past "fashionable" and heading toward worn-out. Her sandals looked as though they should have been replaced a few seasons ago.

Hmm. Maybe not an heiress, then. Which meant he could likely sell her on fame *and* money. He grinned. This was too easy.

She turned suddenly, and Finn almost ran into her. "Whoa there." He grabbed her elbows, his eyes meeting hers as he moved into her space, barely avoiding knocking her down. Mmm. She smelled nice. Outdoorsy. Fresh. Like rain and apple pie.

He glanced at her hands, looking for the coffee she'd had earlier, and found his eyes stuck on the cleavage exposed by her low-cut tank top.

Her knees buckled slightly as he leaned toward her heat, and her face paled.

What could he say? He had that effect on women. Although

the pale face was odd. Usually they flushed. He glanced past her and realized he'd followed her—entranced by her sweet, worn-out butt—straight into a corner. There was no excuse for having followed her this closely. For cornering her. For holding her so close. For ogling her chest.

He gave her a dazzling smile. "Sorry, thought you were my sister."

"You don't have a sister," she breathed. She blinked, eyes wide, catching herself.

Hot damn. She knew who he was. After days of being practically anonymous, he found it refreshing. A relief. Scratch that; it was sexy. Damn sexy.

"How do you know?" he asked with a grin.

"You're a horrible liar." She pushed him away, but he held on tight.

"What do you mean? I'm a fantastic liar. I get paid big money to lie every day."

"To lie?" She crossed her arms in the sliver of space between them, eyebrow raised, her camera bag's strap digging a swath into her shoulder's skin.

She was challenging him. How interesting. He propped a hand on the wall beside her head, leaning close. Her eyes narrowed as he trapped her. Oh, this was fun. He'd forgotten how much fun a challenge was. He'd gotten used to women dropping their panties as soon as he shot them the right flavor of grin.

Time to pour it on.

He dropped his voice so it was low, gravelly. "Wouldn't you like that?"

"What?"

He ran a finger down the side of her jaw and watched, mesmerized, as her eyes fluttered shut and her breathing stuttered. "To pretend to be someone else. Pretend to be mine for the night. Hot for me to touch you in ways that will make you pant."

He ran a fingertip over her bottom lip, closing in. Any second now she'd suck on his finger, pull him into the bathroom….

He didn't expect the slap.

And he certainly didn't expect someone as slight as her to be strong enough to leave him seeing white spots. Wow.

She hadn't even hinted that she was going to move.

Her mouth dropped open in horror, before she clamped her hands over it. He watched as she wrestled with herself, her back pushed against the wall. If he played his cards right he'd bet his new BMW she'd get him ice for his cheek.

But there was something else behind her eyes. Something real. Something he'd forgotten.

Oh…right.

He was one of those big cocky jerks women hated.

His stomach churned and he reached out for her, to let her know he didn't mean it. To show her he was actually a nice guy. A guy whose mother would beat him about the ears if she'd heard what he'd just said to a nice Canadian girl in a nice Canadian town on a nice Canadian holiday.

Instead, he watched as his wild-haired chick slipped past him, fire blazing in her eyes. Filled with longing and regret, Finn placed his palms on the wall and hung his head. He liked her already.

Chapter Two

Hailey handed the tax reassessment form to her sister Melanie, her hands still shaking from slapping Finian Alexander less than an hour ago. Why the hell had she done that? She didn't slap people. But he'd just been so…sure of himself. Intense. Sexual. Cocky. Cornering her and expecting her to fall against his crotch. Women like her didn't want jerks like him, and she'd hated the way her body had responded, singing and vibrating at his touch. Wanting him. Badly. Wanting—no *craving*—to know what his skin would feel like, bared and warm, against hers.

"Do you think we can get them to reassess it before this year's bill is due?" Hailey asked.

Melanie's eyebrows shot up. "Doubtful. Bureaucracy and all that, right? Did taxes go up?" She sifted through the forms laid out on her small round kitchen table, her long legs tucked underneath her. "How much is it?"

Hailey clutched the slender teacup, hoping to hide her shaking hands. "Don't worry about it, I just think we're being taxed too high. No point in paying out, only to have it handed back, right? Plus, I'm not sure they reassess retroactively."

"Do you need money?"

"I'm just trying to save us on taxes. We need to fix the chimney and some other stuff." She pulled the papers back toward her.

Melanie had just graduated with her law degree and wasn't making much money in her first job and had a ton of student loans. In a few years she would be in a position to help carry the burden, but not yet. Letting her know how bad things were would just stress her out, and she'd worry herself into another ulcer. Plus, she'd feel the need to help out and there was no way she could. Not this year.

Other than help find some loopholes that apparently weren't there.

"I can look into it," Melanie said, pouring another cup of tea out of the fine bone china teapot that had been their grandmother's. "But you know, Maya's business degree might be more helpful in terms of ducking through the ins and outs of taxation, red tape, and bureaucracy."

Hailey bit her bottom lip. Maya's nickname, Snap, had been well earned. She made snap decisions which she tended to stick to stubbornly. Plus, she always wanted to wrestle control from Hailey. "I thought your law degree would be able to help us."

"Seriously, you two need to stop competing and learn to work together."

"We work together fine."

Melanie rolled her eyes as if to say, *Yeah, right*. She handed back the forms and straightened the oversize shirt she insisted on hiding her strong build in ever since a summer crush had called her Sasquatch in the eleventh grade. "You can figure this all out. Just follow the red tape. I don't see a way we can one-up the system."

She smoothed down her curly hair and, reflexively, Hailey did the same, finding it knotted and wild from her early morning boat ride from a photo shoot she'd done of a family of loons near the cottage, followed by stalking Finian through the rainy alley.

The bar. She almost groaned. He'd seen her with demented hair. The one time she got to face her crush and she looked like a patient who had escaped from North Bay's psychiatric wing.

"I'll print off a few photos to send with the application to prove it isn't a fancy place with enhancements." Hailey stood, gathering the papers and wishing her sister would read between the lines, guess the troubles they were in, and help her figure out what to do. Hailey was tired of the secrets, the promises, the feeling of obligation and duty. Yet she was the one who had promised their mother she'd take care of the back taxes, not add to them. Nobody had asked her to remortgage her house to finance a photographic show that featured her artistic side, but had never panned out monetarily despite all the awards and accolades. In fact, nobody knew she'd remortgaged everything to keep the cottage afloat. Why? Because it had been a stupid risk intended to buy them another year or two, when things would inevitably be better. But things hadn't gotten better and taxes had taken an insane jump. People were losing cottages or selling them, and the Summer family would soon be joining their ranks.

She pondered telling Melanie what she'd done, but knew her sister would be aghast. Hailey solved problems, she didn't dig herself deeper and deeper into holes. She didn't take risks and fail as she had.

Hailey shook her head. She couldn't do it. She had to keep it a secret. She had to solve this on her own. She couldn't break their trust. And they still trusted her. Trusted her to keep everything safe.

And anyway, she had Finian. The man she'd slapped. Oops.

She closed her eyes for a moment. She should have slept with him and then blackmailed him. She almost laughed. How could you blackmail someone like Finian for sleeping with you when his reputation thrived on exploits?

Her crazy hair was onto something. She belonged in the loony bin.

Melanie was tapping her chin thoughtfully. "Photos might help prove the place isn't worth millions, like those new year-round McMansions Maya is always drooling over. Make sure you show that the cottage and boathouse haven't been upgraded or improved much in the past hundred years. Show that the plumbing and electrical hasn't been changed since it was added a few decades ago. No A/C or jacuzzi tub. The old generator for powering the place, et cetera. And remind them that they don't provide any services like power, water, sewer, or garbage pickup on the island—we're off their grid."

"I'll do that." Hailey grabbed a pen, scribbled on a sticky note and stuck it to the forms.

Melanie shoved her glasses up her nose. "Who is he?"

"Who is who?"

"The guy who has you all shaky."

"It's nobody," Hailey replied too quickly.

Melanie raised her brows.

"It's nothing. I just slapped this guy because he was coming on to me and got in my space and I'm shaken up from it. That's all."

"And?"

Hailey sighed and fell into a chair. Slapping Finian had been stupid. Now she wouldn't be able to stalk him, waiting for her money shot, because he'd remember her and run the other way. She was going to have to face him and apologize seeing as there was no miraculous cottage-saving loophole for her to dive through and she still needed him.

"I was hoping he'd become a client," Hailey muttered. "How about an appeal? Could that save the cottage?"

"Save the cottage?"

"From overtaxation."

"That's something we should have started years ago, if they're overtaxing us," Melanie said.

"What if we sold it?"

"Good luck with getting that by everyone. Besides, Mom will never let you sell."

"We haven't been using it as much over the past several years."

"Yeah, because Maya and I were in school and you were taking care of Mom and starting your photography business. But now we're all here and on our feet." Melanie smiled. "Besides, where would the fairies go?"

"Sorry?"

"The Nymph Island fairies."

Hailey groaned. Tigger's fairies. Their niece believed the island was inhabited by them and had built little fairy houses all over the island, taking up the torch the sisters had dropped when they'd grown up and become too old for such things.

"You should talk to Mom," Melanie said.

"Yeah," Hailey agreed, wondering how much her sister suspected.

Clutching the forms, she headed for her car. She had time to zip over to the nursing home where their mother lived, and see how much wiggle room she had in her promises. If they could sell the cottage quickly, Hailey could at least save her house, her livelihood.

As she started her car, a familiar anxiety grew until it was gnawing at her stomach. It had been several days since she'd last visited their mother, and, sometimes, when she hadn't seen her in a few days, the worry and anxiety got so bad she'd become edgy and distracted, until she had to drop what she was doing and go to make sure her mom was okay.

Hailey let herself into the nursing home, finding the familiar soap smell strangely comforting. When she spotted her mother,

Catherine, in the sunny atrium, she let out a long breath, her shoulders relaxing. She plunked herself down beside her and enjoyed the July sunshine streaming through the windows.

"The rain stopped," Catherine said.

"I brought you a Twix." Hailey placed the chocolate bar on the table beside her wheelchair.

"I think this will be a fine spot to watch the fireworks, don't you think?"

"That won't be for another…" Hailey paused to check her watch "…seven hours, Mom."

"I'm reserving my spot."

"What about supper?"

Her mother stopped staring out the rounded windows that stretched above them. She gave a small shrug. "Not hungry. Besides, you just brought me a snack." She smiled and eyed Hailey's curls. "I see you lost your hairbrush again."

"I was out in the boat. And rain." She tried to smooth her hair using her fingers. "I could take you to see the fireworks if you want." Finian would probably be out being a celebrity-gone-wild somewhere, and she'd miss it, but the idea of her mother sitting in front of this window for seven hours so she could watch ten minutes of fireworks broke Hailey's heart.

"No, that's fine. I'm comfortable here."

"Are you sure?"

"Yes."

They sat in silence, watching a blue jay work peanuts out of a feeder.

"What's bothering you, Hailey?"

Puffing out a big breath, she thought about how much time she and her sisters spent opening the cottage every May long weekend. Cleaning, turning things like the water pump back on, restocking the kitchen, opening shutters, putting on screens, making the beds, removing three seasons' worth of dust and dead bugs and mice, cleaning off the path and dock. Getting the boat back in the water. Paint, fix, repair. Try to keep up with nature, which was unrelenting in its quest to reclaim the 110-year-old structure. And then in October, doing it all in reverse.

The first few years had been fun. It had felt as though they were all finally playing grown-up, and getting to do all the jobs on the list tacked to the back door that their mother or father had always done. But now the thrill of being an adult was wearing off, and the place was starting to feel like a heavy burden. Even though the sisters made cottage maintenance into a party, enjoying margaritas or hot toddies when the day's work was done, it was a lot of responsibility, and the jobs and expenses were never-ending and slightly overwhelming.

"I'm fine," Hailey said finally, patting Catherine's hand. The cottage meant everything to her mother. It was where she'd fallen in love with their dad. Where she'd spent summers teaching the girls to swim. So many memories.

"You're doing an awful lot of sighing."

"Sorry."

"So?"

"So what?"

Her mother arched a gray eyebrow and adjusted her bright orange button-up shirt.

Hailey sighed again. "You know how I promised not to sell the cottage?"

Her mom straightened, her blue eyes flashing.

"I didn't sell it," Hailey assured her quickly. "But it's heading for a tax sale August 30 if I can't find a way to cover the back taxes."

"How much?"

"Trust me, Mom. None of us have that much."

Her mother sagged, her non-stroke affected hand dropping

down to worry her chair's brake lever. "I put you in a poor position, didn't I? Passing it on with taxes owed."

"No, no, Mom. It was me. Taxes went up. There were warnings I ignored, thinking destiny would take care of us and the cottage. There were urgent repairs needed. Maya and Melanie were in school. My photography business hasn't taken off as fast as I thought it would." She gave a shrug, hoping her mother wouldn't take on guilt that shouldn't be hers. It was Hailey's fault the tax bill had grown, not shrunk.

"If it's time for the cottage to move to a new family, then so be it. It owes us nothing and has given us so much. Let the municipality take it." She gave her a wistful smile. "I was hoping you girls would get a chance to follow the tradition and fall in love on the island."

"I think we were, too." Hailey paused. "I know I promised not to sell Nymph Island, but—"

"Hailey, *please*. Let destiny take her course. If it's not meant to be, let it go. It's not ours to profit off of. It's a gift. Always has been."

"But I need to sell it, Mom." Her voice was tight with panic and held-back tears. "I'm going to lose everything if it's seized. If we sell it, I can come away with something."

"What do you mean?" Her mother's voice was barely above a whisper. "Hailey?"

She bowed her head, feeling nothing but shame and failure. "I took some personal financial risks."

Her mom took a moment to recover her composure. Then, with her back straight and voice firm, she said, "Sell it, Hailey Rose. Sell it as fast as you can."

Hailey let out a tremendous sigh that made her ribs ache, and scrunched her eyes shut. If this was what she needed to do, and now had permission, why did it hurt so deeply?

"Look at me," Catherine said gently. Hailey tried to focus on the right side of her face which lacked the permanently sad expression due to the stroke. Today, both sides were sad. "Do what you need to do, Hailey, and know that I will always love you."

Tears in her eyes, the older woman pulled her close. Hailey inhaled her familiar scent, one she linked to home and safety. Her mother trembled in her embrace, needing the hug as much as she did. Hailey vowed she wouldn't let her down. Nymph Island had to stay in the family, no matter what.

HAILEY SET UP HER PHONE'S hands-free system so she could make calls as she drove from her mom's to where she'd last seen Finian. And slapped him. How on earth was she going to recover from that?

She needed a plan. A big plan. And, heck, a big fabulous miracle, while she was at it.

"Simone?" she said adjusting the gadget hanging off her ear. "Any chance you'd be open to me holding a small show in your boutique this month?"

"A show?" her friend asked.

"Yeah. Small photos of Muskoka and nature and things. The stuff that sells, you know? Like the Muskoka chair on a dock with mist all around. The wood boats from the antique show. We can split the proceeds."

"How much do you need?"

Hailey did a quick calculation. Simone's boutique was a two-story house in Port Carling that had been converted into a store. It was still divided into several small rooms, giving her plenty of wall space. Simone had good foot traffic through the summer months, and if Hailey could sell even half of what was hung, she'd be on her way to something. Not a full miracle, but it would at least be a step in the right direction. If she had ten such plans, maybe she could save the cottage. "Space for about fifty?"

"No, I mean how much money do you need?"

"Um, why?"

"Because it sounds a lot like you're selling out. Something you promised you'd never do, and told me I should push you in front of the *Segwun* if you did."

Yeah, that old steamship would definitely take a chunk out of her.

"I'm not selling out, I'm getting my name out there. They'll still be artistic shots. They'll just be ones with more commercial appeal."

"Commercial appeal?" She heard papers shuffling on the other end of the line and she held her breath. "Just checking to see when the next time the *Segwun* will be coming through the locks. The *Wenonah* may have to do, though, as this sounds dire."

"Ha, ha."

"Nymph Island again?"

"Uh-huh."

"You know you could ask your sisters to help, right? Just because you're the oldest doesn't mean you have to take care of everything. They need to start chipping in more."

"They can't."

"Can't or won't?"

"Simone, it's complicated." Hailey rubbed her forehead as she drove along the quiet, tree-lined road, sunlight dappling the hood of her faded red car.

"Did you ask them?"

"Nymph Island's going up in a tax sale if I don't save it by the end of summer." Panic crawled over her and she just about had to pull over. She swallowed hard, bile coating her mouth. "I could lose everything."

"That's heavy. And what do you mean, everything?"

"I mortgaged the house before the Toronto show."

"The dud?"

"Yeah, the dud show that went nowhere. My sisters don't know."

"You've got to tell them."

"Why? So they can laugh and call me Failey all the time, and for good reason? Besides, they'll just freak out and make it into a big deal."

"It is a big deal."

"Only if I fail."

"Right, and you don't fail. Except on your driver's test."

"That's because I was rear-ended! It wasn't my fault."

"Hailey, I know they're going to be over the top, but they're your sisters. They're not in school anymore. Stop making excuses on why you have to protect them."

"Mom put the cottage in trust in my name."

"That doesn't mean you have to solve every little problem. What does Catherine say about all this? Did you tell her?"

"She said to sell it."

"So, then?"

"I can't. I can't be the one who loses it. Not after it's been in the family for over a century."

"There's no question of that, but maybe it's time. Maybe fate or destiny or the man in the moon or whoever your mom talks about wants it back. Lease is up, babe. Let it go. Easy solution."

"I know." Hailey remained silent for a moment. "I just…I want to try. I don't want to give up. And there's nothing my sisters can do other than stress out about it all."

"Hey, I thought I was a Summer sister."

Hailey laughed at her friend's tone. Simone had spent almost as much time at the cottage as the four Summer sisters and had been dubbed an honorary sister with her height marked off in the cottage's kitchen doorway along with the others. But Simone was different. Simone knew everything and wouldn't butt in unless Hailey asked her to.

"You're just getting where you've always wanted to be," Simone said. "And while I hate to say it, the sacrifices you've made for that place are holding you back. If this was a costly time-share in Florida, you'd have sold it by now. The cottage is a sentimental money pit. You haven't even gone to Europe to photograph the Sham-Wow because of it."

Hailey blinked back the tears. "I know," she choked out. "And it's an Apennine chamois. Mountain goat."

Simone's voice transferred into her "let's get our business done" tone, and the tension in Hailey's shoulders vanished. Simone was ready to help. She didn't have to do it completely alone. "So?" she said. "How soon can you have your photos over here?"

"Thursday or Friday."

"Did you want to have an opening?"

"Yes."

"I'll mock up an invite and poster to hang around town and send it over. In the meantime, firm up the date. We don't have a lot of time to save our childhood playground, my friend."

Hailey sighed into her earpiece. "I know." She sped past a grove of trembling aspen, scaring a white-tailed deer back into the brush as she did so. "Hey, if you happened to learn the whereabouts of Finian Alexander, send me a text, would you? And mislead Austin Smith, too, if you can."

Simone whistled under her breath. "This is way worse than you're letting on, isn't it?"

"Can you spread the word? This guy's mine."

"Hails…"

"I know. But it's money, and it's still photography."

It was almost not selling one's soul. Almost.

FINN WAS STARTING TO FEEL the rye and Cokes. All five of them. He was feeling them along with the pull to do something reckless.

The bartender passed him another drink and Finn thought about the woman who'd slapped him. Man, he'd had that one coming. How had he fallen out of touch with the real world and women so quickly? Or was it just a Canada thing that had made her reach out and whack him?

No, he was pretty sure it was him being a jerk. He'd promised himself he'd never let fame go to his head. Looked as if he'd let himself down on that one, too.

He downed half the drink.

He was flunking out left, right, and center.

"From the guy on the end," the bartender said, and Finn's shoulders slumped. A small part of him had hoped it was his nature nut coming by to apologize. Canadians did that a lot. Every time he'd bumped into someone this week, or even came close to bumping into someone, he'd been met with apologies. It had become a game, seeing how many apologies he could collect while wandering down the street. His record was thirteen in one block. One lady had apologized four times for one incident, and he wasn't sure if he could count that as four, but he did. Besides, he was a jerk and it was his game, so his rules.

Finn gave a quick toast to the man who'd sent the drink, hoping he wouldn't come over and start hitting on him with hockey talk. Who the hell followed hockey?

He froze as recognition set in. Son of a...

Austin Smith.

Interpreting Finn's locked gaze as an invite, Austin slid over with his own drink.

"Hiya, Finian. Austin Smith." He offered his hand for a shake and Finn ignored it.

Austin remained beside him, unfazed.

"I know who you are," Finn muttered, keeping his attention on the local concert posters pinned to the walls.

"Anything you need from the paparazzi while you're here in Canada, you let me know. I cover everything in these parts."

"I'm taking a flight out tomorrow."

"That's not what the airlines say."

"Private jet."

Austin laughed and Finn's temperature rose along with his temper. He hated it when the paparazzi knew more about his comings and goings than he did—and it happened. And if anyone would have the 411 on what he was up to it would be this asswipe.

"I get people in the tabloids faster than a Kardashian gets knocked up, Finian. And you know it."

Finn glowered at him. "You give paparazzi a bad name."

"Thank you."

Finn shook his head and downed his drink. Austin was the kind of man who crossed lines, grabbed celebrities, riled them up with angry words—anything in order to get a better photo. Finn still wanted to punch him for the way he'd violated his ex-girlfriend's privacy by flying over her backyard in a helicopter to get pictures of Jessica and her friends nude sunbathing. Finn had never been possessive or overprotective of his ex, but that had driven him wild.

"You know," he said conversationally, "I think there should still be a restraining order in effect."

"That's only for your ex-girlfriend."

Finn inhaled. Nope, he was pretty damn sure he'd sprung for the couple's package on that one. Double-bagged the bastard to keep him from popping up from behind potted palms and making his blood pressure shoot through the roof. The little prick had helped Finn's bad-boy image with all those angry shots he'd sold to the papers, but it hadn't been healthy fun, like the rest of his image building had been. So far.

"Yours expired," Austin said with a grin. "Yesterday." He took a sip of his beer, his eyes glittering with some other tidbit he was holding back.

Finn clenched his hands and waited.

"Oh, and Canada is out of California's jurisdiction."

Of course it was.

Austin dropped a simple business card onto the bar as he stood. He leaned closer. "You haven't been fresh news for almost a week. If you want to change that, I have a few ideas." He tapped the card. "Call me."

Finn stared straight ahead, ignoring the offer. Austin was not the kind of paparazzo he would collaborate with. For one, you had to trust the photographer not to sell you out when you were creating a story together. He'd rather take the time to create a paparazzo out of Nature Nut than shake hands with this guy.

"I have many happy celebrity clients. I can provide references if need be."

"Then why aren't you working for them right now?" Finn said, turning to stare down the large man.

"This guy bothering you, Mr. Alexander?" the bartender asked, his beefy arms folded across his puffed out chest.

"Just leaving."

Finn slipped a twenty into the tip jar after Austin hurried out, letting the bar's screen door slap in his wake. Finn held his breath, staring at the closed door, wondering what to do. What step to take next. It was a scriptless choose-your-own-adventure, and he was at a crossroads, unable to read ahead and figure out which path he ultimately wanted.

He should return to Hollywood.

Instead, he made himself comfortable and ordered another rye and Coke.

"No scotch on the rocks?" the bartender joked, referring to Finn's famous character in the action series *Man versus War*.

Finn gave him a polite smile and a silent *no*. He guessed Daniel Craig, Pierce Brosnan, and Sean Connery had to put up with a lot of martinis—shaken, not stirred—so he could put up with a few scotches on the rocks.

Scanning the bar, he searched for a rowdy group of young men who could swoop him into their festivities, building things up until he'd caused enough trouble to get sold to the celebrity magazines and websites. The bar was filling up, happy hour starting, red maple leaves stamped on faces. But no rowdy men full of testosterone.

He yawned and fought the temptation to go back to his kitschy cottage. He supposed the one good thing about being a bad boy was that trouble usually came knocking. Fame, fortune, and good looks equaled anything he wanted. All he had to do was wait. Wait for it to come through the bar's screen door.

And right now some narrow hips were swaying toward him, and his body perked up. Strange. He usually preferred a fuller figure. Why was this beanpole grabbing his attention?

Beanpole.

His eyes crept up the familiar outfit.

The photographer.

She was back.

He spun back to the bar, sucking his lower lip into his mouth as he rubbed his cheek absently. Hours later, he swore he could still feel the imprint of her slender palm. He lifted his cold glass to the handprint and turned farther from the door. The condensation seeped through his five o'clock shadow, the coolness a comfort.

Why hadn't his stubble been irresistible to her? He knew his blue eyes shone straight out from his face when he was unshaved. He was primal. Real. As irresistible as a plate of fresh chocolate chip cookies outside a pothouse.

Damn sexy. And yet she'd rejected him as if he was a high school loser and she was the prom queen.

He was supposed to be the prom king, making her weak at the knees. *She* was supposed to be just some girl who was happy he'd looked her way. But instead, she'd balked when he'd acted like a pushy alpha who was hungry for one thing and expected to get it.

But there'd been something about the way Nature Nut had reacted that stirred his blood in a way Finn's ex-girlfriend never had. Was it the challenge? The fire within her? The lack of vapidness? This photographer was nothing like Jessica. At first Jess's plastic perfect appearance had thrilled him. *She* wanted *him*. But as time wore on, her fake breasts and piles of makeup had started to repulse him. Yet everyone else found her beautiful.

Maybe that's why he was so turned on by his nature nut. It was her realness. She was the opposite of Hollywood, and every emotion played across her face like a Hot List actor earning her Oscar.

Wait...

His nature nut?

He rubbed his jaw. Canada was getting to him.

Oh, hell. She settled beside him, making him sympathize with the way Miss Muffet felt when the spider sat down beside her.

"I'm not going to slap you," she announced, after ordering a draft beer.

"Okay." His voice squeaked, and he cleared his throat. He needed to regain control. Though he wanted rub against her long, bare legs like a homeless kitten, he knew he had to play a role. Be cool. Intriguing. Debonair.

But she hadn't liked Mr. Hotshot earlier, and chances were she'd hate any role he put on—anything that was less than real.

Finn gripped the bar and rubbed his jaw again. He was screwed.

"I came to apologize," she said, her voice flat.

He spun on his stool to face her. She looked lost, defeated, rejected. Not at all like the fiery woman who had escaped him earlier. He wanted to pull her into a hug to feel her small body against his and make her smile. Make those worries not quite hidden in her eyes flit away like a cloud of butterflies.

"I should be the one apologizing," he said, trying to keep the slur out of his words. Damn. Why did he have so many drinks?

He placed a hand on the bar and leaned toward her. "I'm not the man you've seen in the tabloids. I'm not the man you met hours ago." He turned away. He was already blowing this chance. He was slurring. Obviously there was something wrong with him. Seriously wrong.

"Don't play me," she said, staring at him with serious blue eyes. "I know you don't have a twin brother."

He scratched his head warily, buying for time as he worked to hide the emotions associated with him having a twin brother. The public didn't know about his twin, Julian, and they certainly didn't know about that fateful night when, just a block from home, Finn had lost the man he'd shared a womb with for nine months and a bedroom for sixteen and a half years. "Sorry?"

"Don't lie to me and don't play the role of caring gentleman. I can see it coming and I don't like it. I'd prefer you be straight-up honest. Be who you really are."

"Oh." He pushed his sweaty glass away, contemplating her words. That should be easy. Except he didn't know who he was. He knew who he used to be and who he was becoming, thanks to Derek's hard work. But who he was at this exact point in time… that was difficult to pin down.

"So, I'm sorry." She pushed away from the bar, her beer in hand. A pang of loneliness hit Finn harder than a Jean-Claude Van Damme punch to the gut.

"No." He grabbed her arm a little too tightly. "I'm sorry. Please. Stay." He gestured to the stool she'd slipped off. "Finish your beer. I promise I won't manhandle you."

She cautiously slid back onto it.

He grinned and leaned toward her as though sharing a secret. "Unless you ask me to."

The way she turned, looking shocked and prim, made him laugh. He liked this woman. All uptight and responsible and *real*. He wanted the beauty of her. He wanted real life with her, right here, right now.

Wow. He really needed a vacation if that's the way he was thinking.

Finn shook his head at himself and leaned on the bar. "So, what do you want in life?" May as well start with the core of who this woman was, and work his way out. He wanted to know everything.

Not because he was interested, but because he needed to discover her point of weakness. That's all. A character study, so he'd know how to get her to work with him. A means to an end. A business proposition. Nothing tangled and complicated, or real and deep, such as love or infatuation.

She looked taken aback and kept sneaking glances at him. Judging. Assessing.

Finally, when he thought she'd never reply, she spun on her stool, facing him full on. "I want life and everyone in it to back the hell off so I can make my art. Full-time. That's what I want."

Finn smiled as her body language continued to challenge him. His smile faded when the impact of her words scraped at him like barbed wire. What she wanted felt a little close to home.

He'd wished for the same thing when he'd left film school. After hours of looking up his own ass in acting class, he'd wanted to let loose, make art and be someone. In the end, about to starve, and facing the prospect of returning home a big loser, he'd gone with what paid—action flicks. He liked action flicks, don't get him wrong. But he wasn't creating anything more than light entertainment that would be forgotten a few hours later. He wasn't changing lives or making a statement other than watch out, gas explodes when you're on the big screen and bad guys pop out of nowhere.

But what was causing those worry lines around Nature Nut's eyes? Who needed to back off? When she turned away, her face a mask of agony, he realized he'd waited too long to acknowledge her confession.

"Never mind. It doesn't matter. I'm just in a mood," she said.

"I'm staying at the White Pine Cottages and Estates. Nice place. The Sunflower Cottage. Little sunflower cutouts on it."

"Are you hinting—again—that you'd like to show me your bed?"

Finn choked on his drink. What was it about this girl that kept turning him around?

"I was just thinking, with you a photographer and all..." He paused to clear his throat, and to choose his next words wisely.

She froze as if a polar ice cap had been dumped on her,

encasing her. She didn't move, even to breathe, as she waited for him to finish his sentence.

He gently poked her in the arm and lowered his voice. "I thought you could, you know, take some private photos of me."

"I don't do *that* kind of work." Her voice was cold, her eyes unblinking.

"It's good money."

"Who said I needed money or was a photographer?"

"You okay?" He waved a hand in front of her face. Her cheeks were red, her eyes flashing, but behind it all he saw panic. "I've seen you around, snapping photos, and I thought maybe you could, you know, help a guy out." He was talking too fast, sounded nervous.

"I don't want to photograph you in the nude, okay?" She stood, cheeks flushed.

People turned, gasping and laughing. He was certain at least half of them were wishing they'd caught that outburst on film.

Finn snagged Hailey by the arm as she drew it back as though contemplating throwing her beer in his face. "I wasn't implying that. Geez. Get your mind out of the gutter. I meant publicity stuff." He released her, turning back to the bar, eyes averted. "Do you photograph nature? There's cool wildlife around here."

She was still standing there, ready to attack, although her beer arm was beginning to slacken.

"Like those haunting birds and that turtle with the yellow spots?" He watched her out of the corner of his eyes. Waiting. She was recalculating. "They're probably less difficult than working with a movie star."

"Black shell?"

"Yeah." He dared meet her eyes. The pissed-off look had been replaced with curiosity. "Kind of funky undercarriage. Orangey. With black."

She leaned forward, one hand on the bar, her eyes bright and focused. "Where did you see it?"

Seriously? This woman got off on reptiles. He'd have to remember that.

"In the marsh back there." He waved a hand vaguely.

"They're endangered. I've been trying to spot one for years. My sister needs to prove they're in the area." The photographer gave him a peeved look. "They've just finished nesting so don't go stomping around wherever. You'll squash their eggs."

He held up his hands. "I stay on the rocks when I'm in the marsh and on shore I follow the paths."

"Good." She narrowed her eyes at him and he felt the need to prove he wasn't some city-slicker movie star who would stomp on endangered eggs.

"Strange birds you've got, though." Finn gave a shiver. "What are those ones that look like an anorexic black-and-white duck?"

She choked on a laugh as she took her stool again. "That would probably be the loon." She made a quivering, high-pitched call. "Like that?"

Okay, that sound really shouldn't turn him on, but it did.

"Yeah, like a scared, high-pitched owl crossed with something insane."

Smiling at his description, she pulled out a one-dollar coin and held it up. "The loonie. Named for the loon shown on the front." She turned to the bartender and called, "Jamie? You got an elastic?"

He shot one to her and she snatched it out of the air, wrangling her curls into some sort of bun.

Finn studied the coin as he pretended not to watch her expose a sweeping, pale neck. She was gorgeous. He turned the coin over and handed it back. "That's the bird. What's the story on the toonie? Aren't there polar bears on it?"

"Well, it's the two-dollar coin," she said, as if that explained things.

He scratched his head, thinking. Yeah. "That makes no sense."

"Who said it has to make sense?" She shot him a grin.

He let out a half laugh. Behind him, he could sense a few locals, waiting for him to turn their way so they could smile and say hi, get in on the jokes. Not now. Didn't they see he was picking up a lady? The two of them were finally having a conversation that didn't involve violence on her part. He was getting somewhere.

"Show me some of your photos," he suggested.

She pulled out her phone, then, with cheeks flaming, tucked it into her bag and, instead, slid a glossy postcard his way.

"What kind of photos do you do?" he asked carefully, not looking at the card, trying to figure out why she wouldn't show him her phone. Nude selfies for a boyfriend? He didn't like that idea. Not one bit.

"That kind." She nudged the card.

"Any portraits?" He kept his eyes on hers, but she refused to look at him.

She shrugged. "Only when I'm hard up for cash."

He scratched his cheek, studying her card. "This is an unusual shot." The contrast of light and dark, the way she'd used the deer's fur as texture. It could easily be just another photo of a deer, but she'd somehow made the buck feel real, alive, and as though he might turn his head, step out of the card and give Finn a shove with his antlers. That, he knew, took talent. Patience. Knowing your equipment. The light. The timing.

All the more reason she should work with him. And why shouldn't she? He'd be a great addition to her portfolio.

She faced him more fully, her lips moist and entirely kissable. If she had been even halfway willing...

But he had her attention. About time.

Now he could take it home. Make the connection. Get her on his side.

"I bet you hear a lot of 'how much is a nice relaxing shot that would fit over my new couch? Preferably something that goes with my beige décor and is already framed?'"

She let out a snort, which told him she'd heard versions of that line plenty of times. The hitch in her shoulders relaxed a notch and he took the opportunity to slip the bartender money for her drink.

"You going to the concert tonight?" he asked.

"At The Kee?"

"Yeah. That big old-fashioned dance hall place? I still can't believe the bands they bring out here in the woods. It's unheard of."

"They've been doing it since Duke Ellington's time."

"So, you going? Do you like Vapid Magpie?"

"I do, but they're sold out. I didn't have…" She shook her head.

"Have what?"

"The opportunity to get tickets when they went on sale," she said quickly, taking a gulp of her beer.

"I could get you tickets."

She laughed. "They sold out ages ago."

Finn leaned back, surprised at the edge in her voice. She was daring him, challenging him to surprise her with tickets. He could feel it. She really liked this band. Or she really liked him.

His bet was on the band, even though he wanted to bet on himself.

"Will you go with me if I get tickets?"

She echoed his movements, head tilted.

Damn, she was intriguing.

"Why?" she asked.

He slipped closer, his lips grazing her ear as he whispered, "Why not?"

There was a lot of promise in his voice, and he noted the way her pupils darkened. She was tempted.

But nope, he'd gone too far again. She was closing up like a flower at dusk. Damn. He couldn't be this patient. He had days, not a lifetime. She had too tight of a rein on herself, and it would take too long to get her to loosen up.

But he had a little time. Time enough to see how far he could get tonight. He knew where her line was now and he could patiently play to it each and every time, breaking her down slowly and surely. Reel her in. Push her out, pull her in. Temptation, temptation. Sweet, sweet sexy temptation.

A girl could hold out for only so long.

Before she could leave, he pulled two tickets out of his back pocket, raising his eyebrows in question. It was time for do or die. He wasn't famous for nothing. Strings were something he could pull. And everyone had strings.

"Meet me outside The Kee at nine." He slipped off his stool, leaving her hand outstretched as she reached for the tickets.

Nailed it.

When her face became a mask of something a lot like righteous anger, he went in for the kill. He rested a warm hand on her knee, watched her sharp intake of breath as her eyes fluttered shut for a split second. He tried not to grin. Anger and passion were so closely related that it made the game dangerous. And thrilling.

There would be no boredom in Muskoka as long as she was in his sights.

Meeting her blue-eyed gaze, nothing held back, he said, "Enjoy your life, sugar toes. If you don't let go and enjoy it every once in a while, you're living for nothing." He brushed her ear with his lips, the sensation of falling off a cliff rushing through him as he left her, barely daring to breathe.

Chapter Three

Hailey couldn't believe the gall of Finian Alexander. Where did he get off? She'd slapped his face, come back to apologize, and he'd turned around and invited her to a sold-out concert of her favorite band after she'd misread his intentions.

Going to a concert was almost like a date. But it wasn't a date. He was a rich movie star; she was a nobody. She wasn't falling for this vacation game again. Not after Jake, who acted as though he was totally into her up until the moment he went back to the city at the end of the summer, dropping her and all his promises as if she was just some gal who couldn't take a hint. Why would Finian Alexander be any different?

He was lonely, looking for a fling, and she was the first woman to catch his eye.

Talk about overconfident, if he thought taking her to a concert would convince her to fall into his bed or allow him to exploit her abilities as a photographer. She'd seen him eyeing her photo card, and the rich and famous were always the stingiest. They seemed to believe she should be honored to photograph them pro bono, as if having them in her portfolio was a privilege. Yeah, well, little did they know that she'd won plenty of photography contests and awards without their ugly mugs. Contests that helped pay the bills.

Flopping down in front of her laptop, Hailey clicked the upload button to send new photos to her agent, Cedric Zimmerman. He often sent her a biweekly laundry list of requested nature photos from magazines, knowing she had no interest in capturing celebrity dirt when it came her way. But now she had dirt. Well, maybe not dirt, but dust at the very least. And she wanted to sell it. Fast.

She clicked to add the photos she'd taken with her phone that afternoon, then shook her head. At one point she'd thought she'd seen a glimmer of humanity in Finian's eyes. But that was ridiculous. He was the kind of man who charmed and played the game until he got what he wanted. But he wasn't going to get it from her. He could whisper in her ear in a way that made her nerve endings perk up, but there was no way Hailey was going to fall for his games. Love her? Leave her? No way.

Not now. Not ever.

The way he exuded confidence and sexuality made him just like all the other rich boys she'd met growing up. The summer men. So full of themselves it made her want to slap them in order to bring them down a notch and prove she was more than some plaything to make their pretty lives even easier as they vacationed in their fancy cottages, then left when the summer ended with never a glance back.

It was her time to come out ahead.

Hailey finished the upload and sat back, popping a mint Mentos in her mouth. She checked the time. She could show up at The Kee to Bala. See what he'd do. She let out a chuckle. It might be funny, watching him try to recall who she was, and if he had really invited her. Because by the time the concert rolled around he'd probably have tried to get into three more skirts with the lure of the tickets.

And if Hailey did manage to get inside, she'd ply him with

drinks and wait for him to be the jerk she knew he really was. Then she'd whip out her camera phone, take some unflattering images and sell them. Ta-da! Cottage saved. Happily ever after, while he blissfully resumed his car-crash life.

A message from Cedric popped up on her monitor. *Calling you.*

Yes!

She snagged her ringing phone.

"Tell me the good news," she said. She held her breath and swivelled her chair back and forth, trying to burn off her excitement.

"What the hell are these shots?" her agent asked.

"What do you mean?" She drifted into a nearby armchair she'd picked up from the antique barn on Highway 118.

"You're a nature photographer. A damn good one, and making decent money for your stage of the game. For someone making art."

"And?"

"Don't go blowing your reputation with some half-done celebrity shots."

Ouch.

"These are as good as what I've seen online."

"What are you doing, Hailey? We've spent years getting you into good galleries. I know I hounded you on this whole art thing, but why the hell are you going this route now that you're making a name for yourself and winning awards? Do you need money for some drug habit I don't know about?"

"You sell shots like this all the time, right?"

Cedric hesitated. "I do, but I don't understand."

"Can you sell these?"

He sighed, and she could picture him tugging his ear as he thought how to reply. "You need to shoot a story, Hailey. There isn't a story in these. There's a learning curve to being a celebrity chaser, believe it or not. So, if you are in need of cash, maybe we can set up another show, or find a magazine. Want me to call *National Geographic*?"

"Yes, but there is a story." She needed more than some small show, months down the road, or a few photos for *National Geographic*. She glanced through the pictures she'd selected. They were all beautifully lined up. The light had held out for most of them and the one of Finian rolling up the vintage Jag's window was only a bit grainy because of the clouds, rain, and distance. The one of him holding the door to the bar was slightly blurry because he'd slapped her butt. But the tabloids never seemed to care about quality.

"A man rolling up a car window. Holding a door open for someone. These aren't stories."

"But it's a total contradiction," Hailey protested. "Surely that's exciting?"

"Would you buy a magazine with these on the cover?"

"No," she said with a sigh. "But I'd be intrigued."

"So, be intrigued. Even celebrities who lack manners can hold a door open for someone, Hailey. You need to capture shots of him doing unbelievable things."

Funny, she thought she had.

She narrowed her eyes, staring at the images of Finian. He was a mystery. One she needed to uncover and reveal to the world, one photo at a time. There was a layer he was hiding, and she'd expose it while giving him a nice big dose of reality. Oh, and making herself rich in the process.

"I'm on it, Cedric. In fact," she said with a chuckle, "he's expecting me." And how much more perfect could that be?

FINN SAT AT THE SMALL desk in his rented cottage and stared at the blank page framed in sunflowers in front of him. Sighing, he pushed away his nonexistent plan for pulling Sugar Toes into his devious scheme to get into the tabloids with a new adventure. Instead, he picked up the old guitar he'd had delivered to his room. It looked as though it belonged to one of the employees. Well-worn. Stickered. And completely out of tune. Just the way he liked it.

He adjusted the sound to match his mood, his skills. He glanced at the card Sugar Toes had given him. Hailey Summer. Pretty name. He couldn't believe he'd gotten in this deep without knowing it. Hailey. He liked the way her name rolled off his tongue.

Focusing on the out-of-tune instrument, he ignored how he was slowing down the song as though smothering it. He played "Drooping Flags" by Vapid Magpie, knowing they'd sing it tonight. He played the simple riff again, and again. It was easy enough. If he stuck with the bass, he could almost make it sound untortured.

Almost.

Would Hailey show up tonight? Or would she chicken out? Would he be the man waiting outside the hall to see if he'd been rejected? But the bigger question was, why had he so willingly put himself in this position? People waited for *him*, not the other way around. She hadn't even tried to turn the tables on him. It was as though he'd taken all his power and control, put it in a nice little shopping bag and handed it to her.

He put the guitar away, no closer to having a plan. How could he convince someone like Hailey to use her photography skills against him?

He walked to the window and stared out at the dark blue lake, rocky shoreline and wind-worn trees. If he'd been smart, he would have stirred her up, leaving her pissed off and longing for him. Then her anger could do the rest.

He punched the air, then shoved his hands through his short hair. He needed her to go paparazzo on him. Asking her out had been stupid, stupid, stupid. Derek was right; Finn shouldn't be here alone. Left to his own devices, he'd never get into the tabloids.

Finn paced the room, head down, thinking. He was sure he'd seen a desperate need within Hailey. He'd thought it was for money, but when he'd asked if she did portraits, she'd said only when she was hard up for cash. And she hadn't leaped at the chance to work with him. Hadn't gone all breathy and said *Yes!* Instead, she'd thought he wanted nude photos. He let out a laugh.

Talk about assuming opposite things.

So was she a bad businesswoman? Or was having a movie star in one's portfolio not as big of a deal as he'd thought?

Maybe she was famous in her own right. Maybe she was an incredible, sought-after photographer and he'd insulted her. He touched her card, letting his fingers linger over her name. How many run-ins had they had today? And he'd been so tuned out that he hadn't even asked her her name—not once. How had he gotten used to knowing people before he met them, all of them famous? Or else having people immediately introduce themselves, eager to get on his radar? How had that become normal?

He was losing little things from real life, such as introductions. How to carry on a conversation. How not to be a jerk.

Reality was a sweet reminder of how far he'd climbed. But his new life left him living in a land where nothing was real.

He snatched up his phone as it rang, hoping, for some strange reason, that it was Hailey.

"Finian?" asked the female voice.

His mother.

"Mom, how's it going?"

"I prayed for you at church today."

"Why?" he asked, cringing. There were so many things for her to pray about. She read the tabloids, and while she was usually able to write another story for what was pictured, sometimes she couldn't.

"For your broken heart. Why don't you come home? I'll bake cookies. We'll walk Rex. We'll talk. You must be exhausted."

"Mom, my heart isn't broken."

"You were with her for over a year. Of course it is."

"Mom, did it look like I was actually in love with Jessica?"

"What do you mean?"

"Hey, here's an idea. Why don't you and Dad join me here?"

"What would we do with Rex? I read the papers and they said you—"

"I was in the papers?"

"Last week. This week it's just one-liners here and there saying you're hiding out from the pain. Come home. We'll take care of you."

Finn pinched the bridge of his nose. "Mom..." He tried to be patient. "I'm okay, really. And don't believe what you see in the papers or hear on the news. Any of that. I'm still me. I'm still your boy." Well, mostly.

"My boy who lost his manners. Your hands were all over that girl."

Uh-oh. He knew that tone of voice. He stared at the ceiling, trying to figure out which woman his mother might be referring to. It could have been anyone during the blitz he'd gone on after his breakup. Derek had been elated and said it was the best news he'd heard all week, and that Finn's royalty check would show a nice blip as a result of that bender.

The next day Finn had booked his trip to Canada.

"You know the things you see in the tabloids are usually staged, right, Mom?"

"I had one tough time explaining that to my church group."

Finn swallowed. The wrath was coming down.

"You know that photo was taken out of context?" he said, buying time, cringing, wishing he could hide.

"I doubt she needed first aid applied to her nether regions, Finian."

He let out a short laugh. Yeah, he knew which photo his mother was referring to. He felt his cheeks heat. Not his finest moment. Well, unless you were Derek; then you had that one framed and hung as a fabulous publicity stunt.

"Mom, I'm sorry. I'm sorry." Finn rubbed his hand down his face. This was seriously the absolute worst part of being famous.

"I think you need a new agent. One who doesn't encourage this kind of behavior. I was talking to Adrian and he said you would do well with therapy."

Finn's brother, Adrian, had been there the night Julian died in his arms. He knew what Finn had been through and knew what he was trying to accomplish with his publicity and fame. And yet, Adrian—who Finn had put through rehab, and then college—always sided with their mother in the quest to straighten him out. If they wanted him to keep bailing them out for their medical bills and student loans, someone had to pay the price. They couldn't have perfect, famous Finian Alexander *and* have their financial worries cared for at the same time.

"I'm sorry you feel that way, Mom." Finn made his voice firm. "But you need to realize that this is the nature of being a movie star. I'm okay with it, so you shouldn't let the stories bother you, either."

"They are untrue, Finian. They are slandering you. Creating an image of you that is false! This man in the papers is not the boy I raised. You are better than this."

"Without the tabloids I'd be a nobody, Mom. I'd become that guy who everyone forgets or wonders what happened to."

"Quit complaining about what you don't have, and enjoy what you *do* have. You hear me?"

He sighed. He never won these battles. Ever.

"So, then…" He could feel his mother switching gears, and braced himself a little too late. "Have you met anyone nice in Canada? I hear they wear skirts that cover their goodies."

"Yeah, you'd like her. She slapped me across the face."

His mother clucked. "Already?"

Finn laughed, letting his tension fall away. His mother had forgiven him, and saw the humor in how he was caught between two worlds.

"Yeah. She's got me on the run."

"Sounds like you need to come home and get a refresher on manners and how to treat a woman."

"I have a date with her tonight. If I'm lucky, she might even show up for it."

Chapter Four

Hailey parked her car and, biting her lip, grabbed her purse before she could talk herself into hurrying back home. She had to squelch the intrigue she felt about Finian, and the only way to do that was to hang out with him. Analyze him. Oh, and take photos to sell him out and save the cottage.

Right. No problem.

She nudged her car door closed with her hip, swishing her gray-blue skirt out of the way. With nervous hands she adjusted her necklace and ran a palm over her straightened hair. She joined the crowd that was tumbling out of a bus in front of The Kee. If Finian wasn't already in line they'd never find a place to sit. Although if they did manage to snag a table, they'd spend all night trying to keep it instead of hitting the dance floor, which was her preference. Hailey had to admit it would be pretty cool to dance with a movie star. Assuming he even showed. And danced.

Finian stepped out of a massive cluster of people, waving to her. Hailey's heart hiccuped and she gave a small wave back. There were a *lot* of women around Finian. Like, half the population of Bala. And they had all turned to see who he'd waved at.

Hailey wasn't sure she was going to enjoy hanging out with him all night if these women were going to be sizing her up every second.

Finian stepped out of the throng and grabbed her hand, yanking her into the warmth of the group. What the heck. Might as well make the most of stalking him. She smiled and let her hand linger in his.

"You look hot." His dreamy eyes sparkled, and she had to force herself not to reach out and touch his cheek.

"Thanks."

Hot. Not pretty.

She was in the limelight. With a movie star. At a concert. People were talking about them, heads bent together, trying to figure out who she was. Taking surreptitious photos with their phones.

What had she been thinking?

As if sensing her desire to run back to her car, Finian gripped her around the waist, pulling her into the big building as the doors opened.

Her head felt light. He was touching her. He'd called her hot.

Holy hell, but that was really messing with her head. Big time.

He headed to the bar, setting her up with a drink. She sipped it carefully, promising herself she wouldn't go along for the ride and be his date. This was business. She had to keep her wits about her.

But, oh, he was amazing, and even better in real life than he was on film. He still hadn't shaved, and the way his eyes were set off by the dark stubble on his chin made her want to stare into them for hours.

She looked away, then found herself drawn back to his eyes. There was something consuming in his intense gaze. Primal. As if he had plans for her. Plans that involved getting her into compromising positions.

Hailey studied her leather sandals, tapping the toes together. Normally, she'd run if she got anywhere near a man like this. He was too distracting, making it too easy to get consumed and forget about your own life. Your own needs. Your own wants. He was someone who would love her and leave her, like all those boys who had tempted her and her sisters all through their high school summers.

She was already in too deep with him. She already wanted whatever he was willing to offer.

"What?" Finian asked, his eyes flicking over her face. "What's wrong?"

She smiled and waved off his concerns.

What did it matter, anyway? He'd never…she'd never…

And anyway, all those easy women fawning over him would surely be the ones he'd take home. Not her. Hailey was safe.

She almost laughed at herself. How had she believed even for one second that he'd choose her instead of the buxom babe trying to get his attention?

Oh, right. Because he'd asked her to come with him.

Maybe he thought she was an easy target. Or wanted free head shots.

It was probably that.

She could say no to free head shots.

"Do you like to dance? The band'll be starting in a minute." He lightly touched her elbow, eyebrows raised in question. Nervously, she strode to the spot he'd pointed to, near the stage. Turning, she waited for him to catch up. He was slowly making his way through the crowd as people paused to say hi, offer compliments, and generally distract and waylay him. Hailey rolled her eyes and turned to watch the band's roadies set up, ignoring the way Finian's broad shoulders cut a path, his moves relaxed and confident. There was something about the way he dressed casually in worn clothes that made him seem so real, so "boy next door."

Damn, but she wanted to know what he looked like under that faded T-shirt, and how he moved those denim-clad hips when they were free of cotton. She closed her eyes and told herself to stop thinking about him that way. Finian Alexander wasn't going to take her to bed. And anyway, she'd say no before she played the fool. It would be all right. All she had to do was enjoy the night and live a little while she waited for him to be the screwup he was.

She felt a zing as a warm hand touched her lower back and Finian wrapped himself around her protectively, possessively. She went to step away from his embrace, but realized he wasn't actually touching her, other than that gentle, resting palm. She turned back to the stage, where the band was starting into their first song, and tried to block out the subtle aftershave that made her want to move closer and inhale deeply.

Finian was a good dancer, Hailey discovered. The way he moved with ease, not just shuffling from foot to foot as he swayed to the music. She liked how he'd reach out to lightly touch her, drawing her closer when the crowds started to pull them apart. It felt like a real date. As though she was someone he wanted to be with. He had boundaries out in the real world and she was within them.

His dance was a seduction and she moved closer, intrigued. Every time he prolonged their eye contact beyond a casual, comfortable glance she felt herself flush with heat. And every time he used his body to gently block someone from honing in on them, she fell a little deeper for this version of Finian. She felt safe, protected. Wanted.

Hailey saw a flicker of discomfort in his eyes when wandering female hands brushed his body. He flashed the offender a smile as he spun to slap her on the ass, hard enough to send her back into the throng of other dancers, giggling and with eyes that were filled with excitement and a hint of lust.

These women would rip him to pieces if given the chance. How could he stand it? Hailey's temper was getting the best of her on his behalf, and she didn't even really like the guy.

The band broke between sets, and feeling tired from the tension of watching everyone fall all over Finian, while fighting her own desire, Hailey went to the bar to get another drink. The band was good, but she really needed Finian to do something asinine. And soon. Before she began to think he was human, or began reassessing her no-sex-with-summer-men rule.

With a hand on her lower back, Finian drew her up some stairs that led to an outdoor balcony. He nodded to a bouncer, who drew back a folding screen, revealing a wrought-iron patio table for two.

Yep, she was screwed.

She smiled as Finian offered her a chair in the private, sheltered corner.

"Wow. The bad-boy has some manners, after all. Thank you." Although maybe his manners came out only when he had an agenda, such as getting up her skirt.

"Funny, my mother gave me a lecture on my manners only a few hours ago." He took the seat across from her, and before she could ask about his mom, he said, "So? What's your dream shot? For photography?"

A head popped around the screen. "Hey, guys. Did I hear you want some shots?" Austin held up his camera. "Hailey, you could straddle Finn. Finn, you could put your mouth over her—"

Finian was up in a flash, fists raised.

"Austin, go jump in the falls!" Hailey snapped.

Finian turned to face her, eyes assessing. "You know him?"

"Yeah. Unfortunately."

"Ex-girlfriend, actually," Austin said with a grin.

Finian gave her a disbelieving look that was also full of reassessment. She didn't like it. At all. As her mother used to say, *Who you associate with reflects on you.* And Hailey was associating with trouble, times two.

"It was high school," she said. "Science proves the teenaged brain isn't fully developed until kids are in their twenties."

Austin clutched his chest as though holding a dagger, and grinned when Hailey shoved him back to the bouncer's side of the curtain.

"If you kiss her, Finn, just remember I kissed her first!"

Finian's right hand was still curled into a fist, his jaw tight as he yanked the brown curtain across, just about knocking down the temporary structure. He scowled at the bouncer. "I said *nobody*."

"Sorry, he said he was with you."

Austin shouted through the curtain, "Way to move in on the target and get the good shots, Hailey. I hope it's worth selling your soul."

"I'm not like you, Austin. I photograph turtles, not egocentric jerks!"

"I'd screw him for a money shot, but would you?" he called back.

Hailey moved to the curtain, ready to hit Austin with all she was worth. Finian guided her gently back to the table. "Don't let him get you riled up or he'll have you in the tabloids faster than he came on prom night."

Hailey choked on her laughter. "Good one."

She allowed Finian to seat her again, before realizing what she'd said. "I'm sorry. I don't think you're an egocentric jerk."

"That's fine. You do, and I am."

Hailey studied her hands.

"That's my image, right?" Finian tipped her chin up and gave her a weak smile.

She sent him a grateful one. "I'm sorry about Austin. He's never brought out the best in me, especially since we grew up."

"Me, neither. In California I had a restraining order against him."

"Seriously?" Hailey leaned forward. She'd always thought Austin's stories of ruthlessness were blown out of proportion.

"Yeah. But apparently it doesn't work up here in Canada. Oh, and it expired." Finian cringed. "Think the Mounties would restrain him?"

"Austin can take a good shot from over a hundred yards away. He's like a seagull, and knows exactly where his crap is gonna land. So even if the Mounties did restrain him, your shoulders are still going to get messy."

Finian laughed, rich and deep. Hailey smiled, feeling a bond with him. Someone who finally understood just how much of an annoying burr Austin really was.

"What's your favorite song?" Finian asked. "Of the band's?"

"'Drooping Flags,'" she said, feeling embarrassed. It was a silly song, but the depth of the lyrics got her every time. "And you?"

He paused. "Yeah. Me, too." He leaned on the table, arms stretched toward her. All she'd have to do was place her hands near his and he'd grasp them. Long fingers, wide palms, ready to touch her. Caress her. Lead her into sweet temptation.

She leaned back in her chair. "Same favorite song? You can't do better than that in your quest to get me to like you?"

"You don't like me?"

She swallowed hard. "I mean, we don't really know each other. And the odds of us preferring the same obscure song are pretty out there."

His eyes held a mischievous glint and she had no clue whether she could trust him. Hailey leaned forward and tipped up her jaw in challenge. "Prove it. Sing 'Drooping Flags.'"

"I'll do one better." He got up and went to talk to the bouncer on the other side of the curtain. Finian returned a moment later, grinning.

"What did you just do?" she asked.

"You'll see." He gave her a wink over his rye and Coke, lifting it toward her. "Cheers, Hailey Summer."

FINN LEFT HAILEY in the crowd by the stage. He both loved and hated her discomfort and the way she was wrestling with her attraction. She'd just about swoon, then catch herself and cross her arms, giving him a stern look. And now he was about to take it over the top. He'd either crash and burn and never see her again, or he'd have her naked body panting under him in a matter of hours.

From his spot in the wings he could see Austin at the back of the crowd, his camera at chest level, ready to take aim. Yep, this could get good. Finn could smash the guitar at the end of the show. Jump off the stage into the crowd and bodysurf his way to the bar, where he could drink right out of the keg. That would be tabloid worthy.

He cut a glance to Hailey. *Hailey*.

The way her soft dress was hugging her like a long-lost lover... The way her hair, straightened and glossy, curved over her bare shoulders... She was a vision of simplicity and understated beauty. Someone you could easily miss because of a lack of flash, but when you looked closer, you got drawn in, became lost. There was something undefinably sexy about Hailey Summer, and he wasn't the only one who'd noticed. But it wasn't the cocky jerks, it was the nice guys. Men he hoped to hell wouldn't put the moves on her, because in a contest against a nice guy there was no way Finn would ever win.

And she was his.

Well, no, she wasn't. But he wanted her to be—at least until he figured himself out, and where she fit into his life. Which was stupid. He did flings and relationships that lacked meaning. Hailey wasn't that kind of girl. Hell, she might even have a steady man in her life, and Finn was leaving in a week—even earlier if he couldn't get new dirt out into the gossip rags. He needed to push Hailey into action somehow. Which meant he needed to stop thinking and feeling.

His shoulders slumped as he stared out at her. Somehow this had become a real date, with him trying to impress her enough she'd decide to stick around rather than get her to expose his dark side to the world. The woman didn't even have a real camera on her. Finn had lost his focus. Again.

He gave himself a shake and ground his teeth. He could do this. He could get back in the game. She had a camera phone, right? And there were others with cameras in the audience, including Austin, who was better than nothing—which was what Finn currently had.

He could muck this up, like skydiving without a parachute, and it would still turn out fine. That was the best part of having a persona that was out of control: he had the freedom to do whatever he wanted to woo the object of his affections.

Object of affections? Woo? What was happening to him?

He dragged his hands through his hair, then down his face.

"You okay, man?" asked the lead vocalist.

"Yeah, of course. No problem."

"You sure?"

He gave a short nod.

The band shifted from foot to foot, eager to get back on stage. "Ready?"

"Yeah. Just, uh, take it slow if you can. I'm a…beginner."

Damn. What was he doing? These concert-goers had paid money to see the band they loved, not to watch him flounder and ruin a song.

The lead vocalist grinned as he caught Finn's uncertain gaze going to the front row. "What's her name?"

"Hailey," he replied without thinking. He winced. How did he not know by now to keep his trap shut?

"We're on. Oh, and don't go smashing the guitar at the end of the song. It's Josh's favorite. Just in case you had any ideas." The singer gave Finn a look that made him feel like a kid who'd been scolded for aiming his slingshot at the butt of a rival classmate. Finn pulled the borrowed guitar closer. No smashing of other people's toys. Just like in kindergarten.

Well, they weren't in kindergarten any longer, were they? And there certainly wasn't a principal to keep him in from recess for not playing nicely.

The floodlights brightened as the group hit the stage, leaving Finn behind.

They stirred up the crowd, introducing him at the last possible second. He saw Hailey's eyes fly open as if someone had goosed her good. His hands shook and he wasn't sure he'd remember a chord, let alone how to rip one up with his uncertain digits. He downed the last of his triple rye and Coke, the burn making his throat ache, and then with a smile hit the stage, hand raised above his head. The band was already playing, and he had to concentrate to pick up the rhythm of "Drooping Flags." Every once in a while he'd fall behind, but the band would slow, add a few extra riffs and let him slide back in as if it had all been intentional.

By the end of the song the adrenaline and energy from the crowd had him keeping up, his fingers moving faster than they ever had back in the cottage. Cell phone flashes blitzed the stage and Finn grinned. They let him take the lead vocals and he gave the lyrics a throaty, rough rendition that brought tears to the eyes of a special gal up front. Hailey looked awed, almost stunned, but her arms remained hanging limply at her sides. She didn't take a single photo.

Damn it.

He wanted her to make money off this act, not Austin. She'd do him justice, whereas Austin would turn him into some fame-hungry monster—and rightly so.

Finn flicked Hailey a quick wink, hoping she'd snap to. Her face turned crimson and she slid her arms around herself protectively, toying with a lock of her long hair. The women around her, thinking the wink was for them, almost fell over themselves. This must have been what the Beatles felt like. Awesome. Indestructible. In control.

The band members crowded around him at the mike, belting out the chorus as if they owned it. Finn grinned. He was singing on stage in a concert. With a sweet group. Was being famous awesome, or what?

The song ended and Finn didn't want to give up the mike. Pumped up from the high, he bounced off the stage, forgetting to crowd surf as he headed for the next best thing: Hailey.

He grabbed her in a bear hug and spun her around, knocking into several people.

"That was for you, Hails."

"Hails?" she said, pushing him away.

"Hail Mary, full of grace, you make me do crazy stuff."

"You can't blame me for that." She shrank against his chest as the crowd squeezed closer, people shouting over the music, congratulating him, praising him, snapping photos. Finn protected Hailey with one arm and smiled, then, snagging her hand, drew her to the back of the crowd. People were still snapping photos, slapping him on the back, making room for them to move. Royalty.

He stopped when he knew he was in line with Austin and his camera. Finn swept Hailey into his arms and planted a massive kiss on her lips.

New rumors would be starting tonight. And if she wasn't going to play his way, he would push her until she realized there was no choice. This was his game and it was time he took control of it.

HAILEY, WARM IN HIS ARMS, felt soft and right. In the midst of his fake movie-scene kiss, something twinged within Finn, and he drew her closer. Brought her right in. Nothing fake. Nothing held back. He caught her sweet mouth under his and deepened the kiss, putting all the emotions and excitement of the moment into what he was doing. Hailey trembled and drew back, sucking in air. In her blue eyes he could see her world spinning. It was all up to the universe. They were on a path that wasn't their own.

And one that would likely get him slapped if he listened to his cock. Instead of cringing and waiting for it, he blocked her by leaning in, setting off sparks in her eyes as he dipped in for another kiss. And another. Meanwhile, he ran his hands over the hot, smooth skin of her arms and shoulders, across the silkiness of her dress to the sides of her breasts, feeling her, getting to know her, letting her know it was all right to release her passion. That he would reciprocate.

Finally, she slipped her arms up his chest and around his neck, giving in. He spun the two of them so she was pressed against a wall, maximizing contact as he breathed her into him while they kissed. He was falling into a rabbit hole. One he hoped Hailey would enter, as well.

When would he find a knee in his groin?

He closed in, blocking her just in case. He could barely believe she was tuning out the blaring band, the crowds, the catcalls, everything, and letting herself go free. With him.

His body responded to all the potential a strong woman like Hailey could bring and he ground himself against her. She let out a moan as she pressed against him, asking for more.

Oh, this was getting hot. They were going to have to move somewhere private. Soon.

He ran a hand down her chest, and suddenly she was out of his arms, leaving him propped against the wall, forehead pressed to the paint. She was a female Houdini.

Turning, he pulled her back to him by her hips, cupping her butt cheeks with both hands. She shoved him away, and as he moved forward to catch her again, he walked straight into the slap he'd predicted five minutes earlier.

"Back off," she said.

The women gathered around them gasped.

His hand went to the stinging flesh and he barked, "Hails, what the hell?"

Her hands were bunched into fists and she looked like a bull about to charge. At him. For going too far, too soon. Too publicly. For making her feel passionate and sexual. For being too much.

He didn't know whether to run for cover or wave a red cape at her.

Standing tall, he cornered her again. "You deserve to feel sexy and wanted."

She let out a twisted laugh. "Just because I'm not famous and fake doesn't mean I suffer from poor self-esteem. I have boundaries, you know. And one of them includes not being groped and pawed in public."

Shit.

He'd known that following his cock would get her walls up and maybe push her into revenge via some juicy tabloid photos, but damn. Seeing her look so hurt and disappointed in him was horrible.

She pointed a finger at him. "I mean nothing to a man like you, so don't play games with me, Finian Alexander, because I know when Hollywood calls you back I'll just be a pleasant romp in your memory for about the five seconds it takes to forget me. Meanwhile, I'll be here feeling humiliated for letting you treat me like a piece of meat in front of my whole hometown."

He held out a hand, aware that the audience was hanging on to their every word.

"Hails, come on."

"Don't." She whipped her arm away from him with a glare and stalked down the plank flooring, faster and faster, until she was outside.

Gone.

"Want a shovel? That's a pretty big hole you're digging with Hailey." Austin stood beside him with a large smirk that Finn wanted to wipe off his face, knuckles up.

Chapter Five

Finian Alexander was a jackass. How could she have forgotten that? How could she have let him touch her, all hot and full of longing, and with a passion that made her muscles weaken? Right there in public, with Austin snapping photos. Hailey was going to be just like all those other nameless women with his paws all over her on the front page of *Celeb Dirt!* How had he managed to sweep her up and make her feel special and wanted, when he was so obviously a jerk? She was embarrassed. He'd turned her into a ravenous vixen who wanted to fling him down on the first available horizontal surface and use her teeth to pull the clothes from his body.

Was it the panic of losing everything? Or was he really that irresistible? No, it was his job to be irresistible and sexy, not live in reality where things like emotions mattered. She needed to remember who he was.

But Heaven help her, the way he'd sung her favorite song with that catch in his throat…it had made it that much more meaningful. As though he had grabbed everything from deep within her and pulled it up and used it to make her feel things she'd never felt before. Like he understood. She fought off shivers and chided herself. That was a silly idea. There was no way she had anything in common with a bad-boy movie star.

That was why he was a rising star. He could make women swoon. Even her.

Sighing, she turned her car into the marina parking lot just down from her house and untied the 1970s Boston Whaler that had been in the family for years. The boat wasn't much, but its basic barge-like structure with no cabin was perfect for hauling things out to Nymph Island. She headed out, swiping at the tears streaming down her face. She told herself they were just from the wind hitting her and that she wasn't upset about Finian. Or the fact that Austin had been shooting pictures of them getting hot and heavy, and totally out of control. That one slip-up would be smeared all over the planet by noon tomorrow.

She was a fool. The one thing she'd told herself she wouldn't be with Finian.

Oh, how Cedric would be laughing at her. *Can't get the story? Try creating it.*

Finian Alexander Gets It On with Local Girl.

She wiped the damp crease by her nose and sniffed as she slowed down near the shallows on the leeward side of the island, reveling in how calm the air was.

How had Finian managed to untie a piece of her she always kept under lock and key? How had he slipped under her skin so simply and easily?

But his mouth had felt so right against hers. She'd wanted to push his head down, down, down, and let him spread its heat elsewhere on her body. She choked back a sob. She never acted like this, felt like this. Ever.

No man had ever made her hands shake, just from thinking about the way he'd looked at her with burning desire. Made her knees feel as though they'd lost their strength. And he was a movie star—a man who could, and would, have just about any woman he wanted. He was famous because he could make an average woman feel like a queen. Passionate. Wanted. Needed. Lusted after.

It wasn't real. Could never be real. He was playing his sex appeal games and she'd be a fool to think anything of it. Hailey needed to photograph his troubled side, not feed it. She needed to dig into his layers and…

She needed to stay away. Far away.

She moored her boat at the cottage and sat on the dock, feet in the cool water. It was quiet except for the gentle slap of water on at the underside of the dock, and she closed her eyes and tried to center herself.

She wanted Finian. She wanted money. She didn't want to give up the cottage despite her mother's permission to do so.

But there was no way Hailey could have what she wanted. She was going to lose. Big time.

An owl shrieked, sending shivers up her spine. She eased out a long breath. Across the water, Baby Horseshoe Island sat in the dark, despite it being a long weekend and having a camp for teens on the far side. But because of the high property taxes, she knew many couldn't afford to take the long summer vacations they used to in Muskoka's heyday and that the nonprofit camp had been struggling for years. It was increasingly rare for a family to spend the whole summer out here. Even those who could telecommute.

She sighed and turned to gaze up at the green cottage looming in the dark behind her. How long would it take for Nymph Island to sell? Who would it go to? Would they love it and appreciate its rustic charm? Or would they do like the new owners of JoHoBo across the strait, and renovate the cottage to the point that its heritage and history were completely eliminated? Even the name —a combination of the original cottagers' children, Joanne, Hoskin, and Bobby—had been changed, to Missy's Getaway.

Still in her bare feet, Hailey walked up the long, winding dirt path to the cottage. She unlocked the door using a hidden key, and tugged a note off the clip she'd nailed into the old wood door so visitors could leave messages.

She flicked on a battery-powered light and read the note from a family wondering if the place was available for rent. Hmm. There was an idea. What would a place like this go for per week? She did some quick calculations and realized that even if she rented it out for a crazy amount, it wouldn't be enough to save the island. But it might help. She looked around the kitchen with a critical eye. It had been added on to the back of the cottage in 1960, the old outdoor kitchen having collapsed after a particularly heavy snow year. The whole place would need a bit of cleaning before being rented out.

Carrying a lantern, Hailey walked through the cottage's four bedrooms. The sisters would have to remove their personal effects, which wouldn't take long. The furniture was ancient, but could almost be considered antique. Add that the bathroom still had its original claw-foot tub, and she could sell the place's rustic charm without a problem. A quiet getaway where you could unplug in order to reconnect.

Upstairs was a massive attic that served as a big playroom for Tigger, and held four more queen-size beds. The alcove and small deck, which held a small table and two chairs, wasn't typical in many of the older cottages, and lent a nice openness to the upstairs. The place might not have a large-screen TV or air conditioning, but it had charm in spades.

She returned to the motorboat, inspired by her new plan. Once she was out from around the island and within reliable cell phone range again, she used her phone's screen for light as she dialed the number off the note, hoping she wouldn't be getting the Walkers out of bed.

She introduced herself to the man on the other end of the line. "I apologize for calling so late—"

"No problem," he said in a delicious British accent. "The neighbors at this resort are so loud we won't be sleeping for at least another two hours. My wife, three kids, and I really want to get away from town and chill out on an island if at all possible."

"How many days?"

"Three days, two nights. We'd like to stay tomorrow night and the next."

"We could swing that." She'd have to do a hell of a lot of cleaning between now and then as well as confer with her sisters—although did it really matter if they knew? They'd want to come out for their annual Canada Day picnic since they'd been rained out today, but she could tell them the place was being fumigated and that they had to stay away. Then she wouldn't have to explain or argue or defend the idea. She could just go forward and get this problem solved and move them closer to keeping the cottage. "It's fairly rustic...."

"That's fine."

"No air-conditioning. No television. A generator, solar panels and a battery for power."

"Sounds perfect. Would we have the whole island to ourselves?"

"Yes." She told him the price and closed her eyes, fingers crossed, barely daring to breathe.

"Does that include a boat?"

She scrunched her eyes even tighter. "Yes. You can use mine. But no meals."

"Great. We'll meet you at the marina tomorrow at two."

Grinning, she docked the boat and got into her car, feeling lighter. She had a decent backup plan. The rental money wouldn't go far, but added to the proceeds she'd hopefully get from

Simone's show and she'd be getting somewhere. Plus she'd resume her plan of getting Finian in the tabloids—without her attached to his lips.

Her phone rang and she quickly set up her hands free to take the call. Maybe someone had spotted Finian doing something dumb and she could spin over there and make a mint.

"Hi!"

"You sound happy," her mother said.

"Mom. Is everything all right?"

"Of course it is. I was just calling to tell you the fireworks were great. Best seat in the place."

"Oh, good." Hailey glanced at the sky and pulled out of the parking lot. She'd totally missed the fireworks.

"As well, I was thinking."

"Oh?" She held her breath.

"I think it's time to ask your sisters for help."

"What?" Hailey nearly drove off the road.

Her mother had been so clear and insistent over the past five years that the cottage shouldn't hold her sisters back from what they really wanted in life, knowing it was a burden and that caring for it might mean them not following their own paths. At the time Hailey had been honored that she was chosen to be Nymph Island's main caretaker, but over time she'd become slightly resentful of the burden, yet also strangely protective of it. But now, to let them in on how bad things were because she'd muffed up hardly seemed fair.

"I know I asked you to take care of the place and keep them in the dark on a few things in order to keep the situation simple and easy. But I never dreamed how much the taxes would increase. Or the inflation on maintenance. I'm sorry for placing it all on your shoulders, Hailey. I can see now that it wasn't fair. However, you've still done a good job with what you have and I'm proud of you."

Hailey pulled over to wipe the tears from her eyes.

"But it's time to involve your sisters."

"What good will it do? They don't even have enough money to help cover this year's tax bill."

"Have you asked?"

"I've hinted that the cost has gone up, and everyone kind of goes pale and freaks out a little. Besides, Maya and Melanie just got out of school. Their jobs are crappy, and Daphne is trying to save up to take Tigger to Disney World. I can't just ask them to give me every penny they have when we might lose it all."

"So, then. Tell them it's going up for sale."

"I think the cottage was meant to stay in our hands, Mom." Why else would Finian have noticed her? Invited her out? Strutted about The Kee like a peacock? It was a sign. A sign that Hailey could do this on her own. *Then* she could bring her sisters in. She was the eldest, and the only thing in need of saving was the cottage, not her. "I'll save Nymph Island by August 30."

"It's time to accept help, Hailey. Don't be so stubborn and proud."

"I can do it faster on my own."

"Will the sacrifice be worth it? To you? To your relationship with your sisters?"

"Don't worry, Mom. I have everything under control."

HAILEY SCANNED THE ONLINE tabloids. Nothing. As she'd told her mother last night, everything was under control. Apparently even more than she'd realized. She grinned at her luck and leaned back, taking a sip of her black coffee. Austin hadn't sold the story of her and Finian getting it on at The Kee. Thank goodness.

But then, if this was a good thing, why did she feel deflated?

She shook off the sensation. She had work to do. She wasn't some teenager needing validation; she was an adult in need of serious cash. Like, over half her annual income.

Early that morning she'd taken the boat back across the still waters, removing or tucking away personal effects in the cottage, as well as scrubbing her way through the old building. In a few hours she would be escorting the Walker family out to Nymph Island, but in the meantime she had some serious Finian stalking to do. That, and selecting the photos she wanted to show in Simone's boutique.

After checking her watch, Hailey ran a brush through her hair. She didn't know where Finian would go today or what kind of transportation she would need to follow him, but she guessed he'd stick close to land. Grabbing her camera bag, she glanced in the mirror and adjusted her sundress, then reached for her car keys. It was time to exploit the soul-kissing faker.

She parked her car near Finian's resort and took the boardwalk along the lake, contemplating the marsh at the end, where he'd said he'd seen a spotted turtle. The animal was rare. Like him.

"I want to apologize for being too forward last night."

Hailey whirled, tripping over her loose flip-flop. Finian. Damn him, but it felt as though he found her as often as she found him. And she was the one supposed to be doing the stalking.

He caught her easily, helping her regain her balance. His hand remained on her arm and she tried not to lean closer, to get a whiff of him, to feel his body heat.

"Can I make it up to you?" he asked.

The man still hadn't shaved. Or maybe he had last night before going to bed, and had permanent stubble. She hated how it made his eyes smolder in a way that was entirely too sexy and irresistible. How it weakened her resolve to be a cool bitch who was all about profit. Pair that with how his soft cotton shirt was clinging to his muscles, and she wanted to do a lot more than just capture him in digital.

Hailey plunked her camera bag on a nearby bench and placed her hands on her hips. "You're ridiculous. You know that?"

"I try your patience?"

Damn his pleading look. It made her want to comply, to run a hand down his rough cheek and draw his fine mouth to her own, as well as test the strength of those corded arms.

"Everyone tries my patience." She turned away. She needed to get a grip on herself.

"Wait. I'll walk with you."

Hailey stopped short, a laugh on her lips. Mr. Movie Star sounded so *nervous*. Not smooth or confident. Hot damn, if that didn't make her want her to peel off the layers to see what was at his core.

No. She needed to keep a professional distance. He was an actor. He could apologize and act sincere and still be a jerk. She needed to stay reserved and analytical, so when he shed off those layers she was ready and waiting with her camera. Her camera. Oh hell, she'd left it on the bench. She shuffled back to retrieve it, wondering where he was planning to walk her to. She was supposed to be *following* him. She'd been playing the paparazzo role for a whole minute this morning and she'd already messed it up.

She needed to get back to photographing nature. It, at least, didn't turn around and follow her, and if it ever did, it always resulted in great shots.

He caught up with her in a few long-legged strides. "I was wondering…your nature photos?"

"What about them?" She tried not to let interest and hope creep into her voice. What if he wanted one for his home in Beverly Hills? What if he wanted to pose nude in—whoa…stop right there. Not professional. And not nature the way she usually captured it.

"Do you need a picture of that turtle? That rare one?" He seemed hesitant. Much different from last night, when he'd been cocky and sure of himself as he'd pushed past her limits. "I know where one is."

"You didn't catch it, did you?" She crossed her arms and glared at him. Visions of the endangered turtle swimming in the bathtub at his cottage, looking for a place to climb out and rest, made her breath hitch.

"Do you really think you are the only person on the planet with a brain?" His cheeks had gone pink, and she shifted her weight, staring at him.

"So? What is it you want, Finian? Shouldn't you be doing something asinine for the tabloids instead of trying to tempt me out into a marsh?"

The kindness in Finian's eyes changed, as if he was putting up walls, becoming someone else. "Do you want to see the turtle or not?"

Of course she did. She was a nature photographer, and endangered animals were her prize subjects.

She swallowed and met Finian's eyes. "That's not a euphemism, is it?"

He let out a laugh, so deep and rich it sent tremors up her spine.

Forgiven.

"Why do I have a feeling you're cooking up something shady?" she asked, stepping closer.

"Because you believe what the tabloids tell you." He gave her a bright smile, slightly cocky and bold as he lifted his eyebrows in challenge.

"And why shouldn't I?" She crossed her arms. "Last night you pretty much proved you'd do anything for attention."

The look he gave her was primal and intense. "Are you referring to the attention of my adoring masses, or just yours?"

She wanted to shake him off, feeling claustrophobic as though he'd moved in on her. In reality, he was still a polite distance away and there was no reason for her breathing to be all choked up.

"I'm not interested in gracing the Internet after a night out with you, sporting nothing more than my bra and panties, and strewn across your brawny half-clad body in a public place. Not my cup of tea."

Oh, my. Why did that sound so hot and tempting?

"But it's so much fun." He leaned in, his proximity teaching her body a thing or two about physical attraction and how rich it could be. How strong. Demanding. Natural. And a little something that should be answered to. Right now.

She rested a hand on his chest, blinking to clear the haze of need that flowed through her.

Again, it was no wonder why he was famous.

Hailey straightened, distancing herself as a crowd of women approached and began cooing and fawning over Finian. With grace, he autographed their shopping bags, and then one woman's stomach, his gaze flicking to Hailey as though making sure she didn't sneak off on him.

She turned away, breathing deeply. She needed to focus. She was here to expose his raw underbelly. A celeb gone wild and out of control. Not the real man she saw glimpses of and wanted to get to know.

"Come with me." Finian grasped her elbow, pulling her away from the women, his body tight to hers.

"Where?"

"Trust me?"

"Not a chance."

"Come with me anyway." He flashed her a grin that brought a twinkle to his eyes, and she allowed him to lead her away.

"THEY'VE BEEN SUNNING themselves out here all week," Finn said over his shoulder. He felt like a kid sharing a cool secret with a new friend, hoping she'd be suitably impressed.

The sun felt wonderful on his skin as they skipped from rock to rock through the marsh, just off the small thoroughfare that ran through town.

"It's later than I usually come out, but we might be in luck," he added.

Come on, turtles. Don't make a fool of me.

He jumped to the next rock, turning to hold out a hand to Hailey, who had her unwieldy camera bag slung over her shoulder. She made the leap, grabbing his hand for the landing, her flip-flops looped through the fingers of her other hand, her sundress bunched up to keep it out of the way of her long, slender legs. He couldn't help wondering how strong they were and how they'd feel wrapped around his waist as he…

Wow, this sun was getting to him. His mind was so far in the gutter it would be a miracle if she didn't slap him due to the vibes he must be giving off.

As she moved to the next rock ahead of him, her bag threw her off and she waved her arms frantically to regain her balance.

"You need a backpack," he called, landing beside her and resting a palm lightly on her waist. He liked this game. So many reasons to touch her, get a feel for her body, breathe her in and thrust his fantasies into high gear.

"The one I want is overpriced."

"By how much?" She needed a backpack. The way her bag was swinging and throwing her off balance it was a miracle she hadn't landed in the murky water.

"How'd you discover the turtles?" She turned to check how far they'd come.

"Training. How much are the bags?"

"Training?" She glanced at him with a puzzled frown.

He shrugged and held out his arms. "I have to stay in shape for my roles. It's nice to find something to do outside."

Tipping his head back, hands on his hips, he relished the feel of the sun. This was the life. He smiled at Hailey, his vision bleached from the sun. "Come on. Leaping from rock to rock is good exercise."

Finn took off again, letting out a whoop when he almost fell in, overestimating the distance between two rocks. He heard a laugh behind him and turned to see Hailey shaking her head as she carefully followed his route.

"I can take your bag if you want to try."

"I'm fine." She clung to her shoulder strap, eyes lowered as she eased past him, cheeks flushing as their bodies brushed against each other.

He wanted to run a hand up her arm, kiss her again. But glad that she was still talking to him despite last night's wandering hands, he decided he wouldn't push it. Instead, he'd suffer through the brush of her sweet ass against his crotch as they moved past each other on the rocks.

"So what do you do for entertainment?" he asked.

"Watch your movies," she said with a sly wink.

He stood on a rock, assessing her. Was she kidding? Mocking him? Or revealing a secret obsession? "Very funny."

"You have no sense of humor," Hailey retorted. She let out

another laugh and gave him a playful shove, before catching him so he didn't fall in the water.

She held him near, their eyes locking. He swallowed hard. He knew how she saw him—as irresponsible, full of bad judgment and lacking in impulse control. A man looking for trouble. He'd bet anything she wanted to take him down a notch.

He smiled at her, again resisting the urge to kiss her. Finn could handle her trying to take him down a notch. Anything she did would be just fine by him.

They broke eye contact and resumed moving through the reeds, his mornings sprints over the rocks paying off in nimbleness. Moments later, Finn stilled and held out a hand to prevent Hailey from passing. He crouched and pointed. There on a rock was a spotted turtle, looking ancient and wise, its beady eyes staring straight at them.

Hailey edged closer, her hair wild from the breeze, her gaze focused and intent. She grabbed his arm as she caught sight of the distinctive reptile sunning itself at the water's edge. It looked as though it was communing with a higher order.

"I can't believe it. You know how long I've been looking for one of these?" she whispered. "And there it is, sunning itself with the wisdom of the universe right on the edge of town." She turned to him, eyes full of wonder.

Finn shifted and cleared his throat. It was one thing for him to think the turtle was wise and connected with the universe, but to hear someone else say it out loud…well, it made him uneasy. "You'd better take a picture before it takes off."

Without a word, she let go of his arm and began digging through her bag, matching up camera and lenses, her cheeks pink with excitement.

For a turtle. Finn sighed and scrubbed a hand through his hair. Eager to remain close to her, he resisted placing a hand on her shoulder in case he began caressing the soft, sun-warmed skin. Instead, he brought his head close to hers, as though trying to capture the view she was lining up. He let her curly, out-of-control hair tickle his face as he inhaled the sweet scent of her fruity shampoo.

He wondered what she'd do if he slipped the strap of her dress down to get a better glimpse of the way her chest rounded out before her perfect B-cup breasts. She was so petite, his hands could explore a lot of territory in one small move.

She shot him a frown over her shoulder.

Right. She was creating. Needed head space, physical space. Not some horny dude breathing in her feminine scent and fantasizing about her breasts. *Got it.*

He forced himself to step back onto the rock behind her, watching as she dropped into a squat, lining up her shot. Finn almost laughed at the thought of himself sitting on a rock in a mucky marsh in Canada, excited about sharing a rare turtle with a chick who needed to be introduced to a hairbrush. Some bad boy he was turning out to be.

"My sister Daphne is going to go nuts over these."

"Why?"

Still hidden behind her camera, Hailey whispered, "She's a bit of an environmentalist, and has been trying to prove these creatures live in the area. She's been working on stopping a development across the lake. The spotted turtle is sensitive to water pollution. Big developments bring disturbance, an increase in traffic, and of course, more boats, which means more water quality degradation. All of which is bad for these guys."

"Huh."

So Hailey got off on real-life issues. Who knew? Finn had plenty of those. Such as promises made to charities that he might not be able to keep. A brother who had died in his arms in a gang war. Another brother who'd flipped a switch with only Finn to bail him out.

He stood and tried to catch his breath as memories flooded over him. After twelve years the pain had barely dulled. He tried to focus on the conversation, his voice thick and tight, defensive. "Don't get me wrong, turtles are cool and all, but honestly, would anyone even notice if they went missing from the amphibian lineup?"

She turned to him, eyes round, mouth open.

"Kidding."

Grumbling something he couldn't quite hear, she changed the lens on her camera and took several more shots.

He stared at the sunning turtle. It was like him. Supposedly rare, but would anyone really notice if he went missing from the movie star lineup? Not likely.

"Sorry if I sounded like my sister," Hailey said. "But when you see something as beautiful as this and know it is endangered because its home has become our playground..." She let out a sigh loaded with what sounded like guilt.

"Why does that bother you?" Finn asked, half listening, half caring.

She held up the LCD display on her camera so he could see her last shot. He looked out to the real turtle, then back to the camera. How did she make *that* look like *this*? *That* was boring. *This* was introspective. Her photo had somehow managed to capture exactly how he felt staring at the turtle when he was here alone, lost in his thoughts. Finn took a step back and just about into the muck. He knew from experience that the marsh water looked clean, almost pristine, but there was a helluva lot of deep mud at the bottom. He'd already lost one shoe in here and didn't want to lose another—especially in front of Hailey.

"Nice. Ready to go?" He needed to get out of here. Go be a

badass. Create a new, fictionalized drama. Keep moving forward. And definitely squelch the urge to kiss the serious look off Hailey's face.

He rubbed his stubble in irritation. What the hell was *wrong* with him? How did she keep getting under his skin, jabbing at the places he'd tried to kill off when he entered show business?

He needed palm trees, plastic smiles, and false everything. Not this. This was too real. Too...*feeling*.

He plunged both hands through his hair and trudged back over the rocks, trying to shake off the emotions that assailed him. He needed some decompression time, naked with some bimbo, that's all.

It wasn't Hailey. It was him. It had been months and he was in a weird head space. It didn't help that she was teasing him in a push-pull game, and he was a man in transition. Hell, that was why he'd come here. He needed to sit and chill and not think. He needed peace so he could glide into the next stage of his career. Otherwise he'd get redirected from his goals.

"I'm going to be a while," she called, her soft voice distant.

He paused. What? She'd had her shot. She was like the director for *Desperate Cowboy* who'd kept demanding retakes when he almost always used the first take in the end. Why did Hailey want to hang out in the heat and take more photos? Was she punishing Finn? Trying to gain the upper hand?

This whole "creating" thing she was doing made him uncomfortable. He needed to go to a bar. Art wasn't his deal. Not anymore.

It was going to throw him off.

"I'm leaving," he said, his voice gruffer than he intended.

"Jealous of a turtle and all the attention it's getting, huh?" She straightened, her eyes shaded by her free hand. She came a few rocks closer, moving carefully. She lifted her lens, fired off a few shots of him standing peeved on a rock. In Canada. Great. Good luck selling that to the tabloids. It was time to find a real paparazzo.

"I'm not wearing sunscreen," he snapped.

Without looking, she reached into the bag resting against her hip and flung a bottle at him. SPF 60.

Ever Miss Practical.

"I'm going to move over that way and see if I can get some head-on shots. Maybe catch it swimming. Thanks for bringing me out here."

"There are no rocks that way."

She shrugged.

"What about the eggs?"

"They're not in the open water, Finian." Hailey rolled her eyes.

"And leave you out here in the sucking mud? What if you drown?"

He could barely believe she was dismissing him. Didn't she know who he was? He was Finian Alexander. A movie star. You didn't dismiss him after he showed you the thing you'd been seeking for years. And you sure as hell didn't casually snap off a few shots as if it was a joke. You would pay at least as much attention and care to him as you did to the turtle. "You can't stay out here alone."

"You sound like my mother," she said, her tone odd.

"You ever heard of a hairbrush?"

"Really like my mother," Hailey muttered, her tone flat. She self-consciously drew her curls into a bunch, twisting them into a knot, her cheeks pink again. She stepped off the rock and waded through the marsh to face the turtle. What was wrong with this girl? She was dealing with mud between her toes and indeterminable squishy depths for a turtle. A freaking turtle.

Dammit. She was making Finn feel like a girl. Out in a marsh waiting for someone, being ignored. Insulted. He didn't like it. Not one bit.

"Your mother's a smart woman," he called.

"Watch what you say." Hailey sloshed through the marsh, and in the process scared the turtle into the water. She lowered her camera, her face hard, the hem of her dress wet.

Good. She'd missed her shot and was pissed at herself. And him.

Hands on his hips, he smiled, waiting for her to turn to him.

"You're a big jerk, you know that?"

"Yeah, I do. It's been amply noted by the general public."

She splashed toward him, her head cocked to the side. "And yet you are so proud."

"Damn straight. It pays the bills." He shook his head, sighing as he held out a hand to help her out of the muck. What was it about Hailey Summer that always pulled him between two worlds, and made him ruin her mood? Not meeting her eye, he wrung out the hem of her dress so the moisture wouldn't spread. "Your feet stink."

"You need to shave."

"You need to kiss me." He grabbed her and, in the middle of the marsh, showed her just how under his skin she'd gotten.

Chapter Six

By the time Finn pulled Hailey out of the marsh he was ready to take her back to his cottage and run his hands over her body and through her hair—hair that was surprisingly soft and fine, causing all that fly-away business he so often saw. He wanted to finish exploring all that potential he'd felt under her dress last night at The Kee.

He was practically dragging her as she laughed, stumbling along as they hit the dock, his eyes on his small cottage still yards and yards away. She'd let him kiss her again, her mood turning, her playful side coming out like a ray of sunshine.

A car peeled up beside them as they cut across a small parking lot, and Finn tugged Hailey behind him, afraid the paparazzi would distract her and dampen the mood they were building. He hustled her along as a woman, half hanging out the silver minivan's window, hollered, "Did you get it?"

"Get what?" he asked suspiciously, keeping Hailey hidden behind him.

Hailey shoved him aside, yanking her camera out of its bag. "Sure did."

Seriously? "Um, we have plans," Finn said pointedly. Specifically, consenting adult plans, and this soccer mom with the hippie vibe was totally going to dampen the mood.

The woman, who had the same petite frame as Hailey but seemingly without the height, waved a hand burdened by massive rings. "Show me."

Hailey moved to the van, holding out her camera's LCD.

"How the hell do you know about the turtle already?" Finn demanded.

"Hailey texted me," the woman stated.

"Oh, Finian, meet my youngest sister, Daphne," Hailey said, without glancing his way.

She could barely give him the time of day because of that damned turtle. What had he been thinking taking her out there?

"Nice to meet you," Daphne said, her eyes on the camera's screen.

"Yeah, pleasure is all mine," he muttered. Sulking, he took a few steps away to see if Hailey would notice. Nope. Not even a glimmer that he was missing.

He was definitely feeling like a means to an end right now. He turned to face the breeze coming off the lake, eyeing Daphne out of the corner of his eye. She was a modern-day hippie, wearing lots of beads and an embroidered smock. Add in the fact that her silver Dodge Caravan had a bright red flower painted on the hood and plastic flowers wrapped around the antenna, and it was pretty obvious she took nature as seriously as her big sister did—more so, seeing as Hailey was looking for turtles for her.

Derek would be laughing his ass off right now if he knew who Finn had chosen to be his paparazzo. Yet the way the two sisters appeared to be opposites gave Finn hope. Maybe Hailey would find him—an opposite—just as intriguing and worthy of helping as she did her sister. And if not, it wasn't exactly horrible hanging out with her.

"You found this?" Daphne asked him, looking up at last.

"The turtle?" He ran a hand through his hair and tried to act casual. "Yeah. Why?"

The van door was flung open and he found himself being hugged by what resembled a python. Every time he tried to exhale Hailey's sister squeezed tighter, until he couldn't breathe at all. A smaller creature that he could only imagine was her offspring hugged his legs with all her might. Just when he thought he might actually pass out from a lack of oxygen, they released him, as if by unspoken agreement.

Finn inhaled and steadied himself. That mother-daughter team could take out unsuspecting spies with their killer grips.

The offspring began bouncing around on the asphalt, her fluffy party dress flouncing as she sang, "Mommy found the spotted turtle. Mommy's going to save them." She paused to give Hailey a hug for good measure, then climbed back into the van. Clicking the seat belt across herself, she announced, "All ready, Mom."

Panic slipped under Finn's skin as Hailey slid the little girl's door shut and climbed into the passenger seat beside Daphne. She couldn't just leave. They had unfinished business. They were about to go to his cottage and get it on. He was going to convince her to work with him.

But the women weren't even talking, they were moving as though this was all part of some prearranged plan.

Hailey had found what she wanted and was ditching him. The idea left him with a surprisingly hollow feeling that echoed throughout his being.

"Well?" the hippie asked him.

He stood on the asphalt, feeling like a third wheel.

"Are you coming, or what?"

"Where?" He glanced at Hailey, and knew that it didn't matter what the answer was, he was going where she did. He climbed in next to the child bouncing in her booster seat.

"You'll see." Daphne pulled out of the parking lot in a move that would make most soccer dads hard with desire, and had Finn falling out of his seat.

"You might want to buckle up, mister," the young girl said. "Mom's like a race car driver. And they wear helmets."

STANDING IN THE PUBLIC PARKING lot near Bala Falls, Hailey nervously ran her hands through her hair, accepting an elastic from her sister. Thank goodness Daphne and Tigger had come along. Hailey had become so swept up in Finian's kisses in the marsh that she'd forgotten herself. And that would have been a complete failure seeing as she wasn't supposed to be exposing him to the tabloids in a kiss-and-tell sort of way.

She wrestled her hair into a ponytail, the humidity of the warm day making it go nuts. The only thing worse was January and February, when she wanted to shave her head rather than deal with the static electricity that made her hair stick to her face.

"Don't break it!" Daphne squealed, just before the taut elastic snapped in Hailey's grip. "Why do you always pull it so tight? That was my last one."

"Sorry." Hailey grabbed a silk scarf from the front seat of the van and tied it like a headband to keep her hair at bay. Why hadn't she used product like she had for her date at The Kee? Oh, right, because she didn't want to be noticed by Finian. That had worked well.

Out on the rocks he'd cupped the back of her neck while kissing her, his hands delving into her hair in a move that had made her fall against him, eager for the contact.

Some self-restraint she had.

She snorted, and turned to find Finian standing in the parking lot, listening to Tigger with rapt attention. Her niece took advantage of his focus, talking faster and faster, as though she expected him to suddenly look at his watch and declare that she'd used up her allotted talking time for the next two days.

Instead, he let the girl take his hand and lead him into the throng of Daphne's people who were enjoying a picnic before they launched their protest.

"They keep saying a parking lot isn't a heritage site," someone said as Hailey passed them.

"Those rocks..." added another.

"What are we doing here?" Finian asked through closed lips as she drew nearer.

"This? This is the picnic and protest I was trying to duck out of." She checked her watch. She had a little more than two hours until she had to meet up with the Walker family at the marina. It was going to be tight. "I'm supposed to take photos for Daphne, but I have to be somewhere soon. Help me out and tell me if you see something that would look good in a pamphlet."

"Like that human pyramid?" he asked, pointing to five protesters who were wobbling and laughing as they tried to stack themselves into a vertical triangle.

"Sure." Hailey swung her camera up and took a few shots. "What else, wingman?"

He pointed to the protest signs leaning against a picnic table. He picked a wild daisy from the tall grass near the edge of the park and laid it across the top of the table.

"Nice eye," she said. This was going to be easier than she thought. With Finian's help she might make her appointment with the Walker family with time to spare.

"Oh, my God, you guys!" Daphne squealed to a nearby group, and Hailey moved closer, raising her camera to capture the excitement in her sister's dancing eyes. Daphne paused, holding everyone's attention as she hauled Hailey and Finian over. "You'll never guess!"

The group pushed forward, eager to hear her news, whispering to each other.

"Is Finian Alexander our new spokesperson?" one woman squealed.

Finian flashed Hailey a panicked look.

"No, Liberty, he's not. But this man..." Daphne pulled Finian as close as possible. "Found..." She let the anticipation build. "... the *spotted turtle!*"

The crowd gasped, their round eyes focusing on Finian.

"Here! In Muskoka!"

People squeezed in on him, a thousand questions flowing in rapid-fire succession.

"And Hailey got photos of it!" Daphne called above the noise.

The crowd surged toward Hailey, who held her camera bag against herself for protection, looking for a way to escape.

"The spotted turtle lives in Muskoka!"

The group began moving toward the parked cars, excitedly making plans. Hailey exhaled in relief. There was nothing like being squished in a mob to make a woman feel claustrophobic.

"Wait!" They all stopped moving and fell silent as Daphne held up her hands. "We can worry about that tomorrow. Today we have this." She flung a hand with flourish to the *Stop the Hydro Electricity Plant!* sign hanging above the protest picnic. "Tomorrow the turtle."

The protesters refocused, heading back to the tables.

"Wow. If I ever need crowd control, I'm calling your sister," Finian whispered in Hailey's ear. She smiled and nodded. Her sister was definitely using her powers for good.

Her smile faded. Oh, damn. She'd just hauled Finian to a rally. She was supposed to be introducing him to drug dealers and tempting him with street racing, not *this*. She was also supposed to be stalking him from afar.

She sucked at being a paparazzo.

Daphne gave Finian a tight squeeze that made his cheeks flush. "Thank you, Finian Alexander. Now, let's set you up with a veggie dog. You must be hungry."

"*Veggie dog?*" he mouthed over Daphne's head, making Hailey laugh.

Her smile froze when she spotted Austin at the sidelines, carefully lining up a shot that had Finian in front of the protest signs.

She quickly tugged Finian in the opposite direction and pressed her body against his, distracting him so he wouldn't turn around, giving Austin the shot.

Being a good paparazzo was much harder than she'd realized.

OKAY, THIS WAS GETTING ridiculous. Everyone was all over Finian, and Austin was everywhere. He was going to scoop her, leaving her with nothing. Hailey didn't think Finian had seen Austin yet, as he was still smiling as if he was king of the world. Although who could blame him? He was a friggin' hero for finding the turtle. Plus, he was sexy and irresistible, and definitely worthy of being the center of everyone's attention. But what was she, the one with the photographic evidence they needed to stop the development—chopped liver?

She inhaled, trying to settle her frustration.

Okay, all right…it was jealousy ripping at her, pure and primal.

And it wasn't because Finian was the only one getting the credit. It was about all the women fawning over him. Which was a silly waste of energy. There was no reason for Hailey to feel jealous or possessive. He was a sexy movie star, so of course women fawned over him. She was just some girl with a camera.

She held her heavy camera against her shoulder and looked around it at the way Finian was grinning that big perfect smile, as if he and the fawners were the only ones at the picnic. She inhaled a shaky breath, watching how he gave each woman a light touch as he turned to chat with her. Nothing too intimate or encouraging, but enough to show that he wasn't passing her off. That he was listening. Caring.

Hailey ducked behind her camera again and fired off a few shots, struggling to keep her cool. It should be *her* receiving his smiles and touches. *Her.* Not random women who were supposed to be marching around shouting "Heck no, we won't go."

She swung her lens a few feet to the right, to zoom in on Austin who was looking frustrated as some large hydro power trucks lumbered between his hiding spot and Finian. She smiled and turned her attention back to Finian who was now giving out cheek kisses to the group. Why wasn't he kissing her? He wasn't even looking her way.

With deliberate moves, Hailey set up her tripod, barely refraining from breaking its legs. What was her problem? It was as though she liked him or something. She glanced up at Finian again. Oh, hell. He was looking her way. She gave him a weak smile, grabbed an organic drink from the picnic feast to her right and jammed the straw down inside the juice box. He started to come over and she fumbled with her setup, aiming her camera in random directions, snapping shots that would likely be out of focus, as she tried to act natural.

Her heart tore into action, pumping harder the closer Finian came.

Be cool. It's okay. He came here with you. Of course he's going to stop by and say hi. He doesn't want to be abandoned here without a ride back, that's all.

"Hi," she said, as he grabbed her around the waist, his gaze focused determinedly in the distance. He pivoted her and pulled her along with him and she barely managed to snag her camera, still attached to its tripod, as he hurried them to the edge of the group. He didn't stop moving until they were hidden under the branches of a weeping willow. Then he released her, ran a hand through his disheveled hair and let out a "whew." There were bags under his eyes she hadn't noticed earlier. For all the fun he'd seemed to be having, being mobbed, it appeared, had drained him instead of filling him with energy like playing at The Kee had.

Last night he'd been jazzed, with waves of alpha excitement and energy coming off him, and Hailey had been a sliver too close to taking him to bed because of it. The only thing that had stopped her were thoughts of her sister Daphne, and more specifically, Tigger. Of how her little niece had come to be during a one-night stand with a summer boy after a Kim Mitchell concert at The Kee.

Add in the fact that Hailey had had her heart broken by a summer boy—a man she'd thought was different from the rest—and she was a little too sensitive about summer romances and the way Finian kept drawing her into his sights.

On the flip side, he was hot, intriguing, and his attention was totally flattering. Plus she needed him to want her near so she could photograph him when he finally showed his wild side.

Finian stretched out in the grass and yawned.

She stood above him, watching him tip his head back, eyes closed, content. He was so different from her in almost every way. His life was on autopilot. No cares. No worries. It was a miracle they even spoke the same language.

"What?" He opened his eyes, and she dropped to the ground beside him, feeling unsure. Finian reached over to run a hand down her bare arm, giving her the shivers. "You look bothered."

She flashed him a bright smile. "Nah, I'm fine." She scanned the area. "Where's Tigger?"

"With her mom," Finian said, without glancing around. Sure enough, Tigger was bouncing along beside Daphne, her fancy dress swaying in time with her movements. In fact, the girl was bouncing more than usual—vibrating, really.

"Ah, crap."

"What?" Finian mumbled, his eyes drifting closed.

"Someone gave her sugar."

"Is she diabetic?" He sat up abruptly, his eyes wide as he sought out Tigger in the crowd.

"No, she just gets hyper. She'll be fine. Once we scrape her out of the clouds."

"She said it would be okay."

Hailey laughed and shook her head. She reached over and tapped Finian's nose. "You were scammed by a five-year-old."

"I'm losing my edge."

"Her mother restricts sugar like it's cocaine, so she's developed ways to get treats from unsuspecting people in order to get her fix."

"Interesting analogy." Finn shot Hailey and enigmatic look.

"Yeah, well."

They both stretched out on their stomachs.

"Are you an addict?" she asked quietly.

"No, but I know people who are. Or were." Finian swallowed hard, his eyes filled with pain.

"I'm sorry." She laid a hand over his and he met her gaze.

"For what?"

"For causing that expression on your face."

The sounds of the crowd grew in the background. It was getting close to protest time.

"Does your sister do these sorts of things often?"

Hailey nodded. "She views protecting Muskoka's environment as her duty."

"I can see why the two of you get along."

"I recycle, choose products based on their impact on the environment, and drive a car with a small carbon footprint, but I'm not Daphne. I mean, I go to more protests than the average Joe, but it's not my thing in the way that it's hers. It's not a major part of my identity." Her attention was drawn to her sister, commanding the growing rally with vim. "But I'd do anything for my sisters."

"I meant that you both step in to take care of others."

"My houseplants are all dead."

"Funny."

"Not really. I feel guilty every time I look at them."

"But it seems like you feel responsible for a lot." His face scrunched in a frown. "Never mind. I'm probably projecting."

Still on her stomach, she locked eyes with him. There was a lot going on in behind those amazing blue eyes of his, and she didn't have a clue what it was. There was a layer in there she hadn't managed to unearth yet. She saw glimpses of it right now, but it kept vanishing. Was it an act to up his appeal and intrigue, or was it something real he was trying to hide?

"You need to have more fun," he said at last.

"And what would you suggest?" she said with a laugh, adding a hint of flirtatiousness to her voice, hoping to see his hidden layer again.

He hunched forward on his elbows, the shade of the tree dappling his torso. "Come here." His voice was low and full of meaning.

Rolling her eyes, she leaned forward so their faces were closer.

She was playing along only so she could snap pictures of him and his version of "fun." Nothing else. She wasn't curious. She wasn't into him.

Right.

He watched her until she began to feel self-conscious. Was the dappling sun making strange shapes on her face? She shifted to pull away, but Finian pressed his warm lips to hers, gently grabbing a lock of her hair to keep her close.

He was doing it again. Pulling her in, drowning her in feelings she'd only read about in romance novels.

"Hey, lovebirds."

Hailey snapped away from Finian, feeling guilty for being the stupidest woman on the planet by falling for his moves. Again.

But damn, he was a fine kisser and it felt so real.

She snatched the protest sign from Daphne and, without looking back, hurried off to meet up with the rest of the group.

"And you, hero boy," she heard Daphne say to Finian, "if you're good and wave this sign for the next half hour, I'll let you come to our cottage picnic tomorrow."

Oh, crap.

Hailey turned to see Finian nodding and smiling. Not tomorrow. And there was no way this man was ever going to see their cottage.

"Been in the family for four generations," Daphne was saying, as Hailey made her way back to them under the tree. "It's almost in its original state which is very rare for a cottage of its age," Daphne added.

"I'd love to see it."

Hailey thrust the sign back at Daphne. "I forgot I have to be somewhere. And the picnic is off. Trixie Hollow is being fumigated this week." She turned to glare at Finian. "I think it's time you stop following me around."

It was time he learned who was stalking whom.

Chapter Seven

Finn held his phone away from his ear and winced. Derek was pretty much ready to sell him out to the first women's hygiene company to hint at an offer that he do a commercial.

"You're not Angelina Jolie, you understand that? You can't pull off this 'save the world' crap."

Finn inhaled, knowing if he shut up and let Derek blow off steam his agent would get over yesterday's protest a heck of a lot sooner. Although shutting up certainly hadn't worked with Hailey at the protest. She'd suddenly gone from all kissy under the tree to running away, and Finn couldn't figure out why. He'd totally kept his hands off the goods this time.

In the end, he'd watched her hoof it across the park, her sister hot on her trail. He'd seen them have words before Hailey had taken off to someplace where girls went to have a hissy fit on their own, and Daphne had reappeared to give him a long and silent ride back to his lonely little cottage. Once there, he'd sat on the deck overlooking the lake, and drunk enough beers to give himself a headache come morning. All night he'd wondered where Hailey was and if she'd seek him out again.

Which was what pathetic losers did.

And apparently, he was as pathetic as they came, because her words about him not following her had hit hard. All night he'd wondered how many of their "bump ins" had been his fault. Did she really think he was following her around? Because his feeling was that it was *her* following *him*.

He half listened as Derek strived to rant and rave Finn down to the size of a gnat.

"You can't go around waving Save the Whales placards."

"I think it was for a heritage site and a hydro electric thing," Finn corrected, rearranging little sunflower candle holders on the mantel of his cottage fireplace.

"You just undid months worth of work with this stupid stunt. I thought you knew better than this, Finn. A lot better. I thought we shared the same goals."

"We do."

"I have three kids to feed and an ex-wife to support."

"I know." Finn let out an anguished sigh. This was supposed to be the easy life, not him in the middle of a web where if he bounced hard enough everyone else fell off.

"You have charities depending on you."

"I'm aware of that." He shut off his mind as he moved to the table to tap through the links and images Derek had sent him. Finn knew damn well how spectacularly he was failing; he didn't need help feeling just how deep it was.

The photos that had made it online last night were ones of him looking cozy in idyllic Muskoka. Enjoying himself. Content. Kissing Hailey.

His heart squeezed tight and his protective instincts hit the red line. His hands squeezed into fists and he cursed whoever had broken into her private life like that.

"How'd they get that shot of Hailey?" he demanded.

"The girl? Come on, Finn. You know nothing is private."

But this was a private moment between the two of them, and she wasn't a superstar kissing him for attention. She was trusting him every time she let him get close, and he'd broken her trust by letting his life invade their world. And he knew better. A whole lot better.

This was no longer about stirring her up so she'd go paparazzo on him, but something else. Something he couldn't figure out. Maybe the beginning…the beginning of what?

"And for Christ's sake, Finn," his agent said, voice tired. "If you're going to roll in the hay with a local, tell her to brush her hair—she's going to be in the papers."

"It's the humidity, Derek. It gets frizzy."

"Don't you dare go falling in love with some nobody, you hear me?"

"I'm not in love." He stared at the photo, unable to peel his eyes away. It was a beautiful picture and definitely one to keep.

He sighed. Hailey didn't need the world on her because her hair wasn't perfect, because *she* was perfect. The world wouldn't understand. The world wanted fake perfect. You could be anyone as long as you were glossy on the outside.

Finn needed to find Austin. He needed to tell him to back the hell off, because Hailey wasn't equipped for Finn's world and he wanted to spend more time with her—out of the limelight.

He flicked to the next shot. It was one of him holding hands with Hailey's niece. Tigger's face was so bright and open and trusting. Not knowing he was a man ripping down the tracks of self-destruction and that he'd just ripped away her anonymity, thrusting her into the mean old eyes of the public gossip circles.

What had he done to Hailey and Tigger?

Finn continued to stare at the photo of him with Tigger. He looked like any guy his age out in the world, finding his place, as well as happiness, family, and friends.

Not the image he'd been working toward, but somehow it still felt right. This tightness in his chest left him when he was with

Hailey and her family. The tightness he hadn't even known he'd been carrying.

"Last time we talked, you said you had things under control, Finn."

"I do."

"This is not under control."

"Give me more time."

He banged through the rest of the photos. What about images of him in the alley looking for a joyride? Him on stage at The Kee? Outshining the band everyone had paid to see? Why weren't they here?

"How much more time?"

"I've got a plan. I just need a little time with the Canadian paparazzi."

Derek laughed. "There is no Canadian paparazzi. I'll send someone in."

"I've got this, Derek." An edge was slipping into his voice. "These pictures are barely anywhere, and this is just a ripple of intrigue. I know the world isn't ready for this kind of turnaround in my personality and way of living, but this is…this is the setup, okay? Trust me. The world will be waiting for me to mess this up."

"And you will."

Finn nodded, head bent low enough that his chin grazed his chest. He would.

But this time it was going to hurt.

FINN WIPED THE SWEAT from his brow, leaping from rock to rock, the reeds slapping at him as he went down his now-familiar path through the marsh. He was already faster than he'd been earlier in the week. More nimble, too. A few more days of this and he'd get the starring role for *Ninja Fighter*. Then he'd make it.

Just one more movie. That's all he needed to set him up where he wanted to be. Then everything would be easy. Everything would fall into place.

Taking a wild leap, he soared through the air, landing on both feet. Forced to bend low to keep his balance, he hovered over the rocks, pumping his arms. He could sense the power in his muscles and knew the exercise would make him feel great for the rest of the day. Well, until he caught up with Hailey and tried to convince her to be his. His personal paparazzo. Not *his*, his.

Because her as his paparazzo—even though she seemed peeved at him—was the only way to go without either pairing up with Austin or leaving Canada. And Finn wanted more downtime.

But what would she do when he showed up again? Accuse him of stalking her? Slap him? Kiss him?

He stumbled and recovered, moving on through the cattails from rock to rock, disturbing birds whose sudden flight no longer fazed him. Great training for his reflexes. He was ready, ready, ready.

Nothing could faze him. Nothing could throw him off. He could have ten ninjas jump out of the reeds and he'd stay strong, not wavering in his straight line to the docks and boardwalk, which were approaching in less than twenty strides.

Fifteen.

Ten.

Finn skipped a rock, moving fast, arms pumping. He glanced up to judge the distance he still had to cover.

And there she was. Hailey.

He missed the third last rock and splashed into the marsh, his momentum throwing him into the water, where he sank to his elbows in the muck.

"Finian?" Hailey's voice drifted over to him, curious.

Embarrassed, he pulled his hands out of the muddy ooze, surprised they didn't make a sucking sound.

"Hey," he said lightly, rolling onto his back in the shallow water, letting its coolness wash away his heat.

"You weren't disturbing the turtles, were you?" She stood on the edge of the wooden boardwalk that connected to the docks, hands on her hips.

"Just taking a nice morning swim."

"In your running gear?"

"I was hot."

Hailey rolled her eyes and turned away. Hot damn, she was a vision today. It was as though she'd received a memo from his agent about her hair. This morning it was smooth, silky—even better than it had been at The Kee. All that fine hair hanging low on her back, a slight wave to it that shimmered in the sun. Her legs looked longer and sexier from his water-level vantage point, too. He was going to have to stay in here for a while to hide his growing erection if he didn't distract himself.

He scrambled onto the dock, focusing on her hair. As amazing as it looked cascading down her back, he kind of missed the wildness of her berserk curls. He scraped muck off his watch face, hoping it was not only water resistant, but also marsh bottom resistant.

Beyond Hailey, a man who had to be a reporter was talking to Daphne and Tigger. Finn's heart lifted, as did the corner of his mouth. Perfect. He liked reporters. And male reporters were almost always ruthless about revealing dark secrets and bad behavior. Female reporters only sometimes—but he usually had to have a one-night stand with them first. Finn's attention drifted back to Hailey. She'd made it pretty clear she wasn't interested in that type of thing. Which meant if he did take it that far…well, then maybe she'd blast him in the tabloids. But probably not. And anyway, he had other things in mind first.

He studied the local reporter, all crisp in his ironed shirt and neat haircut. Eager for something bigger than this small town.

Finn jiggled up and down to shake some of the water off himself. He still had lots of mud stuck to him—hardly a great look—but maybe he could pick a lover's spat with Hailey and get the reporter to catch her slapping him or something. Finn could line it up so she'd have her back to the camera and could stay anonymous, but he'd be in the news and she'd have her privacy.

He sidled up to Hailey, assessing the situation. She didn't move away.

Would she forgive him for picking a fight?

Man, he was losing his edge. That was the last thing he should be worried about. Or even care about. They were both playing a game for money and fame. Surely she knew the stakes. She wasn't just some girl who appeared around him all the time with a camera. She couldn't be. She had to be waiting for her moment. In other words, she was stalking him as much as he was now stalking her.

He turned to her, wanting to touch her hair.

"Over your snit?" he asked.

She frowned and moved two steps away.

"What were you mad about, anyway?"

"Just..." She let out a sigh and looked the other way. "You wouldn't understand."

Suddenly, he was hit in the midsection and squeezed so tight he had trouble breathing right. "Whoa there, Tigger!" he gasped.

The girl pulled away, her face wrinkled in disgust. "You smell, Finian. And you're all wet."

"True and true. Did you know my friends call me Finn?"

"Fin? As in what fish use to swim?" She gave him a doubting look as if to say *Why on earth would you let people call you that?* "People call me Tigger, but my real name is Kim."

"And why do they call you Tigger?"

"You gave me sugar, you figure it out."

She flashed him a sly smile, and he laughed and gave her that one.

He pointed toward Daphne, who was still talking to the reporter, but was starting to come their way. "What's your mom doing?"

"She's talking to Rick. Did you and Auntie Hailey have a fight?"

He glanced up at Hailey from his crouch. She was ignoring him, her arms crossed as she stood outside the circle Daphne and Rick the reporter had created near the water's edge. "That's a good question."

"I ask good questions. Why'd she leave the picnic yesterday?"

"I think she was ready to go home."

Tigger shook her head. "She always says goodbye to me."

"Oh. Sorry, kiddo."

They both turned to study Hailey, who looked pretty, but had smudges under her eyes.

"She looks like she needs a friend, Finian Alexander." The five-year-old wrapped her arms around his neck, apparently no longer caring that he was wet.

"She does." He sighed to himself. There went his plan to get her mad at him for the reporter. It seemed that was the last thing she needed. "What's the interview about?"

"About the turtle you and Auntie Hailey saw."

"Are they going to try and save it or something?"

"Public awareness is the first step," Tigger said seriously.

Finn gave her a light hug. She felt good. Warm. Full of life. It made him want to have a whole houseful of kids. And of course, a wife who loved him. Really loved him.

"You're a smart cookie, you know that?" he asked.

The reporter moved closer, his pace increasing as he recognized Finn.

Finn lightly pulled Tigger's arms from around his neck and stood, preparing himself.

"Finian Alexander! Rick Steinfeld." The reporter pumped his hand enthusiastically, then snapped a few shots of Finn at close range. "I heard you were in our neck of the woods. Let's get some of you together." He pushed Hailey into the shot. She was frowning at Rick as if he'd just placed her in someone else's family Christmas photo.

Finn slung an arm around her, drawing her close to his wet body. This girl really needed to lighten up. She'd probably never gone photobombing—incredibly cool when you were as famous as sin.

Oh wait, they were the ones who'd discovered the turtle. No photobombing required here.

He grinned at the camera and noted Hailey was shooting him a peeved look while trying to lean away.

"So, you told him about us, huh?" he said through the smile he kept aimed at Rick.

Hailey tried to shrug out of his hold. "There is no us, Finian."

"Us finding the turtle together. But if you want another kind of us, I can probably oblige you. I think you'd enjoy being the girlfriend of a famous man once you got a taste of it."

Her cheeks flushed and he pulled her closer.

"You're so full of yourself."

"You could be full of me, too, if you play your cards right." He shot her an over-the-top seductive wink and waited for her to get physical. To his surprise she broke out laughing. So much for the reporter catching her shoving him into the water or slapping him.

She bit her bottom lip, her mouth stretched into a large grin. "Does anyone ever stay mad at you?"

"You were mad at me?"

"You're all wet." She pushed away, looking at her now-damp outfit.

"I'm worth getting wet for." He shot her a lewd smile.

She laughed and gave him a massive shove that caught him off guard. Some ninja-ready actor he was.

"Where do you store all that confidence?"

He put on his best Austin Powers voice, thrusting his hips towards her. "Do I make you randy, baby? Do movie stars make you horny?"

Her smile faltered and she sighed, stepping away.

"Oh, come on. Where's playful Hailey? Why so serious? Life is fun and easy."

Her eyes flashed as she crossed her arms over her chest.

Now they were getting somewhere. That spark in her eyes. Kill him, but it made him want to push all her buttons.

Naked. In bed.

He cozied up to her, ready to take their beef to the next level. The one where they fell on each other and caused fireworks with their heat and passion. Oh, yeah, mark his words, she'd be a wild thing in bed.

"I heard you found the turtles?" interrupted Rick.

"What?" Finn struggled to pull his focus from Hailey. He gave her a last look as if to say, *We're not done here, sexy woman. Oh, yes. You will be mine.*

"Daphne said you found the spotted turtle."

"Yeah." Finn sized up the man. He looked about the same age as Hailey, and he hoped Rick wasn't another ex-boyfriend. Finn didn't need another man around that he wanted to kill on principle.

"You found it with your girlfriend, Hailey?" Rick looked from one to the other, pen on his notepad, lips ready to smile. He flicked a lock of hair out of his eyes and flashed a thumbs-up at Hailey, who seemed about ready to slap him. Oh, man. Maybe not an ex if he didn't know to clear out when that look came down the pipe.

"Yeah, my girlfriend." Finn put an arm around her shoulders.

"We're *not* dating." Hailey's eyes flashed as she flicked his arm off her.

"You don't want to be associated with me now?" he joked, his voice low and sultry.

"You're not my type and I'm looking for more than a fling."

"You think I'm not capable of something other than a fling? I just came out of a year-long relationship, I'll have you know."

"On the rebound. Even more not my type."

Finn faced Hailey. "What is your problem with me?"

Hailey brushed him off and addressed Rick, "I have photos of the turtle and Finian simply—"

"We'll pay you the usual rate for those, Hailey," the reporter said. "Make sure they're suitable for the paper. None of that artistic crap." Rick waved her away and Finn could see the man had stepped on her pride. He was so getting slapped. If not by Hailey, then by Finn.

"So, what's the scoop between the two of you?" Rick looked from Finn to Hailey again.

Finn opened his mouth, but Daphne pushed her way between them. "We're having a rally for the turtles on Saturday. We want to stop the Oakview Estates planning meeting. We can't let them go ahead."

"Right." The reporter made notes. "So, Hailey, what was that photo in the tabloids about?"

"What photo?" She stared at him with a blank expression.

"The one of you and Finian kissing?"

Finn met her eyes. Uh-oh. His get-Hailey-pissed-off-so-she-reveals-you-in-the-tabloids plan might take off earlier than expected.

HAILEY STRODE AWAY from Rick and Finian, resisting the need to break into a run. Daphne blocked her on the boardwalk, hands on her hips.

"I'm sorry," Hailey blurted, realizing she'd inadvertently stolen the limelight from Daphne's cause—the whole reason they were here in the first place. She'd called Rick this morning to interview Daphne as a favor, and as a peace offering to her sister for the way she'd taken off from the picnic—even raising her voice when Daph wouldn't let her flee to go let the Walkers into Trixie Hollow.

"What's up with you? Your moods are all over the place."

"Sorry. Just stress."

"And him?" Her sister pointed to Finian, palm raised. "One second you're looking like you want to drag him to bed, and the next punch him."

Yeah, that about summed it up.

"He gets under my skin, that's all." *And gets me in the tabloids, evidently.*

"I'll say."

Hailey turned away from Daphne and dug her fingers into her waist, hunching forward. Why was everything so difficult? This was supposed to be easy. How was she going to blow up Hollywood and take that cocky life-serves-me expression off Finian's face if Austin was going to pop up and scoop her every time? How was she going to catch Finian doing wild and crazy bad-boy things if she was always hanging off his lips?

She wasn't cut out for this. She hadn't even snagged a photo of him on stage at The Kee.

She strode over to the men, determined to set Finian straight and get things back on level ground.

"Rick, you came here to talk to Daphne about the turtles, so, Finian, you should kindly go finish your jog or swim or whatever you were doing."

The reporter opened his mouth and Hailey shot him a look.

"And Finian, I'm not your girlfriend."

"Okay."

"You can't call me your girlfriend to reporters." When she turned to Rick, shooting him another look, he smiled and tipped his head, then headed off to catch up with Daphne.

"Can I still kiss you?" Finian asked. He took a step closer, and panic pierced Hailey's muscles, making her want to flee. Was he going to kiss her right here? Right now?

He was near enough that she could smell the muck on him. Damp and earthy.

"You're wet and you stink."

"You did something new with your hair." The way his voice was soft and kind, it was easy to forgive him way too quickly. In fact, she couldn't quite figure out why she'd been so peeved a few seconds ago.

Hailey smoothed a hand over her hair, bothered and flattered that he'd noticed the extra effort she'd put into it. Oh, who was she kidding? She'd driven all the way to Bracebridge to get new hair product last night, when she should've been prepping her photo show.

"You're just too damn likable, you know that?"

"I try."

"That's so bad boy."

"Yeah." He swallowed and looked away.

She rubbed the bags under her eyes and sighed. She needed an injection of caffeine. Or an injection of life, at the very least.

"Known him a long time?" Finian asked.

"Who? Rick? Yeah. Since high school."

"Another ex-boyfriend?"

"No. I worked with him on the school paper. Austin, too. After graduation Austin fled to Hollywood to make it big, Rick went to McGill, and I...I stayed around."

Hailey hugged herself, wishing she could have gone somewhere exciting and wonderful instead of sticking close to home and backfilling the holes in her photography knowledge with online courses, books from the library, and tips from other photographers kind enough to help her out while she struggled to get her family through their days.

She let out a long sigh. She needed a miracle to get her life back on track.

Finian sidled closer, his breath warm on her shoulder. She had to fight the urge to lean into him, to pull comfort from his presence.

"I should hate you, you know that?" she murmured.

"Why?" He looked hurt.

She shrugged. "I don't know. I've been trying to figure that out."

"You're a complicated duck, Hailey."

She stared at him. There was just something about him that not only messed her up inside, but also calmed her. Maybe she needed to stop fighting it. Whatever it was.

"Come work for me," he said.

"What?"

"What?"

"I'm sorry?" She shook her head. It sounded an awful lot like Mr. Movie Star had just offered her some sort of job.

He gave her chin a gentle chuck. "You Canadians apologize a lot."

"I'm sorry, but we do not." She placed her hands on her hips and squared off. Realizing she'd apologized, she let out a soft laugh, her anger gone like a drop of water falling on a hot skillet. Her laughter turned into guffaws. "Are you the only handsome and charming one in your family or are there others?"

The angles and shapes of his face were arranged as though someone had the camera in mind when they'd created him. If the whole family looked anything like him, a group portrait would be stunning. A photographer's wet dream. Not that he was asking her to be his personal photographer. He probably had something menial in mind, such as answering fan mail or styling his hair.

"Are you asking if I have a brother? Because you never answered my question," Finian said, his eyes serious.

"Work for you?" Her laughter bumped up a notch.

"Yeah." He crossed his arms, his broad shoulders widening as though the indignation of her laughing at him was puffing him up. "I saw the pictures you took of the turtle. If you can do that for an ancient-looking reptile, I can only imagine what you could do for a guy like me."

He gave her a cocky grin, but his eyes were flat. There was something there that looked an awful lot like longing playing peekaboo behind his amusement and teasing. But it couldn't be. Guys like him didn't long for women like her. What the hell kind of trick was he trying to pull?

He was confusing. One minute lighthearted. Then it was as if she'd done something wrong joking about a brother. And now there was longing. And hurt. Fear of rejection.

Hailey didn't have time for mind games and men jerking her heart around.

She cast her eyes downward, giving his crotch a shrewd

assessment. "I'm sorry, but if you want to get back together with your ex-girlfriend, you're going to have to take selfies. As I've said, I'm not that kind of photographer."

HAILEY PRETENDED SHE DIDN'T NOTICE Finian come up to her car, laughing at the way she'd stalked off. Instead, she kept her head bent, reading text messages from her network stating they'd seen Finian near the lake here in Bala. Her system was working even if she seemed to be invisible to everyone, considering she was out here *with* him.

And why did that make her feel so frustrated, angry, and put out?

And why did she just act like a raving bitch and intentionally misinterpret his sincere job offer? What was wrong with her?

Finian's shadow crossed her lap and she flicked off her phone's screen. She gripped the steering wheel as he crouched beside the car, arms crossed on the door frame. He smelled good. Even under the marshy scent.

She blinked back tears. Why did he have it so easy? Why couldn't it be her?

Ignoring his presence, she started the car, its power steering belt squealing. Add another item to her list of things she couldn't afford.

"Can I tell you what I desire?" he asked her.

"There are 1-900 numbers for that."

She bit her lip and blinked long and hard. Resisting his appeal was turning her into a bitch. She needed to stop slapping him, stop saying things that weren't like her, and cease running away from him every time they got close.

She turned to face him. He looked amused, if anything.

"Why don't you think I'm a bitch?"

"Who said I don't?"

"You continue to talk to me, and yet every time we meet I say something awful and run away or else slap you."

He shrugged, his arms still crossed on her door. "I'm from Hollywood. Standard behavior."

"You're kidding, right?"

"Hailey, you're not a bitch. It's me, okay?" He looked away, his eyes dark. "Don't go twisting yourself into knots for a big jerk."

"See?"

"What?"

"Useless jerks don't say nice things or care about other people's feelings."

"They don't?"

"Nope."

"All the more reason I need your help, don't you think?"

He smiled, his eyes lighting with humor. No matter what she said to him or how many times she'd slapped him, he responded with forgiveness or a smile. It made her want to crawl out of her car and hug him just for being him.

Heaving a sigh as if she was doing him a massive favor, she said, "Okay, fine. What's the deal? What do you *desire*?"

She held on to her steering wheel for support and turned to face him when he didn't speak right away. The proximity of his bright eyes was too much. The way they shone and delved into her soul, whispering to her secrets, coaxing her into feeling okay…it was unnerving.

She didn't want to see that unless she was behind her camera, protected.

"What? What do you want from me?"

"I have a feeling you can give me something the rest can't, Hailey."

Chapter Eight

Freshly showered and wearing clean, dry clothes that he couldn't help wishing was an Armani suit to wow Hailey, Finn climbed into her old car, after securing a bag of wardrobe changes in her trunk. He still couldn't believe she'd agreed to take a few head shots. It wasn't his full-on paparazzi proposal, but that could come soon enough. He needed to play this through, slow and sure.

He smiled to himself. There must be some dazzle left in his crooked grin, after all.

Plus two birds, one stone. New pics for Derek to hand out to his peeps, and Finn got to keep Hailey close enough that maybe he could finally figure out which button to push to get her to play paparazzi.

He frowned as he buckled his seat belt. Of course Hailey hadn't played paparazzi yet. Around her he'd been like a puppy asking for a belly rub. And when he'd stirred her up enough to make her slap him, he was simply being a jerk and not a celebrity worth noting.

"Are you paparazzi?" he asked.

She choked in surprise. "Am I what?"

"You know." He made camera clicking motions. "Paparazzi."

"Do I look like I am?"

"No, not really." He slouched in his seat and took in her slight frame. Her lower lip protruded in a pout as a pickup truck pulled out in front, almost cutting her off. The determination in her eyes as she floored the rattling car in order to pass the guy surprised Finn and he let out a chuckle. She fixed her attention on the rearview mirror and kept the car pushing up a hill.

"Good." She finally answered when they reached the top.

"You don't want to make a lot of money?"

"Everyone wants to make a lot of money," she said quietly.

Finn ran a hand over the dusty, faded dashboard. "You need a better ride. I can practically see the ground whizzing by through the floorboards. And the way this thing is rattling, you'd think it was a space shuttle breaking through the atmosphere."

"Some of us have to actually break a sweat in order to earn something like a car."

"What's with that chip on your shoulder? Do you think I was born with a silver spoon in my mouth? Because I wasn't."

She flicked her attention to him for a moment before returning it to her new favorite, the rearview mirror.

"Well, you sure act like you were."

"That's because I'm somebody special." He winced and inhaled the car's dusty smell. He couldn't stop being a jerk, could he? Outside, tall trees and waving grass fell away suddenly as they blasted through an impossibly pink granite rock cut. "I'm sorry I sound like an entitled prick."

Hailey's attention flicked to her mirrors again. "Sorry."

"For what?"

"For what I almost said."

"Do you always look this antsy and serious when you drive?"

"Only when I'm trying to ditch Austin Smith."

Finn turned to glance behind them. "Good luck. You'll never lose him."

"You've obviously been hanging out with the wrong kinds of drivers." She raised an eyebrow, a naughty smirk dancing across her lips, and his blood raced, ready for action.

She floored the old car, rocketing around a corner as she poured on the gas down a sudden open stretch. Farmland in the middle of what he'd believed was all bush and water and massive rocks.

She flew through an intersection and Finn braced himself as other drivers honked at them.

"You know it's okay if he takes pictures of me, right? It's kind of what makes a movie star's world go round."

"Don't worry. I know what I'm doing."

"I'm sure that's what Princess Di's driver said, too." Finn sent a cautious glance through the rear window. Austin had had to slow down at the intersection, his balls evidently not as large and steely as Hailey's.

She spun them onto another paved road. Unprepared, Finn failed to brace himself in time for the momentum and force of the turn, and fell against her. He swallowed bile and wished his headache would go away.

She shot him a look.

"Sorry," he said.

The road dived down a steep decline, where the ditches were thick with trees again. Hailey lurched into a hidden driveway, throwing gravel as she took the sharp turn. She performed a perfect brake turn at the bottom, spinning the vehicle so it was aimed back up the drive, but out of sight of the road. She threw the car in Park and rolled down her window.

"Wow." Finn's heart was racing so hard he'd fail a stress test. He forced himself to pry his left hand off the dash and his right hand off the "holy shit" handle near his head—a grip usually reserved for old ladies struggling to exit the passenger side.

None of the stunts he'd ever done in his career had scared him like this. Those scenes had been strictly choreographed by professionals. Not real or completely spontaneous.

A car sped by on the road above—Austin—and Hailey's lips moved as she silently counted to seven. Then she poured on the gas, roared up the driveway and cut back the way they'd come, leaving the other photographer behind.

As they hit the main highway, Hailey kept pushing the speed limit. "He'll guess where we're going, so I need to get the car hidden and us tucked away before he shows up. Otherwise he'll pester us all day. He can be quite unrelenting."

A spark of protectiveness Finn usually reserved for family members ignited a blaze of jealousy. "What? What did he do?" Had Austin pestered Hailey into something she didn't want? She'd said they'd dated, and the prick had said he'd kissed her first. Finn had managed to block that image out of his mind, but now it was all he could see. Austin kissing Hailey. Austin being pushy with her. Being an unrelenting jerk until she gave in.

"Oh, he's just like a dog with a juicy bone. Won't give it up for anything." She waved a hand dismissively.

"I've never seen anyone drive like that before…. Have you had to, uh, lose Austin before?"

"Are you okay?"

"Have you?"

"No, but it was fun." A smile flickered.

Finn relaxed into the seat. Austin was trying to get under his skin, and had succeeded, and Hailey was tired of men like her ex-boyfriend getting in her way of making her own dreams come true. Finn needed to get a grip.

"So? You normally drive like that?" His voice came off high-pitched.

"Yeah. Of course. I often have paparazzi following me." Hailey shot him a grin, her body at ease. As relaxed as after he'd kissed her under the tree last night. Only last night…

"You need to kiss me more," he said, letting his hand trail a line over her shoulder.

Hailey cranked the wheel, then straightened it just as suddenly, gasping as she avoided hitting a steep rock cut where the road zipped between high walls of pink-striped Canadian shield.

"Sorry," he gulped. "I'll preface something like that next time, so your surprise doesn't kill us." The sad thing was that he probably wouldn't mind her killing him as long as she was with him in his final moments.

She cleared her throat. "Squirrel. I was avoiding a squirrel." She tucked a stand of hair behind her ear and he saw her swallow hard. "I, um, didn't want to squish it."

He bit back a grin. Oh, this was going to be a fun day of him stripping in front of her for his wardrobe changes. He would play to her every line, and watch her blush and squirm, and loving every moment of it. Before the day was through she'd either be in his bed or selling his images to the gossip sites.

FINN WATCHED HAILEY move around her one-car garage with the confidence of someone who knew where everything belonged. It was a pale yellow, clapboard building with an old, swing-up door. He'd expected her to pull the car inside, but instead, she'd driven right up onto the grass and into the backyard where she'd left the overheated vehicle out of sight. Then she'd led him through the old two-story house, his bag of clothes in tow. As she went, she'd grabbed drinks from the fridge, a package of trail mix and some fruit, popping them in a reusable shopping bag. Other items that he guessed must be props were added to the collection. She moved fast, her actions sure and confident. Finn had wanted to check out her digs and all the photographs hanging on the warm-colored walls, but he could barely take his eyes off this version of Hailey.

She'd then gone flying out the front door, across a wide porch and down onto the lawn, just about leaving him behind. Her place had reminded him of his grandmother's house, where he used to spend his summers, playing dress-up and dazzling her with a new play every evening after supper. Warm, welcoming, and somewhere you felt safe being yourself. Because he sure as hell couldn't be that "pansy acting boy" in the rough place where he'd grown up.

Her small garage studio was like the house, warm and welcoming. Area rugs covered the concrete floor in layers, track lights ran above, extra handheld lights and tripods hung in organized rows on racks and hooks below. The space had been drywalled and painted white. Finn moved toward a large worktable set in the corner, a rack of matting sheets and picture frames stacked vertically to the side. She seemed to be in the middle of a large project, judging by the reams of computer labels, piles of photos, and inventory lists. A large computer sat under a white sheet that she whipped off, showing a snazzy Mac Pro. Next, she moved on to unlock a cabinet beside her computer. It was filled with cameras, lenses, and other gear. She was definitely the real thing if her equipment was anything to go by.

But for a woman who didn't do many portraits, she had exactly what was required. The backdrop, the lights, the tripods.

"You have equipment for portraits?"

"As I said, I do them when I'm hard up for cash. So, yes, I do."

"I'll make sure my assistant pays you promptly."

She stuck out her tongue, thinking he was joking, as she unloaded her ever-present camera bag, tossing battery packs onto their chargers.

This girl was serious, a hard-core pro with a system and a plan. Organized and effective. Exactly what he needed. She would understand what he required. And when the moment was right, he'd present his own plan for what he wanted leaked to the press.

He eased himself into a worn armchair that looked as though it had been built in the 1930s and had seen a lot of sitting. The cushion was saggy enough to pull him in deep, which felt comforting after their crazy ride across the countryside. His headache had been coming and going all morning, but now it was forcing a major comeback. A quick rest here in this chair, head tipped back and eyes closed, would do the trick. That and a glass of water.

Something stirred the air beside him and he opened his eyes, realizing he'd drifted off for a few minutes. Hailey stood over him, camera poised.

"Sorry, I didn't mean to wake you."

He rubbed his hands over his face. Hailey was still perched over him, focused intently on something she saw. Saw on him? Within him?

He wiped his face again in case he'd drooled during his nap.

She crept back, placing her camera on the nearby worktable. She'd set up a backdrop in the middle of the room, the corners of the sheet tied to hooks set in the ceiling. She was ready, and he was the superstar keeping her waiting.

He jumped out of the chair, catching a can of Coke she chucked at him.

"You look like you need a pick-me-up." She leaned against the table, cracking a can for herself.

Not diet Coke. Interesting woman.

"Thanks." He pointed to the Mentos she was eating. "Haven't you seen those YouTube videos where they mix Coke and Mentos to make rockets?"

"I think that was diet Coke."

"Still. Aren't you afraid your head is going to explode?"

"Yeah, like, every day. It's called living on the edge." She tossed him the pack of Mentos and rearranged a few pieces of equipment.

He threw the mints back to her without taking one, and moseyed over to her worktable, waiting for her command. He glanced at her for permission before flipping through the stacks of enlarged images she'd sorted into piles. The first seemed to be "please anyone" shots he'd seen around town in stores, posters, and hotels. Typical stuff the tourists wanted for a memento, such as a windswept tree, close-up of a chipmunk, an old wood boat gleaming in its berth, or a canoe tied to a weathered dock with mist floating around it. All pretty shots, but not particularly original for these parts. In his peripheral vision he saw Hailey lift her camera and focus it on him.

The next pile was still distinctly Muskoka, but the images were slightly more unusual. Another shot of the steamship *Segwun*, but taken from a low vantage point, with some sort of filter to make the great ship appear dominating and brooding. Massive.

He compared it with the bright and innocent shot from the first pile, hardly believing it was the same boat, taken by the same photographer, likely on the same day.

He flipped through more shots, laughing at a photo of a cow. Instead of focusing on its face, nuzzled up close to the camera, Hailey had shot focused in from behind, catching the cow's head turned inquisitively, as if to say, what are you doing back there? A vet would think this was hilarious.

Finn's nature nut had a sense of humor.

She moved the armchair he'd napped in so it was in front of the background. "Ready?" she asked.

"As ever."

She adjusted a few lights as he made himself comfortable in the chair again.

"Are those photos for a show?" He pointed to her worktable.

She nodded, silent.

"I like that your studio is unpretentious."

Hailey blinked at him.

"It doesn't scream *I'm an artist!* It reminds me of a buddy from film school, Bruce."

"Are you still in touch with him?"

"Not really. Not since I chose the more commercial route."

"Do you miss him?"

"Sure. We always miss those we leave behind, don't we?" Like his two brothers. One alive, one dead. Finn shook his head, thinking how much different his life would be if he hadn't chosen to follow the fickle stream of money, and how he'd simply traded one kind of deficit for another.

She stood in front of him and reached up to adjust a light, her knee brushing his. "I'm glad you didn't shave."

He rubbed his chin self-consciously, inhaling her scent. "Actually, do you have a razor?"

"Later. I need some shots of you awake in this thing. Then we'll get into more traditional head shots, etc." She adjusted his arms on the chair, moving him into a take-charge, I'm-in-command position. Hell, he felt powerful and manly just sitting this way. He grinned up at Hailey and moved his arm from where she'd placed it.

She readjusted it on the armrest again. "That desperate for a woman's touch?" she asked, and gave him a playful pinch.

Finn flinched, laughing. "It's like in those improv games where someone else directs your body." He'd always hated them, but for some reason, the way Hailey moved his body didn't bother him.

She was respectful and had that cute, thoughtful expression when she posed him.

"I'm sorry." Hailey stood back. "I could try and direct you verbally, but I don't know what I want yet. Do you mind?"

"Not at all." He flashed her a killer smile and she hesitated, cheeks flushed, before she adjusted his position ever so slightly, her cool hands sure, her touch tentative yet firm.

She vanished behind a large camera, tweaking, making adjustments. She took shot after shot, her physical directing changing into verbal commands as they fell into a rhythm. Her body relaxed and her moves became more fluid.

"That's good, take a break." She finally arched her back and twisted a lens off the camera she'd been using.

"We're done?"

"Nope. But I need to think through what I want next. Do you have a list of specific shots you need?"

He knew the laundry list Derek would want, but couldn't bring himself to interrupt her flow to get stagnant pictures everyone else had. They would be like the pile of commercial shots she had on her table, and he wanted to be in the other pile. Finn wanted to see what she could do. He wanted to be someone who stood out and wouldn't be overlooked. Plus he wanted to know how Hailey saw him.

"Give me something different, Hailey."

"Can do." She finished her Coke, her head tipped back, exposing her long throat.

"I haven't met anyone who consumes sugar in a long time," he commented and she shifted her weight in a way that caused him to apologize.

"Canada's getting to you. That's twice in the past two hours that you've said you're sorry. A new record, I presume."

He laughed and fell back in the chair, his legs splayed. He liked this woman. Liked her wit and willingness to poke at him. None of that skittering about to appease him as some women did.

"So, um, how bad were those shots in the tabloids?" she asked.

"Of us?"

He left the chair, moving closer, trying to figure her out. Was this his chance to ask her to collaborate with him and sell stories to the tabloids? Because right now, those rags felt miles away from this moment. From Hailey. And they were the last thing he wanted to think about.

"I'm tired of trying to stay one step ahead of my reputation," he said. "And I'm tired of having to strategize my relationships with people and commoditize our time into something that can be leveraged in my career." He shook his head and stepped to her worktable. "I'm sorry. I didn't mean to say that. I meant..." He drove a hand through his hair. "Don't pay any mind to what gets printed in the tabloids. The people who truly love you will understand."

"Understand what?"

"All of it."

"What are you saying?"

"What are you asking?"

They stared at each other for a few moments.

"Okay, fine." He crossed his arms. "The lighting in the shot was kind of crappy. And it was grainy, but those kinds of shots are the ones that the audience really goes wild for. They tend to think they're seeing something that's—"

"No," she said impatiently. "I meant, like, was it...*bad*?"

He stared at her, his heart catching. She was afraid to be seen kissing him and didn't want her private life smeared across the planet. She also probably didn't want to be associated with the likes of him. Honestly, he couldn't blame her even though the knowledge hurt worse than being smacked by a microphone boom.

He rested a hand on her elbow and watched her struggle with her emotions. They were flipping across her face, one by one. Fear. Frustration. Curiosity. Maybe a touch of anger and pride, as well.

"I'm sorry, Hailey. I didn't mean for you to be a casualty."

She straightened. "I'm not a casualty. And I'm not a victim. But I don't like being part of some stupid publicity stunt."

He clenched his jaw. "I know that. The photo wasn't my idea."

"And you're not too good for me, Finian Alexander. Your fame doesn't define you. You're just as human as everyone else."

He grabbed her by the elbows and brought her close enough to kiss, not sure what move he should make, only knowing that she'd successfully crawled under his skin once again.

Her eyes flashed as she pushed him away. "Show me the photos. I need to see what everyone in my world is going to be talking about—because trust me, they will be."

HAILEY OPENED A BROWSER on her computer and Finian reached over to take the keyboard, sending shivers up her arm.

"There." He propped himself against the desk, his jaw set, eyes on her.

Slowly, she turned her attention to the webpage.

"Oh, wow." There she was stretched out in the grass, kissing Finian. Her heart raced and excess heat leaked up her throat and across her cheeks.

There it was for the world to see. Her. Kissing a movie star. Like in some romantic comedy where the famous guy falls in love with some girl wishing for a real life. Hailey nearly sighed.

It was a beautiful photo. Yes, a tad grainy, but gorgeous nevertheless.

Finian's eyes roved over her, assessing. "Think how much that photographer got paid."

"For exposing our personal lives." She shoved her chair back, and stood.

He gave her a smile, a glint in his eyes.

"*My* personal life," she corrected.

"If you're with me, Hailey, it comes with the turf."

"I'm not *with* you." She stared at her computer. This was fiction. Not real life. Real life was gritty and full of obligations and duties and burdens. It wasn't being swept away and falling in love. Or, in her case, lusting over a guy who would leave her once his vacation was up, and then never think of her again. "If this was my personal life, it would imply that you and I are something."

"We're not?"

"What's my last name?"

"Summer."

"Okay, that was probably an easy one. Middle name?"

"Something…classic, strong, feminine."

"Rose."

"Told you so."

"What's my favorite color?"

"Something soft, like a cream or light yellow."

"How did you know?"

"The color is everywhere."

"My point is that you don't know me. You don't know what I like. So, pretending that this photo actually means something—"

"I know you like this." He cupped the back of her neck, pulled her body against his and gave her a long, lingering kiss.

Yeah, okay. He was right. She liked that. A lot.

She pushed him away. The kiss—*kisses*—had been errors. Signs of her temporarily leaving reality and getting swept into the distraction that was his life. He starred in movies that distracted people across the world from things like the bills they had to pay and the turtles that needed saving. And that was his life, too, one big, easy distraction, where he always won against the bad guys.

Not her world. Not at all.

"Leaving reality is your thing, isn't it?" she asked. "Acting as if there are no responsibilities in the world?"

"That's my job. Not who I am."

She yanked her hand away when he tried to take it. "Don't you get it? I'm a real person, Finian. Living a real life." Her phone's screen lit up with another Finian-spotting text, and she flipped it onto its face. "You can't just sweep in here and decide that I'm somehow yours. I'm not. And I never will be, because I live in the real world."

He grabbed her hand again, this time more firmly. "I like hanging out with you, Hailey."

"I never said I didn't like hanging out with you, Finian. But that's not the point."

"Then hang out with me." His jaw was tight with an emotion she couldn't identify. There was a sincerity in his eyes that couldn't be faked. Or could it? He hadn't won any Oscars yet, but how could she be sure what was real when dealing with an actor?

He waved an arm to encompass her studio. "This is nice. No, not nice. Refreshing. Real. Genuine. Like you. I didn't realize how much I needed downtime, Hailey. Time out of the spotlight." He flinched, as if struck by his own words. "I need grounding, Hailey." He fell into the armchair, his palms rubbing his face. "I need to touch base and figure out where I'm heading."

She sighed and crossed her arms. She wasn't here to ground him or be his base to touch. As much as she wanted to hang out with him and see if something real happened between them, she knew they were from two different realities and needed different things in their lives.

He needed fame and downtime. She needed money.

She turned away as his cell phone rang in his bag. "I have to empty my memory stick. Please change into something more badass." She glanced at his jeans and T-shirt. "Maybe add some black leather. Oh, and don't shave. Not yet."

She needed a reminder of who he really was. Not this mixed-up man with sincere eyes who liked hanging out with her. He was too tempting. Too *real*.

She focused on her computer, her hands shaking as she began transferring photos to the hard drive. Behind her, Finian answered his phone.

"I know," he said. His voice had a certain reserve she hadn't heard before. Kind of like a husband preparing for a dressing down. She almost turned to look, to make sure his ring finger was still bare.

She slipped to the tabloid page as the photos transferred, hoping Finian wouldn't notice. She took a screen shot of the article and read the headline. Finian Alexander Mending Broken Heart with Local Gal. The one line below simply said, "After last week's breakup with movie star Jessica Cartmill, Finian Alexander takes up with an unknown woman in Canada to distract him from his broken heart."

This was what Cedric had been talking about. Making a story from nothing, because in reality Finian didn't seem to be even a speck brokenhearted. And if he was, Hailey certainly wasn't helping him through it.

She sighed and rested her head on her hands. Damn that Austin. He'd probably gone home with a nice little finder's fee for putting her in the tabloids.

She pivoted, watching Finian. He'd removed his shirt, his new outfit draped carelessly over the old armchair. He was amazing without a shirt on, having the right amount of muscles, and a nice trail of belly hair that led her eyes down to his crotch. His free hand was clenched into a fist and his shoulders were tense, making the muscles flicker under his skin as they flexed. She quietly grabbed a camera, lining up black-and-white shots. The harsh shadows from the lights by his side left striations along his corded arms, the muscles bulging as he fought for control of the conversation, his emotions, or whatever other demons he was wrestling.

The dark side. It was real.

She set her camera on her desk and turned away as he began moving around the room, touching objects, before stopping in front of the stacks of photos for her show. She was dying to know what kept drawing him back there. This was the third time she'd noticed him drift to them.

He rested a hand on the table, leaning over the photos, eyes focused almost as though he was falling into the top image. Or pulling strength from it.

She shook her head. She was reading too much into it. He just needed something to focus on while he listened to his caller.

"I don't care if he can't offer me my usual rate," Finian said. "He's an old friend."

Hailey didn't mean to eavesdrop, but she found herself leaning closer, trying to hear the other side of the conversation.

"I don't think doing something like that would affect where I am on the pay scale. And it doesn't set a precedent. It would be a completely different kind of project. Plus, I happen to think I'm at a point where I can branch out." He paused, then his voice tightened. "I know you are the expert and I pay you to advise me, but last I checked I got to choose my projects."

He gave another sigh, shoulders dropping in defeat, the fight gone. "I know. No, I appreciate you weighing the two sides of an offer. I know. I don't have to say yes, but he's good." Another pause. "Yeah, but I was a nobody once, too, and he's going somewhere. I'd like to help him." Finian was looking at the ceiling now, and Hailey glanced up, as well. Nothing thrilling up there. Not since she'd insulated and transformed this place into her studio, at least.

Finian turned off his phone, gently setting it down. The room was too quiet, but Hailey was afraid to say anything. Finally, he turned to her with a sigh. "You wanted badass?" His voice was laced with fatigue and resignation. He held up a leather jacket. "With or without a shirt?"

Chapter Nine

Hailey led Finian into her house. She wanted to tug the leather jacket off Finian and run her mouth down his bare chest, pry his faded jeans open and…

Whoa! She fanned herself and let him into her en suite to shave for the upcoming shots she had planned.

There was something about photographing a sexy man and having him shoot her smouldering looks that did funny things to her brain. It didn't help that he had a wicked sense of humor and had her laughing half the afternoon, making it almost impossible to take a nonblurry shot without the aid of a tripod.

"Okay, sexy beast, here's some shaving gear."

"Mmm. I like it when you call me that." He slid a hand around her waist and she bit back a smile, trying to hold on to her slipping professional persona. Hailey wanted to turn in his arms, have him lift her onto the vanity, and then grind against him while consuming him with her mouth.

She handed him a pink towel, a pink razor, and shaving cream. She giggled as he held them out.

"You expect the bad boy of Hollywood to use these?"

She grinned. "Real men can handle pink."

"Yeah?" He shrugged off his leather jacket, his eyes on hers.

She broke contact to let her eyes feast on his bare arms, chest, and back. Heavenly.

He filled the sink with hot water, his moves sure and confident, falling into a routine. He filled his left hand with lavender shaving cream, letting out a sigh that made his shoulders hunch forward ever so slightly. "Purple? Really? Are you trying to kill me?"

"I think lavender will look great with your complexion."

He smoothed the cream between his hands, his eyes twinkling with mischief. Her own smile faded and she eased toward the door. *Uh-oh.*

"I happen to think…" He took two steps toward her, traveling into her bedroom to pursue her. "That *you* would look good…" Two more large steps. "…in *lavender*."

She squealed and turned, fleeing into the upstairs hallway to get away from him.

He cornered her there, but she dropped to the floor, crawling between his legs to escape into the nearby sitting room. He turned, just missing her as she scrambled, laughing, into the room, ending up trapped in another corner.

Knowing he had her, he licked his lips, moving slowly. Agonizingly slowly.

Her chest heaved as she waited, giggling, half cowering. With two quick moves, he trapped her hands in one of his and lifted them over her head, against the wall.

Gently, he drew a line of shaving cream down her cheek with his free hand, then leaned back, assessing her. "It does suits your complexion, sugar toes."

"Yeah?"

She bucked halfheartedly against him and he pressed in closer, licking her mouth in a slow, languid move that had heat pouring down through her belly and into the space between her legs. She dropped her head back, and his mouth moved to her neck, kissing, nipping, and holding so much promise she moaned, wishing he'd take her to her bed.

His mouth returned to hers and she poured her passion into him, their hips grinding together as they slid down the wall and onto the floor. They rolled, leaving her on top, and as his shaving-cream-covered hands began tugging at the hem of her shirt, she whipped it off. His eyes were dark pools of lust and longing, and Hailey froze, doubting herself.

What was she doing? She was supposed to be his photographer. He was paying her as a professional. Not for a good time where she could give in to her longings. Especially since this could never be anything more than a fling.

She lowered herself to him, trying to listen to her body and its needs, instead of her mind and its wants.

His hands moved up her skin with purpose, cupping her breasts. He let out a grunt of pleasure and she arched her back, allowing herself to grind against his hardness as he caressed her.

God, this was good.

The doorbell rang and Hailey sucked in a breath, determined to ignore it. She ran her hands down Finian's chest, showing him she had no plans to stop.

The front door's hinges creaked as it opened.

Hailey scrambled for her shirt.

Finian, smiling, wiped her face with what was now a bare hand, removing a trail of drying shaving cream. With a wink that looked a lot like a promise, he headed to the bathroom as she checked her shirt for telltale handprints.

"Hailey?" called Simone. "Are you home?"

"Simone?" Hailey quickly adjusted her shirt and smoothed her hair. "I'm upstairs."

"I'm just dropping off invites for tomorrow's opening." Her friend appeared at the top of the stairs. She cast a glance around the sitting room, her dark brown eyes on the lookout. "Why do you have shaving cream on your forehead and shirt?"

"I was, um, shaving my legs."

"Am I interrupting something?"

"No, nothing," Hailey said quickly.

Simone gave her a sly grin. "Okay, well, here are your invitations. I'll see you tomorrow to hang the pics?"

"Yup."

Simone handed Hailey the stack of postcards and headed down the stairs, saying, "Don't do anything with him that I wouldn't!"

Hailey closed her eyes. She was going to end up in the tabloids again if she didn't get control of her lust and longing for the man she really shouldn't have.

FINIAN WAS BY FAR the best subject she'd ever had model for her, and it wasn't just because he was the sexiest man she'd ever seen, or that every time she thought of his kisses her hands shook. She'd taken over a thousand shots of him during the afternoon. An insane amount, but she'd loved every second of it. And if she was honest, she loved having him to herself.

"If all people were as easy and fun to photograph as you are, I would *so* be in the portrait business for life."

Finian smiled and let out a huge yawn from his spot on the studio floor, where she'd been snapping a few candids of him, freshly shaved.

Okay, so she'd kind of gotten off track with the standard head shot thing. Way off track. She blamed the way he'd revved her engine during his shaving session for that.

"I'm sorry." She leaned forward, pressing a hand to his forearm. "I've exhausted you. You should have told me to stop."

"I never tell a beautiful woman who's having fun with my body to stop." He sent her a wicked grin and she slapped him with her camera's shutter release cable.

"Ooh. Whips? I would never have guessed."

Hailey gave him a playful shoulder shove and laughed as he rolled over on the fake bearskin rug, exposing his bare abs. She stood and went to her desk so she wouldn't be tempted to straddle him, and put her equipment away. When she was done, she grabbed the items she needed to show him the afternoon's photos.

"Do you want to see the pictures? Say yes," she prompted. She'd found parts of that layer she'd been looking for. Deep within him. The real Finian. And she'd captured it. "You're going to be pumped. Blown away."

"Yes. But no to whips and chains. Not my thing."

"Ever tried it?" She waggled her eyebrows and laughed when he blushed. "Your reputation is completely inaccurate. My, my. Wait until I tell the world."

"Image isn't everything. Or is everything. I can't remember anymore." He rolled back onto his stomach, propping himself up on his elbows and yawned again. He played with a tuft of the fake fur under him. "This rug feels good."

She tore her eyes away from his near-nakedness, where she'd had him pose like a nude baby on the rug, with a worn pair of jeans gracing his legs and hips. She'd wanted to ask him to take off his pants, to really play up the parody but hadn't had the courage.

She locked the cabinet that held her camera equipment. "I had fun today."

They were completely different people, living in different worlds, but they'd connected and bonded for a few hours. And somehow that had chased away her demons so she could enjoy life—her life—if only for a little while.

"Thank you," she said, nudging his shoulder as he joined her at the computer.

"It was fun, wasn't it? But you don't need to thank me. Anytime you want to have fun, I'm your man."

"I'll bet."

"Hailey." He gripped her face between his hands. "Look at me. There are two Finians. I know you've seen both, but you keep assuming the one in the tabloids is the real man. He's not. This man, here, is real." He placed her palm on his bare chest, her fingers trembling. "I'm real."

She bit her lips and worked to keep her emotions at bay. She knew this was the real Finian. It was just hard, the way she was developing feelings for him, because she knew the other—show business—Finian was the one who ruled both lives. And where did that leave her?

Leaning back, she broke contact and turned to her desk. "I kind of got sidetracked with the shoot, but there are some good pictures in here that you can probably use for other purposes. Promo or your website or something."

Sidetracked was an understatement. She'd slipped further and further off track as the afternoon progressed. The more Finian got into it, roaring with laughter, shooting her playful looks, scowls, and more, the further she'd slipped.

"Does it sound weird to say that I feel I know you better now?" She always did after photographing someone, but this was different. He'd let her into himself. Trusted her like nobody else had.

"Maybe it was the way you grilled me about my family and my life as you took photos," he joked.

"I was getting you to open up." She'd caught various emotions, whether in his expression or in his body language, which often revealed more than words. His family was close and meant the world to him. That had translated into a softening of his pose, and made the creases in his face vanish. Talking about his agent and career created instant tension, as well as lines at the corners of his mouth. Jessica Cartmill? That had been interesting. His face had remained practically blank when Hailey had asked how his ex was doing, how they'd met. No flash of love, devotion, happiness, or even pain. It was odd. Really odd. Spooky, almost.

"I feel as though I know you better, too," he said.

"Shall we?" She collected the supplies she needed and opened the garage door.

"I thought we were going to look at the photos?" He slung his bag over his bare shoulder.

"Do you work out a lot?"

"Are you usually this ADHD?"

She laughed. "Let's get a snack. I'm famished. Plus, we can watch these on my TV in the house. Bigger screen."

She led him back to the house, tugging his hand to draw him over the threshold faster, in case Austin was lurking outside somewhere. She set Finian in front of the large monitor she used as a television in the living room, and plunked her bag on an armchair.

In the kitchen she made popcorn over the stove, added butter and salt, grabbed two beers and headed to the living room, where Finian was stretched out on her cream-colored sofa, eyes closed.

She grabbed her phone and, unable to resist, snapped a couple shots. He was peaceful, handsome, and more youthful looking now that he'd shaved. Quietly, she set up the monitor so they could flick through the images together, then waved the popcorn under his nose to waken him.

His eyes cracked open and he focused on her blearily. "That smells like it needs to be in my stomach."

"Real butter." She plunked the bowl on his chest and shoved

his feet off her end of the couch. She sat, using a mouse to advance the images, her hand brushing his as they shared the bowl of popcorn.

"This is weird."

"What do you mean?" She pulled her hand back, wondering if he'd noticed that she always went for popcorn at the same time as him. She was definitely out of practice at flirting.

"All these photos. Sitting here watching and eating popcorn. Feels surreal."

"Don't you watch your own movies?"

"If I can help it, no."

"You're kidding!"

"I don't like watching myself on screen. It feels…" He gave a shrug and sank down lower in the cushions, his long legs stretched out in front of him.

"My mother recorded my outgoing voicemail message for me. I don't like the sound of my voice when it's recorded."

"Nobody does."

"Not everyone's heard my voice, you big jerk."

Finian smiled and tossed a few pieces of popcorn her way. "Someone once told me it's not all about me. Maybe it's not all about you, either."

Hailey snatched up the popcorn bits and tossed them back at Finian, who caught them in his mouth, leaning toward her, his shoulder pressing into hers as he lost his balance.

"I thought you loved the limelight and seeing yourself on the big screen?"

"I like the consequences."

"Having the paparazzi jump into your love life?" She felt her cheeks flush as he glanced over at her, his eyes a bright, inquisitive blue. "Not with me. I'm not in your love life. I mean we're not—I'm not…you know."

"The lady doth protest too much, methinks."

Hailey rolled her eyes and began advancing photos, jumping to some of her favorites near the end—the shots where she'd caught the other side of him.

Finian swallowed, head tipped back. "These are..." He ran a hand through his hair, his eyes stuck to the screen where he was revealed, uncovered. Raw and laid out for the viewer. Real. So very real.

He swallowed again.

Hailey bit her bottom lip and refrained from saying anything. Could he see who he could be? The side of him that she'd begun to adore? The world would eat this up and it would pull him to a higher level of fame. Something he must surely want.

His hands clenched into fists, his eyes flickering darkly. "But they're art."

"Of course they're art," she snapped, rising off the couch. "What did you expect? Department store family portraits in front of a fake cloud background?"

Finian laughed, raw and brutal.

"Don't be an ass." She flicked her shirt so that it hung straight. "I thought this was what you wanted. Something different. And now you're laughing at me. How perfect. Thanks for the reminder of who you really are."

"Head shots," he choked out.

"Yeah, head shots." She marched out onto the porch, slamming the door behind her.

How had she let herself believe for a few short hours that she was someone interesting? Someone special? Someone he liked hanging out with, as though they were on the same page? She'd thought he understood what she was doing, posing him in unconventional positions.

What a waste of a day. Anger and frustration welled up inside her.

The worst was that it was an amateur move not asking for a specific list of the shots he needed. He'd said he wanted something different, and she'd stupidly assumed he'd expected something other than the plain, boring standard fare which lacked interest or uniqueness.

Why had she tried to make art with him? She was supposed to be saving her cottage. Finian was Hollywood, and despite what she wished him to be, he was still an actor who wanted the easy way out. He didn't want gritty. He didn't want real.

And he didn't want art. He wanted plastic. But she had given him his real emotions, served up in digital.

She opened the door to her house, shaking her head at the still form still staring at her television. She leaned in, and said, "I've got work to do in my studio. Let me know if you see a boring pic you want me to send to your agent and let yourself out when you're done."

FINN FLEXED HIS HANDS and reached for the garage's doorknob before changing his mind. What could he say to Hailey? How could he make up for laughing at her, then sitting there like a stunned dork instead of running after her?

Sucking in a breath, he yanked open the door and rested his shoulder against the frame. "There's a fund-raiser ball at the Windermere House tonight. Want to crash it with me?"

She was at her worktable, the obvious agitation in her moves leaving him uncertain.

"I don't crash parties. Especially ones like those."

She didn't even deign to look his way. Not good. But was it because she was feeling unsure, or was she still pissed off?

"Besides," she continued, "I'm not the kind of girl who has things she can wear to something like that. If I were to take you up on your gallant offer, which I am not."

She looked up at him, her eyes filled with pain.

"I'm sorry I laughed. I didn't mean to."

She nodded, head bent again. She was more unsure than super pissed. He raised his eyes upward in thanks. He could coax unsure into sure. The problem was, that she was back to being tough Hailey. Real-life, hard-nosed Hailey. Not the woman he'd chased with shaving cream, making her laugh and squeal until he'd been so turned on he'd had to concentrate way harder on his shaving than he should have in order not to cut himself.

That Hailey had glowed. All her burdens had lifted and she'd bloomed. But now she was closing her petals as if expecting a storm to break her stem.

"Please," he said, his voice low. He wanted this woman at his side. To keep him from being the big jerk he was so used to becoming. To be the man she saw through the lens of her camera. Bigger in soul than he felt.

He wanted to be someone who made eyes twinkle for, all the right reasons, when people saw him coming. The reasons that made Hailey's eyes light up before she caught herself and acted indifferent to his arrival. Not the reason Hollywood twinkled. Not the way people expected the worst when they saw him and wondered what buffet table he'd break when he fell over drunk, or which lucky woman would get laid upon it so he could feast on her mouth for all to see. Arrogant prick. That was who he'd become.

But with Hailey he was himself. His old self. And it felt okay to be that person. Really okay. Safe in ways it had never felt with anyone else—even his family.

In fact, he felt so okay that he'd even argued with Derek over the artsy role his film buddy, Bruce Proust, had offered. Last week it would have been a flat-out "No, thanks," as the offered role was something he used to do before Hollywood. Something Derek told him would do no wonders for his career. It was as though Finn had killed that part of himself—the artistic, creative side—in order to succeed in Hollywood. But this afternoon Hailey had dug it up, breathed life back into it and shown him that it had been merely hiding out, waiting for a safe place to play. She'd quite simply captured the art side of him and presented it as if it was obvious.

Everything he was wrestling—who the world thought he was, who he thought he should be, who he was, and who he wanted to be—she'd ensnared for him to ponder. At first he'd been so stunned it was as though someone had dropped a grand piano on him. All those emotions. The light and angles. The way he looked. The way he held himself... It was art. Art that he had believed could no longer apply to him in his fake world of Hollywood and false images.

Finn hadn't known what to say. How to react. Sitting there, he hadn't been able to rev his engine out of the rut of stunned-ocity he was facing. But now, maybe he could make up for his lack of response. He could take her out, bring to light that blossoming Hailey he'd been so smitten with earlier. Return the favor by bringing a part of her back to life.

Plus he felt a strong urge to keep her close until he figured himself out. On the other side of the sealed door was his real life, and Hailey was the key to the lock he didn't even know he'd been trying to pick.

She cut him a glance, her posture stiff. Professional Hailey.

He adopted a formal business tone. "I'd like photos of myself in a tuxedo."

She gave a small harrumph. "Fine. Put it on and we'll snap off a few uninspired poses that will lack originality right here, right now. No need to take me out in public in order to do so. I'll only want to artify you."

Finn swallowed and shut his eyes. Regret speared through him and he moved to where she was standing, turned her around and laid his palms on her shoulders, making her face him.

"I'm sorry if you thought I was laughing at your photos. They are amazing. I wasn't expecting it, and it hit me, Hailey." He took a hand off her shoulder, placed it over his heart. "It hit me here." He moved his hand to his head. "And here. I don't expect you to understand, since you don't know me. You only know who you've let yourself believe I am."

"I know who you are."

"No, you don't."

She turned away, picking up her camera. "Come on, let's get the shots over with so you can go crash your fancy party."

"The tux isn't with me."

She heaved an impatient sigh, hand on hip.

"And I'd like shots of me..." His mind ran through various ideas. He needed her with him tonight. At any cost. "In crowds. And in the night, outside. And...a dark lawn. The whole man-of-mystery thing." He frowned at her shaking shoulders. "What?"

A laugh burst out. "Finian Alexander, bad boy of Hollywood, the world's hottest bachelor, are you afraid to go alone?"

He straightened his back. "No, of course not."

She gave him a look of challenge, arms crossed.

He came near, crowding her, almost hating himself for the way he planned to push her buttons. "What about you? Are you afraid of coming with me?" He eased closer until their shirts brushed. "Afraid of walking into the limelight?" His voice dropped an octave. "Afraid of being seen with me?"

Hailey gave a shaky laugh and leaned back against her table, hands braced against it, her chest pushed out in an effort to get away from his looming presence.

Oh, he had her. Had her bad.

His groin tightened and he refrained from touching her, having her. Consuming her.

"Are you?" He let his breath roam over the exposed skin at her neck.

She crossed her arms, bumping against him, chin raised. "Fine."

"You'll come with me?"

"If only to keep you from making me claustrophobic." She pushed him backward. "When does this monkey business start?"

"Half an hour."

"Half an hour!"

"You're with me. We can be fashionably late." He sent her a wink. "Don't forget your camera."

"Photo shoots outside the studio cost double."

"That's fine." He leaned over her again, all smiles, knowing he was too close and loving every second of it. "My last movie was a blockbuster hit."

"And I can tell that fact did not go straight to your head."

He grinned at her. She was fun. "Let's get ourselves outfitted like the sexy beasts we are."

HOLY DYNO. HAILEY WAS…she was…*every*thing.

The one English class he'd taken in college had told him not to use more than one adjective when describing something, but, hot-damn, adjectives were all he could think of while staring at Hailey move across her sister's living room to the entry where he was waiting.

Breathtaking.

Stunning.
Out of this world.
Gorgeous.
Curvy.
Unbelieveable.
Delicious.
A fifteen on a scale of ten.
Bedable.
Hot and sexy.

He'd dropped her off at Maya's house—another of her multitude of sisters—so she could get decked out while he borrowed her wheels to go get himself a monkey suit. Obviously his invitation had gone to her head as she'd been like a giddy teenager when he'd dropped her off to raid her sister's closet. But a crazy transformation worthy of a sci-fi show had happened in the thirty minutes he'd been out. She was mellow, graceful and demure. And she'd shined up, big time. Soft makeup and lipstick that made her shapely mouth luscious in all the ways that turned a man on and made him think of things south of the border. Hair in soft curls. A red dress—quiet, serious Hailey in a knockout dress. It hugged her curves, its swooping neck bunched with lots of extra material, creating soft folds across her chest. Her shoulders looked strong and entirely kissable. That hint of cleavage he knew would keep him close all night, wondering, waiting. Hoping.

He wanted to take her home. To his parents. To his bed. He wanted to kiss her, and have that kiss last for the next fifty years.

Instead, he lifted her hand and lightly brushed his lips across the back. "You look utterly amazing," he told her.

She let go of his hand and he was unsure where to put his own. He needed to touch her, hold her. He quickly leaned forward, brushing her cheek with another light kiss, unable to move away.

Her cheeks flushed, the color spreading across her chest. She took him in with careful, quick glances. "You look nice, too."

"He looks hot, Hailey," said her sister. "Come on, admit it. You want to bump uglies big time."

Finn shot Maya a grin and she gave him a double thumbs-up. He was going to have to tell his friends about Canadian women, because he could only imagine what these hotties were like in the sack. His groin tightened as extra blood hurried to the area, in case he should decide to listen to the devil on his shoulder and take Hailey behind the bushes lining her sister's yard.

At the car he offered Hailey her keys. She paused, then accepted them. It was almost as though she expected him to drive. Interesting. She liked to be pampered and taken care of. He could do that.

Easily.

"She's wanted to go to one of these things since she was a kid," Maya called after them. "Make sure she gets the full experience!"

Hailey grumbled something about sisters that he didn't quite catch and carefully slipped behind the wheel.

"Maya's nice," Finn said, settling into the passenger seat.

"Yeah, she's all right." Hailey's eyes darkened as if she was holding back a secret, but before he could figure it out, she turned to check her blind spot, then pulled out onto the tree-lined street.

As she drove them to Windermere he eyed the silky material of her dress and the way it moved with her, creating shadows and curves and lines any man would admire.

And she was Finn's. For the night.

Sort of.

He was going to have a hell of a time reminding himself she wasn't his, because his body had kicked down into full-on primal mode, where he was hers and she was his and he'd do whatever he had to do in order to protect that.

He rubbed his cheek in anticipation of the slap he knew he'd get before the night was through. Oddly enough, he was kind of looking forward to it.

Chapter Ten

Oh hell, she was nervous. Hailey had tried to park away from the dazzling Windermere House, seeing as her car's rusty old body was an obvious indicator that she did not belong and never would at this fancy event—unless she was working it. However, Finian, always so full of confidence, had directed her to the valet with an assurance that had been thrilling and comforting. That was, until she had to hand over her keys to the surprised attendant. And of course, it had been a guy she'd gone to school with, who'd done a double take.

Finian, cupping her elbow, led her into the old hotel, ignoring the valet.

"This place looks great for its age." He gave a short nod to a person manning the door, and quickly breezed past before the man could ask to see their invitation.

"It was one of the few original hotels from the late 1800s, but when *The Long Kiss Goodnight* was filmed here in the 1990s, the place accidentally burned down. It was rebuilt and restored to look the same, but there are subtle differences."

"Hmm."

Finian swept her into a large room where the ball was being held, acting as though he owned the place.

"You have crashing down to a science."

"How do you think I met the producers and directors I wanted to schmooze with?" He shot her a wink and pulled her onto the portable dance floor.

Hailey pulled out "calm, cool, and collected" and tried to take in the place without gaping. She'd been through the entire hotel once before, as a kid, and had been wowed by it then, but tonight it was in full splendor, from the gowns to the intricate appetizers to the delicate decorations. She could imagine the years of old money moving about this room. Lady Eaton and her friends. And now newer money. People like Martin Short, Bill Murray, Kurt Russell and Goldie Hawn could magically appear to rub elbows.

She let out a sigh as Finian, her own movie star, kept his hand on her lower back, guiding her across the crowded dance floor. She liked having his hand there. His body heat pressed into her and she allowed herself to stay close, to not push away. And his tuxedo? Hot damn. She'd thought he'd looked good this afternoon without a shirt on, stretched out on the floor of her studio, but that was nothing in comparison to the way he looked decked out in black. She'd have to stop staring at him or the dampness in her panties was going to get out of control. Sex appeal? Hell, yeah. He was the sexiest man in the room.

"I forgot my camera in the car," she whispered.

"Later. Right now we live large."

Hailey tipped her head back, and Finian took advantage of her position and dropped her into a gentle dip, spinning her slowly in a half arc before pulling her up into his arms.

"You're a good dancer" she told him.

"You know what they say…."

She raised a brow in question.

"Good dancers make excellent lovers."

Hailey laughed and resisted the temptation to glide her hand up the nape of his neck and pull his face closer to hers.

"Shall we take a break?" He led her to the bar with a hand still on her lower back, announcing that she was with him. She smiled as women noticed him. Noticed her with him. The crowd parted as though they were royalty. A girl could get used to this.

"Why are we here, exactly?" she asked, as he handed her a flute of champagne.

"Publicity. I can't hide out from my broken heart forever." He gave her a wink, and they moved to the side to enjoy their champagne.

A voice loaded with surprise broke into their conversation, "*Hailey?*"

Hailey kept her back to the woman, furiously trying to think of something entirely engrossing to say to Finian so he would lean in close, blocking out Polly, her ex-best friend and almost-rival. But the woman stepped around, facing them.

"I *thought* that was you, but then all those years you said you'd never go digging for gold. I just *had* to come see for myself." Polly placed a highly manicured hand against her silicone-enhanced chest and gave a tinkling laugh. She waved a finger at Hailey. "You naughty girl, I *knew* you'd succumb."

Before she could retort, Polly slipped her highly toned body between Hailey and Finian, gripped his arm and pressed her chest against him. "Honey, you just *have* to watch Hailey. She'll tell you one thing, then do the other." She gave a coy wink.

Hailey pulled her away. "Finian is my client. I'm photographing him. This is an *assignment*."

"Then where's your camera?" She sidled up again with a smirk and assessed an amused Finian. "He's *not* a bad catch. Made several mill on his last movie."

"Finian, meet Polly Pocket."

"Pollard," Polly corrected. "Thank you."

"Polly's been digging for gold since sixth grade and no longer understands the social complexities of friendship. Only financial commodities—she won a lot of awards as an investment advisor before she got married. We used to be close friends." She turned to Polly, who hardly looked real other than for the stress lines beginning to show around her eyes. "Polly, meet Finian. He's pretty much full of himself in ways you'd enjoy. However, he also has a tender side I've come to appreciate."

"I was going to say you're complete crap at introductions," Finian murmured. "But that's probably the nicest thing you've said about me." He gave her a light peck on the cheek that made Polly turn an unnatural pink. Possibly due to the shade of envious green mixing in with it.

"I didn't see your name on the guest list, Hailey. I'm sure I would have remembered seeing it. Yours, *too*, Finian." She tipped her head, eyes hard, jaw clenched. "I'd hate to think you were *crashing* a *charity* event."

"I never go by my real name at events like this." Finian leaned close to Polly, grasping her elbow and sidling close enough that her perfect posture softened. "You know how it gets."

Polly tipped her chin up. "Of *course*."

Finian stood beside Hailey, allowing the other woman to politely excuse herself. He rested his shoulder against Hailey's, his warmth easing into her as they looked out at the crowd of beautifully dressed people, while sipping their expensive champagne.

"Sorry about Polly."

"Never apologize for someone else's problems."

Hailey froze as a cluster of sparkling-eyed women rushed toward them. Finian, spotting them, spun around and placed a hand on the wall behind Hailey, blocking her in. Her body heat rocketed and her pulse throbbed as the room shrank down to just the two of them.

"Don't look at them or they'll interrupt," he said, his mouth close to her jawbone.

She darted a glance to the crowd of women hanging behind Finian, waiting. Lurking.

"You are such a contradiction," she whispered. He wanted to be seen out in public, but didn't want the attention? Could she dare think he wanted to spend time with her?

No, of course not. Those were hungry dames who would suck his evening away. It wasn't about her. It was about staying sane.

"I think you are the contradiction." His breath came as warm puffs against her cheek.

Her longing ratcheted up a notch. Why did it seem as though one moment she was angry with him and the next moment she was ready to wrap her pulsing, naked body around his?

She raised her face, taking in his beautiful lines. The angular jaw, the lips…the lips that were closing in on hers.

Oh, here it came.

Hailey almost forgot the flute of champagne she was holding as he kissed her slowly and sweetly. Her body pressed against him, and his arm wrapped around her waist, reeling her in so she could feel every inch of his body against hers. What had he done with his glass? And why the hell did she care? They were propped against the wall, locked together, sharing heat, his mouth on hers. And he'd chosen her.

Hailey.

Chosen her for his summer fling.

No.

She wasn't that girl. She couldn't do flings and she didn't need a broken heart. Not again. She'd learned those hard lessons, and one of them was to stop things before they went too far. She gave a gentle push against Finian's chest and he started to move away.

But it was fun breaking her own rules. Thrilling. And she was sure her old brokenhearted self would understand that if a man like Finian came along, you went along for the ride. Even if you knew the consequences.

You broke the rules for men like Finian Alexander.

So she kissed him again, harder, letting her passion and need enter into it. He immediately returned her passion, making her very aware of how close he was and how much his body wanted exactly what she was dreaming of.

She broke the kiss, gasping. "I crave you, but not here."

He stepped back slightly, but still way too close for her to be able to breathe or think straight. The man was all-consuming.

And he was going to break her heart as if he'd dropped it from the top of the CN tower. But the funny thing was she couldn't summon the energy to care. It would be worth it. Entirely.

Hailey leaned her head against the wall, dared to look into his eyes. Saw exactly what she was feeling reflected back at her, full force.

Oh, she was in trouble.

Big, big trouble.

HAILEY LET FINIAN SWEEP her back onto the dance floor instead of upstairs to a room with what would surely be an exquisite bed. The champagne, her need, and his consuming presence were making her head spin. She laughed, the skirt of her sister's borrowed dress flaring out in a way that made her feel sexy and free as Finian twirled her—and straight into the arms of Austin.

"May I cut in?"

"No." There was a possessiveness in Finian's voice that made

Hailey pulse with longing. Finian tried to tug her back, but Austin held strong.

"Austin, I don't want to dance with you."

"Just for a few notes," he said.

Finian released her and crossed his arms. Hailey almost laughed. She'd bet anything he was going to stand right there and count the measures before reclaiming her. Her only regret was that he hadn't fought longer or harder for her.

"Interesting approach," Austin said, his body an uncoordinated wreck as he tried to lead her around the floor.

"What's interesting? Your approach to dancing?"

Austin gave her a smile as crooked as his bow tie. "Getting in close to Finian so you can expose him. Sell him out. Be there to capture the images of him at his worst. I never knew you had it in you."

"Shut up, Austin." Hailey pushed him away. "And you'd better not take any photos of us tonight."

She ran her eyes down him, on the lookout for a camera. Someone like Austin...who knew where he might be hiding one? For all she knew, he had a camera in his shoe and had already taken a photo up her dress.

"I'm on a date." He raised his hands in professed innocence. "I'm not working."

"You're always working."

"Watch out, Hailey." Austin lowered his voice, gazing in Finian's direction. "He'll use you faster than you can use him."

"He's not like that."

Austin turned her in that direction. Finian was surrounded by a mob of women who were gushing, taking photos and generally petting him as if he was their long-lost puppy. "Maybe you'd better go rescue him before he begins to like it too much and you get busted for crashing this thing."

"Austin, no photos, okay?"

"Tonight only, but if something juicy happens I will break my promise."

"Deal. Now scoot."

He bowed, releasing her to go save Finian and try her hand at being Cinderella for one night.

THANK GOODNESS FOR HAILEY. Finn made a dash for her, breaking through the mob of women. He'd never had so many tush grabs or offers of "servicing" in a five-minute span in his life—even in Hollywood. There was something scary about these done up, perfect broads. It was as though their husbands ignored them and they hadn't been let out of their cages in months. But he got why rich men went after younger women—they were still halfway real.

Real like Hailey. Not like Jessica.

"I'm getting hungry. Are you?" Hailey asked as he fell into step beside her, his body curled around hers in a way he hoped would ward off any further advances.

"Are we leaving?"

She'd been a radiant beauty only moments before when they'd been dancing, and now she was closing up again. He glanced over his shoulder to see if he could spot Austin and get a hint for the trouble he'd stirred up.

"You can do what you want, but I need to eat," she replied.

"There are a few munchies here. Do you like shrimp?"

Her pace increased as she spied the exit.

Finn picked up his own pace in order to steer her in the opposite direction.

"I know just the place," he said.

"This way is closer to my car."

"Trust me."

"I think we've already established—"

He spun her into a hard kiss to stifle her objections.

"Do you want this night to be memorable, Hailey? Or do you want to traipse back to that life of yours that gives you frown lines?"

She paused as if deciding whether to be offended or not, so he pulled her into a French kiss, his hand on her left butt cheek. He consumed her in the crowd, then, snatching her hand, tugged her, breathless and unresisting, out of the hotel and down the sweeping, lit up lawn to the lake's edge. Where docks lined the shore he found the man he was looking for, waiting in a boat.

"You forgot to take pictures of me," Finn murmured in Hailey's ear, and her steps faltered.

He shot her a grin as a uniformed man came up, holding her camera bag. Right on time.

"What the hell?" She whirled around.

"The valet. He's allowed to have the keys to your car." Finn slipped a bill in the man's hand and took Hailey's bag.

"I said I was hungry," she snapped, snatching it from him. "I've been working for you all afternoon and need to eat."

"You weren't working a few minutes ago." Finn moved closer and her cheeks flushed. She began walking toward the hotel again, clutching her hips in a way that reminded him of a runner with cramps.

"There's nothing to eat in town at this hour unless we go back to the hotel," she said.

Not what he had in mind, nor what he had planned.

"Hailey, do you trust me?"

She turned. "No."

"Good. Come on." Finn held out his hand and she hesitated before walking carefully toward him.

He led her to the large speedboat with the waiting driver. When Finn stepped onto its deck and offered his hand to her, she hesitated, her hand trembling ever so slightly.

"To Port Carling, please," he said to the driver, when he had Hailey settled on board. The man gave Finn a nod, and within seconds they had cast off and were heading across the calm lake.

Hailey's eyes sparkled in the moonlight and her lips curved into a small smile as the boat's breeze flipped her hair. Just as he'd thought. She could be swayed and dazzled by a little special treatment. He leaned closer and laid a kiss on her lips.

He was getting further away from his original plan to piss her off so she'd expose him, but it felt right being with her. He couldn't intentionally hurt her, but maybe if he got close enough she'd understand what he needed to do, and would help him. They could be a team.

He kissed her again, wanting to stay in this moment with her. She was everything he no longer deserved, and everything he thought he'd left behind.

She leaned against him, the cool air whipping around them as the large craft picked up speed.

"You're cold." Finn whipped off his tuxedo coat and draped it over her shoulders, drawing her closer in the process. She was a beauty. Pure. And someone he could only lose or hurt.

He gave the top of her head a kiss, wrapping his hand in her soft curls.

What if he took over his life again? What if he risked it all and took a long shot? A long shot that could maybe, one day, make him a happy *and* successful man. Would he be able to rebuild his old community like he'd promised? Or would he lose everything, including Hailey?

"You look sad," she said.

"Then I guess I'm not doing it right."

FINN MANAGED TO SHAKE his melancholy by the time they hit the docks in Port Carling. It was time to show Hailey how fun it was to let loose for a night. To be free and have a good time. Hand in hand, they walked the short distance up the hill, meeting up with the sidewalk that took them to the restaurant overlooking the locks. Gently, he ushered her inside.

"Hi, cutie." The server sidled up to Finn and he almost laughed at how obvious she was.

"Table for two, please." He slipped his tuxedo jacket off her shoulders and caressed her exposed shoulder.

The waitress, eyes on him, led them to a table by a large window.

"I'll bet you'd like your usual drink? A scotch on the rocks?" She batted her lashes.

Finn blinked. The usual? He'd never been here before.

And he hated scotch. It tasted like spider piss.

Oh, right. Famous. And it looked good in a glass. Fit the image, blah, blah, blah.

He gave a short nod, not bothering to fill her in on his true tastes.

"What would you like?" he asked Hailey, annoyed by how the server's back was angled to shut her out in order to gain more attention from him—the person she presumed would be tipping her.

"Just water for now," Hailey said, her head buried in the menu.

"We have a nice sparkling water," the waitress said. "I could add a refreshing slice of lemon."

"Tap water," Hailey clarified, looking up, hands splayed across the table's linen cloth.

"We have a—"

"Tap. Please."

Finn hid his smile as the waitress hurried off. He closed his heavy menu, watching Hailey frown at her own. Her eyes skimmed the right column, then the items. Next page. Skim the prices, then the items.

He reached over and closed her menu, ignoring her downturned mouth.

The server appeared. "A scotch on the rocks for you, sir." She did a little curtsy as she lowered his drink. She set down Hailey's water and turned back to Finn. "Now, what can I get you for an appetizer? I think you'd enjoy the roasted tomato and whipped goat cheese spread on our fresh sourdough. It's fresh and delicious. Shall I bring that out along with a side of hot smoked salmon on our homemade crackers?"

Finn gave a wave in agreement. He didn't care what they ate as long as Hailey was happy and stopped frowning at the prices—which really weren't too bad, compared to the places Jessica usually tried to take him. In fact, this converted house was casual, yet sophisticated in a way he'd come to equate with Muskoka.

"No, thank you," Hailey piped up. "Unless you wanted that, Finian?"

"I'm cool either way."

"Great, I'll go put that in."

Hailey vanished behind her menu again and Finn resisted the urge to tip it down.

"That color looks nice on you," he said when she finally closed it. "The red brings out a certain…life in you." The lights above them were dimmed and the soft glow highlighted the natural strands of gold in her curls. She looked healthy. Alive.

But she could look happier. Less uncomfortable.

"What's your favorite color?" she asked.

"Beige."

She placed her fists on the table, eyes twinkling. He took a sip of his drink, waiting for her to call him on it.

"I can't believe your pants have yet to burst into flame," she said.

"My pants?"

"Liar, liar, pants on fire," she sang. "Hanging on a—"

"I am familiar with the reference. I did have a childhood."

"Since when?"

"Since ever. I wasn't born famous and fully grown. I grew up in a crappy rented town house, with loud neighbors who did drugs and had fights on the communal lawn. I learned to ride a bike without training wheels, teased and fought with my brothers. Got my heart broken at the prom. The usual. I am real, you know."

"So, then..." She placed her hands under her chin, the picture of innocence. "Which parent are you closest to? Your mom or your dad?"

"Why does this feel like a test?"

"Because it is."

"Really?"

"No. Quit stalling. I won't tell the parent who loses that they didn't make the cut."

"Everyone has a parent they feel the closest to."

"And the winner is?"

"My mom. And you?"

"I've never met your mom, so how would I know she would be my pick?" Hailey winked over the rim of her water glass.

"What's in that water? It's turning you into a tease."

"So?" he asked. "Are you dodging my question? You're like honey, all sweet and innocent, pulling me in."

"Better to catch Hollywood flies that way."

He leaned forward. "Have you been following me?"

"So, my dad's dead—accident when we were teens—and Mom had a debilitating stroke a few years back. The parents I grew up with are no more, and the roles have been reversed. So your question of which I'm closest to doesn't really apply."

"I'll take that as a yes. I'm flattered."

Her mouth tightened into a thin line. "This is real life, Finian. This is what it looks like. What it feels like."

"Why do you always call me Finian?"

"Last I heard, it was your name. Or is that another thing that's been faked about you?"

"What's fake about me?" He grabbed her hand, keeping her at the table. She was preparing to put distance between them again.

He wasn't sure why he cared what she thought or why he felt so insulted by her comment, but it was as though her answer could sweep away everything he'd worked toward like the swoosh of the final curtain.

"For one? Your bad-boy image."

Finn placed his palms on the table, stared at her. He glanced away, then back at her, letting out a massive sigh. "Come on, more details. Please." He must have given her a pathetic look because the tension in her gorgeous shoulders eased and her chest expanded, thrusting up a hint of cleavage. But all he could think about, other than how sexy she was, was that he depended on her answer as though it were his last meal. "Is it obvious that it is mostly faked?"

"To me it is."

"Gimme more."

"Manners?" She sent him a saucy look.

"Mother, may I, please?"

Hailey snorted, but the corners of her lips curved into a smile. "The hints add up, the more I get to know you. And honestly, when was the last time you've done something bad? It's not in your nature. It's merely a role you're playing."

He stood, hooking his fingers under the table as though he was about to flip it over.

"Don't!" She held out a hand, eyes wide with panic.

"Just kidding, Hails." He sat again, arms resting on the table. "Could you help me?"

"With what?"

"Building up my image again. We could work as a team." He held his breath, forcing himself to remain quiet. He had just one shot at this.

She laughed, rich and deep, as if the laughter was bubbling up from the depths of her soul. She placed a hand on her chest, her eyes merry. "Me? Hardly."

"You're a photographer, aren't you?"

The merriment vanished.

"Help me with my image, as a photographer, Hailey. Please."

"See? Bad boys don't say please."

"You're helping me already."

"Finian, I'm not the kind of girl who creates images for movie stars." She played with the edge of the tablecloth. "That's not my thing."

"That's not what I'm asking. I'm asking you to take photos. Sell them. Make money." He leaned closer, lowered his voice to a whisper. "A *ton* of money. A win-win partnership."

She averted her eyes, something warring within her. "Let's talk about it later, okay?"

"Promise?"

"Promise."

The server arrived with plates racked up her arms. "Here we are." She began sliding appetizers onto the table.

"Wow." He gazed at all the food. "This is a lot."

"I'll get you more serviettes. Would you like fresh pepper? A glass of wine, perhaps? We have a lovely Bordeaux that would go nicely with the dip."

"I'm fine, thank you."

"Would you like another finger of scotch?"

He shook his head.

"I've put in an order for our surf and turf, as well."

"Oh, I think this will be plenty for me," Hailey said, her eyes round.

"Yeah, we're good. Thanks."

"Oh. Okay." The server's shoulders slumped in defeat.

"This is lovely, though. Thank you."

"You don't want to miss our desserts. Save room for that. In fact, I'll bring you a dessert menu, as well as the wine list, so you can see what you need to save room for."

"Thank you."

Hailey's eyes flicked over the appetizers as though tallying the cost. The skin between her brows pinched and she reached for the small purse she'd set beside her plate.

"My treat. After all, I broke some labor laws today by not allowing you the time to get fed properly. This is my appeasement."

She opened her purse, fingering through its contents.

"No, really," he insisted. She paused, her blue eyes assessing him. "Haven't you been on a date before?" he asked.

"It's been a while. And I thought we were working?"

Chapter Eleven

"We're going to what?" Hailey took a step away from Finian, her stomach pleasantly full, as a light breeze picked up off the lake back at Windermere. It was a perfect night. Full moon. No wind.

But it sounded as though Finian had just said they were going to go—

"Parasailing." A few helpers came down the hill to the docks, and before she knew what was happening, they had pulled the string of buoys out of the swimming area and she was standing barefoot in the small beach's cold sand.

"I've never done this before."

"Me, neither," he said with a grin. "Well, okay. I have. But not here. And not tandem."

"Tandem?"

"You and me, sweetheart."

"Sweetheart?" She gave him a playful shove. "Isn't that sexual harassment?"

"What?"

"We're working right now. Although I have no idea how I'm going to photograph you if you're strapped to my back, sugar buns."

He let out a laugh, allowing the attendants to strap him in, his arms wrapped around her waist.

"I'll show you sexual harassment," he growled in her ear.

"Is that a promise or a threat?" Her voice came out breathy with desire, and she didn't know whether to squelch it or run with it.

The helpers began doing up the harnesses.

"Wait! I'm wearing a dress." She squealed and tried to turn away from Finian.

"Don't worry, it's dark out. Nobody will see your underwear. Live free, Hailey."

She closed her eyes. If only her whole life was like tonight. Then she might believe in living free. But she'd already done a hundred things she'd never dreamed of. Well, not quite a hundred, but the night was far from over and there was so much potential in the tentative connection between her and Finian.

"On three," said the parasail assistant, "I need the two of you to run across the sand for liftoff."

This was going to be interesting. Running with Finian strapped to her back?

"One, two, three…"

Hailey took a step forward and they were launched into the air as the sail behind them lifted.

"Wow!"

It was as though she weighed nothing, like an angel, or one of Tigger's fairies. Finian held her close, his warmth protecting her from the cool, soft air swirling around them as they quietly floated above the lake. The moon glanced off the water's surface, racing them as they soared along.

"Look, our shadow," Finian said in her ear. Her dress's soft fabric danced across her smooth legs, as sensual as his husky voice.

"I wish I had my camera." Even though she knew the camera couldn't pick up what she saw—the small glimmers, the reflections, the way she felt—Hailey would have something tangible to hold on to. Something to remind her that this night was more than just a dream. A dream she'd want to repeat every night for the rest of her life.

Finian's arms tightened around her and she allowed herself to believe that he felt the same way she did. That he'd never done this or felt this way with another woman. That she was special. That she was his.

He kissed her ear and she pointed in the direction of Nymph Island, telling him stories of her life as they glided along, letting him into her world one island at a time.

THE BOATMEN LET THEM DOWN in the damp sand, the assistant easily catching them. Hailey felt graceful, beautiful, alive. And maybe a little bit in lust with Finian.

The helper unstrapped them and the cool air hit her back as Finian stepped away from her. She turned to face him. "You were nice and warm." He wrapped himself around her again as the boat puttered off, the moon's reflection dancing across its wake. She let out a small sigh of contentment, safe in Finian's warm embrace. She never wanted this evening to end. Ever.

"Let's walk," he said, taking her hand.

She let him lead her to their shoes, her camera bag resting in the sand beside them, Finian's tux jacket draped over it.

They wandered up a quiet, narrow road, away from the water.

Finian let out a laugh and stepped into a yard. "Check this out." Under a window was a flower bed filled with petunias, whirligigs, and gnomes.

"Finian! That's private property!" she hissed. She ducked

behind a large tree just off the sidewalk, wishing the streetlight above her would burn out.

What the hell was he doing? Trying to prove he really was a bad boy?

And if so, why did she want to run away more than snap a photo of him?

"This guy looks like Santa!" He waved the gnome at her, a clump of dirt falling from its joined feet. "Doesn't it?"

"Someone's going to see you!"

She was pretty sure that even in Hollywood people didn't go picking up lawn ornaments, willy-nilly. Although that could explain why the big homes were gated.

"Come on, Finian!"

The window directly behind him opened and Finian, unfazed, chirped a hello.

A gray-haired woman poked her head out. "What are you doing with Alfred?"

"Alfred?"

"The gnome in your right hand, buster." She leaned out farther and Hailey hid behind the tree again. Naturally, Mr. Everyone's a Fan of Mine So I Can Do Anything I Want had to choose Mrs. Star's house. This was going to get back to Hailey's mother faster than the time she and Austin went egging houses.

"Put him right back beside Georgie, please. They're brothers and don't like to be parted."

"Did you ever notice he looks like Santa?" Finian held the gnome up in the light cast from her house.

"Of course I did. Why do you think I bought him? Say, has anyone ever told you that you look like that Finian Alexander fellow you see in the movies?"

"Of course they have. Mostly because I am Finian Alexander."

He beamed his bright smile up at the window and the woman wobbled before catching herself on the frame.

"Well, damn! I'll say." She turned to look into her house. Turned back. "I'm going to need to take a photo or else my sister Elsie over in Blueberry Springs won't believe me. Don't move a muscle."

Finian flashed Hailey a smile and she shook her head, wishing she could move back onto the sidewalk where the dew wouldn't chill her exposed toes.

"I hope you don't mind that I came onto your lawn," Finian said when Mrs. Star returned, camera in hand.

"Of course not," she purred, aiming the device. A bright flash went off and Hailey winced. Mrs. Star's photo was going to be awful. Finian was going to have major red-eye and be completely bleached out.

He posed with the gnome again.

My word, the woman was blinding him with that flash. Hailey took a step forward, her heavy camera bag slung over her shoulder.

"Who's there?" Mrs. Star called out.

"Just me, Mrs. Star." Hailey stepped closer. "Hailey Summer."

"Hailey? Are you hanging out with Finian Alexander?"

"I'm afraid I am."

"What on earth are you doing with the likes of this young man?" She reached out to pat Finian on the shoulder. "No offense, but you don't have the best reputation, and Hailey here, she's a good girl. I've known her mother most of my life."

"None taken."

Mrs. Star patted Finian's cheek. "How you got such a bad reputation, I'll never know. Although you did waltz right into my yard like you owned it. You stick close to Hailey. She'll set you up all nice again."

"I'll do my best, ma'am."

Mrs. Star turned back to Hailey. "I bet Elsie five bucks it wasn't you on that celebrity show. I told her you'd know better than to kiss a man like Finian Alexander—not that you couldn't get him. You are a lovely young thing, and look at you, all dolled up. But I thought you had more sense in that head of yours than to get tangled up in this Hollywood disaster."

"Mrs. Star, would you like me to take a photo of you with Finian?"

"Oh, yes, please!" The woman patted her hair and leaned out.

Hailey took out her camera and snapped a few shots, laughing when Mrs. Star pretended to kiss a shocked-looking Finian, who was hamming it up, making the woman glow.

"You are just too special," Mrs. Star finally said, giving Finian a big kiss on the cheek. "Isn't he special, Hailey?"

She nodded, not daring to speak over the sentimental lump that had formed in her throat. If only…if only he would stay, so she could explore just how special he was.

"Now, if Hailey doesn't mind," said Mrs. Star to Finian, "let's get one of you without your shirt."

HAILEY TURNED OFF HER CAR and leaned back in her seat. Tonight had been amazing. Even though she was parked outside Finian's cottage so they could part ways, she still didn't want the night to be over. Not yet.

Without breaking the silence, Finian drew an arm around her shoulder, pulling her to him, his lips finding hers in the darkness. Her hand stroked his cheek as his tongue delved into her mouth. She moaned in contentment and wished she could press her body against his warmth.

"You're cold," he said, tipping his head so his forehead rested against hers.

She was trembling, but it was from something other than the cool night air seeping into her car. Something much stronger.

He broke their embrace and was out of the car, opening her door within seconds. "Come."

She hesitated.

"Trust me, Hails."

She placed her hand in his, meeting his eye. "I trust you."

"Good." He led her into his cottage, where he started a blaze in the fireplace with an ease that surprised her.

"Where'd you learn that?"

"In *Desperate Cowboy*."

"Oh, right." For some reason she'd never thought of him actually having to possess the skills he displayed in his movies.

Finian disappeared, then returned with an afghan in yellows and browns, sporting sunflowers like pretty much everything else in the cottage. He wrapped it around her shoulders with care, tugging her close enough to kiss. Then he was gone again.

Hailey watched the fire crackle, wondering what she was in for. Well, she knew what she was hoping she was in for. She was in his cottage at two in the morning after a night of…hell, she didn't even know what to call their night. Perfect. It had been perfect. And she was here now because she wanted more. A lot more. She wanted everything he was willing to give.

The overhead lights flicked off and Finian slipped onto the couch beside her, supporting her as he offered a glass of wine.

She toasted him in the firelight. "Thank you."

"You are welcome."

The held each other's gaze over the rim of their glasses and Hailey leaned into his strength.

"Did you have a nice night?" he asked.

"I did." A smile crept onto her face and she snuggled closer, wishing she could run her hands all over him, explore him, get to know him intimately. She wanted to know absolutely everything about him.

She placed her glass on the side table and then took his, placing it beside hers.

"You don't like it?" he asked.

Wordlessly, she held the blanket around her shoulders, standing so she could shift onto his lap, straddling him. Through the material of her dress, she could see her hard nipples, and knew he could, too. Instead of being embarrassed by how much she wanted him, she slid farther onto his lap, letting her heat rest over his erection. His eyes darkened as he grabbed her hips, pausing as if double-checking to see if she was making the moves he thought she was. She pressed her chest against his, their eyes not breaking contact. With a quick pivot he had her on her back, his body pinned above hers. She wrapped her legs over his ass, drawing his hard-on against her wet mound.

She let out a moan and, grabbing his shirt, tugged his chest down to meet hers. She wanted him. He propped his elbows under her armpits and cradled her head in his hands.

"What do you need, Hailey?"

"I need you." She lifted herself so she could reached his lips, diving into him, showing him how much she yearned to feel his body, his passion, his desire. "All of you."

FINN SAT ON THE EDGE of his bed in the Sunflower Cottage and glanced at the sleeping form behind him. He quickly looked back at the wall so he wouldn't crawl back into bed.

What had he done? This kind of partnership wasn't going to do a thing for either of them, especially with him destined to head back home in less than a week.

Hailey would never expose his dark, underside now. Not unless he did something evil like betray her trust. And he couldn't do that. Not to his Hails.

She was too good. Too real. Too honest. Too everything he didn't need in a paparazzo. But everything he needed in a girlfriend. Sighing, he slipped back under the covers, tucking his arms around her, drawing her close. She felt good. Warm. Friendly.

He needed a girlfriend like her. Always had.

He whispered a thank-you into the air in case the God his mother believed in was real, and with care and attention, began kissing his way up Hailey's exposed arm, liking the way he could make her lips curve into a gentle smile.

She was no longer trying to run away. She was his. Here in bed. With him.

Forever.

There was a loud bang on the front door as Hailey rolled over, pulling him down into a full-mouthed kiss that had him hard and ready to yell, "Action!"

She ignored the door, pressing her body against him. He did likewise, spreading himself over top of her, nudging her inner thigh.

"Finian!" called a woman's voice.

His head popped up. "Holy hell."

Hailey froze under him.

"It's my mother." He rolled off Hailey and rubbed a hand down his face. "I think I was supposed to pick her up from the airport."

"Finian?" called his father.

"Shit. They're both here." He popped out of bed, yanking on a pair of jeans.

His mother banged on the door again and Hailey scrambled into action, falling off her side of the bed, her bare butt exposed.

Finn reached across the bed to give it a light slap, and she squealed and ducked out of reach, tucking the fallen sheet around her torso.

"You're so bad," she giggled, her hair tumbling across her forehead.

He shot her a wolfish grin, brushing the curls off her face. "That's what I keep telling you."

FINN SETTLED HIS PARENTS at the small table on the deck that overlooked the calm lake, where the eerie loons were calling to one another. He placed a mug of coffee from the small one-cupper in front of his mother, and set up the machine to make one for himself.

"Sure you don't want a coffee, Dad?"

"I'm fine, thanks. There was free coffee on the plane. I had my fill for the day, plus some."

Finn glanced at the French doors that led into the cottage. Where was Hailey? Had she slipped out the back? Or would she hide out until his parents left? Maybe come in here with bed head, and dressed in her killer sexy dress as if everything was normal? Or would she slam through the front door as though she'd just arrived? Maybe he should have taken his parents for a walk so she could escape.

"What in heaven's name are those?" His mother leaned over the railing, gawking at the lake. "They are strangely gorgeous."

Finn lined up his sight with hers. "Loons."

"They sound atrocious, but I like it. Chilling and haunting." She hugged her arms around herself for effect and sat at the table again.

"Hailey said they're the bird you see on the one-dollar coin."

"Such colorful money," his mother replied, tucking her blond bob behind her ears.

"Monopoly money," added his father.

"It makes a lovely rainbow. And who's Hailey? Is she the girl you were telling me about on the phone?"

"Yeah."

"Can we meet her?"

"Um, maybe." He glanced toward the doorway.

"I'm so glad you invited us. We set Rex up with the neighbor and were off. You were so right. We needed a vacation. With your father's health—"

"I'm fine, dear, quit worrying," his dad said, leaning back to tuck in his plaid shirt. "Finian, I tried negotiating a better deal for you with the cottage manager."

"Thanks. But it's okay, Dad. I can afford it."

"With all those charity events you have planned in the fall? And your donations? That's a lot of money you've promised, son. People are counting on you."

"I know." Finn tried to ignore the way his chest tightened, and instead focused his attention on the doorway.

Last night he'd seen Hailey's phone light up in the night, and had checked the screen in case it was something worth waking her over. Turned out it was a series of texts from various people, all stating where they'd spotted him. Him. Finian Alexander. She *had* been tracking him and following him. In order to get him into bed? He didn't think so. But was she paparazzo? If so, she sucked at it, plain and simple. Which left stalker fan. But that didn't fit, either.

So who was she? What did she want?

He was missing a piece. And it wasn't just the piece of his heart she seemed to have stolen in the night.

"I tried getting them to switch the booking to my name so I could get you a senior's rate," his father continued.

"You're not old enough."

His father flipped an ID card in his direction.

Finn spit out his coffee and laughed. "You're kidding me, right?"

His mother sighed and threw up her hands. "I told him he'd gone too far, but he couldn't resist. He likes the way people give him a second glance and ask to see his driver's license."

"What? It's a nice feeling. It's like being carded at the bar."

His mother blew on her cup of coffee, and as her eyes lifted, Finn felt the earth shift ever so slightly. *Hailey.*

"Hello. I'm Hailey Summer."

Hailey slipped past him, reaching out to shake his mother's hand. She was a vision in her red dress and wild hair—which looked as though she'd brushed it, then dampened it, causing major havoc. He grinned up at her and lightly touched her waist, loving the way the fabric felt over her curves.

His mother looked slightly in awe and stood up in front of Hailey, one hand over her chest.

"I know she's pretty, Mom, but you're staring." Finn pulled Hailey close and kissed the side of her head, inhaling her scent.

His mother blinked and gave herself a little shake. "I'm so sorry, it's just that I'm such a fan of your work."

"Uh, what?" Finn asked, his grip loosening.

"A fan?" Hailey echoed.

"Yes! The way you make wildlife come alive is simply incredible." Finn's mother tugged on his arm. "Have you *seen* her work?"

"Um, yes." He pushed a hand through his hair and met Hailey's eyes. "She took some photos of me yesterday. She, uh, revealed a side of me nobody else has."

Hailey was changing his life just by being in it. He pulled her close again, not wanting her to be farther than a breath away.

"Consider yourself very lucky, Finian." His mother gave him a look mixed with awe and wonder. "You don't realize what you have."

Finn rested a hand on Hailey's lower back, guiding her to a chair. "I think I do."

"No, this woman has won some impressive awards and doesn't do portraits any longer. How you managed to snag her..." His mom blinked, taking in Hailey's wardrobe. Her attention flicked to Finn and back. She gave a small smile.

"Hailey, this is my mother, Daisy Alexander. Apparently one of your biggest fans. Don't give her your phone number or she'll call you with career advice every day."

His mother gave him a playful smack. "Oh, Finn."

"It's a pleasure to meet you, Mrs. Alexander."

His father gave Hailey an eager handshake. "I'm Bob, by the way. So, I'm guessing you're the girl who's been slapping some sense into our son."

Finn cringed as Hailey shot him a look, her face matching the hue of her dress. "Dad..."

"I can tell by that shit-eating grin of Finn's—pardon my language—that he'd do just about anything for you." Bob lowered his voice as though Finn wouldn't be able to hear. "Maybe we could borrow your influence to work through a laundry list of grievances his mother has. Namely, his image."

"Dad..."

Hailey was angling in her chair as though she was going to bolt. His parents were worse than the paparazzi that would undoubtedly start hounding them once word got out that he had a new crush.

All he wanted was a moment with her to solidify what they were before his real life interfered.

"Hailey and I have a few things to do today—"

"So? Will you work with him?" his mother asked Hailey.

"I've asked her to work on my image already, Mom, Dad."

"I don't think I'm the right woman for that job," Hailey said quickly.

"Good money in that, I suspect," his father countered.

Finn sighed. Ever since he'd started making enough to pull his family out of debt and out of that shithole community he'd grown up in, plus get his dad some proper health care, all his father had been focused on was money, money, money.

For Finn it had been money and fame. And with his focus on that, all the seven deadly sins had begun to line up, one behind the other. But that was it, wasn't it? Own a sin or two or be a nobody who never did anything or went anywhere. Be voted most like to sit around with a thumb up his butt. Or in his case, voted most likely to become a starving artist.

Anyone could change their destiny. The process just might not look pretty.

"Can we see the photos you took yesterday?" Daisy asked.

"I don't have them with me," Hailey said.

"I have the ones you shared through online storage." Finn ran to grab his tablet from the bedroom, flicking it on. He hurried back to the deck, worried he'd offered his parents a chance to give Hailey the third degree. Instead, she was sipping his coffee, sitting beside his mother, getting the scoop on his childhood temperament. If it had been anyone else, he would have felt exposed.

"Finian's always liked turtles," his mother said, reaching for the tablet. "But I didn't predict this environmentalist side."

"What environmentalist side?" he asked.

His father shot Hailey an appreciative smile. "You're a good influence, my dear. You really should work with him."

"Oh, Bob. They don't want to mix business with pleasure," his mother said with a sly smile.

"So? The turtles?" Finn asked.

"The tabloids are all over the whole turtle thing, Finian," Daisy said. "That article with you down by the water has gone viral."

"The article?"

"It was all about you saving the turtles. It started in the local paper here."

"My sister is going to love you," Hailey said, reaching over to give him a light hug.

He slipped from her grip. Derek was going to be livid. Two environmentally slanted news items in less than a week. Finn pinched the bridge of his nose and inhaled slowly. This was how his career tanked. And Hailey was smiling as though it was the best thing in the world.

"Oh, Finian." His mom leaned over the tablet. "Look at how handsome you are. Hailey, you are incredible. Look how you've portrayed my boy. You really see him."

That, it seemed, was exactly the problem. She saw him, but not his career.

He stormed into the cottage, at a loss on what he should do.

"What's wrong?" Hailey asked, joining him.

He pointed to the tablet she was carrying. "I need you to fix my image."

She grinned. "You're on."

Chapter Twelve

Well, helping Finian fix his image was proving to be a particularly bad idea. Photos she'd taken in her studio as well as out in public were spread over her worktable. And every single one of them he'd rejected. She had to check in on the Walkers, and get her show to Simone, and having him spend the past hour rejecting everything she'd suggested was starting to get to her.

"I hired you to fix my image," Finian said, arms crossed. He looked so serious and business-sexy. If the world could see what he looked like right now he'd never have trouble finding work again. Too bad he was impossibly difficult.

"I don't get it, Finian. You want me to bury the turtle stuff in an avalanche of bad-boy disasters? That's not fixing your image, that's building on what you already have." She blinked back her disappointment and hurt.

"Who's going to pay money for this version of me?" His cheeks flushed as he waved a gorgeous photo of himself hunched on the rocks, looking concerned over the rare turtle in the background. The perspective was dead-on perfect. "This isn't going to rebuild the damage you've caused to my image, Hailey. Don't you get it?"

Tipping her head up, she fought the tears.

"I'm sorry that being seen with me did damage to your precious image. God forbid you be seen with someone wearing clothes."

"Hailey, don't be a drama queen. You know what I mean. Two environmental articles in a span of two days. That's not what the public imagines when they think of Finian Alexander. It's incongruent."

She shook her head, her disappointment a heavy weight in her chest. She'd thought he'd seen the beauty and art in what she did, and had falsely believed that he wanted it for himself. For his image. To build and grow out of this phase. Instead he was asking her to bury the real things that had happened while he was with her. He was rejecting her and the things she stood for.

She'd seen him maneuver last night. He'd held her up like a princess, while other people ran around, making his life effortless. He'd had locals take them parasailing, and wait in their boat while the two of them ate supper. He'd been polite and charming, but it was obvious who was being catered to, and there was no equal footing. And now she had put herself in a position where she was the assistant, hired to make his easy life perfect again. Not his girlfriend or equal.

Hailey puffed up her cheeks, then blew out slowly. But she was a professional. She could handle this. This wasn't personal. This was his image. His career. His car-crash disaster. It was his choice. Not hers.

"Finian, we can't work together. We have two very different visions, and I don't want to fight with you."

She couldn't believe she was giving up a good paycheck by saying no to working with him, but Simone was right. Hailey had let the cottage and its needs lead to enough career sacrifices. And now it was leading to friction between her and the man she liked. She closed her eyes, knowing that once her family saw the For

Sale sign on Nymph Island, she might regret this moment. But it was still the right move to make.

"Hailey, I hired you because you can do anything with that camera. You can *capture* my vision."

"I don't care how much money you have, Finian, I have a reputation to protect, as well. I live in the real world where it took years to build up to who I am today."

"So have I."

"Everything depends on my reputation."

"Same here."

They stared at each other as a breeze wafted through the open garage door, stirring papers.

"Then you understand why I can't work with you."

He let out a growl and pushed away from the worktable.

"Who do you want to be, Finian?"

He shook his head at her, his eyes filled with something she couldn't identify.

"I know you see the other man you could be. You didn't hire me, an award-winning nature photographer, to create some stupid fake drama. So why are you chickening out?"

Finian moved closer, loosely wrapping his arms around her shoulders. He kissed her lips with a gentleness that scared her. He rested his forehead against hers and sighed. "Oh, Hailey."

"What?" She pushed away. That was a break-up voice. A you-don't-understand-me voice that would soon say, "It's not you, it's me."

"Don't you want to be more than some car crash that people stare at, grateful it isn't them?" She could barely believe she was pleading with him. When had she begun to care so much about how others viewed him? Was it when she'd slept with him?

No, it was before then. When she'd seen his exposed,

vulnerable side, asleep in her chair. It was then that she'd felt the need to protect him. Not only from the world, but from himself. She had to convince him to see it her way. That the bad-boy persona was killing him. That he could be himself and get further.

Finian placed a hand on the back of his neck and stared at the ceiling, his T-shirt pulling across his muscular chest.

"Don't you see who you could be?" she asked. "You could make a difference in this world. Use your power for good instead of evil."

"Dammit, Hailey."

"I'm serious."

"You don't know me."

"Funny, but I think I do."

"Well, you *don't*."

"Are you afraid the world won't accept the real you—the man I've grown to care for?"

His eyes flicked to hers and his breathing halted.

She continued, "Are you afraid they'll chew you up and spit you out?"

"Yeah, pretty much."

"But don't you want to be more? Don't you want to prove to the world that you're more than what they see? That there is a real man under this artificial shell? What's holding you back? Why won't you be that deep and meaningful man I see, and who can change the world?"

"This is exactly why I need this bad image, Hailey. Don't you understand? It's my chance to making a difference."

Hailey scoffed and crossed her arms. "How?"

"The place where I grew up, Hailey. I made promises. Big promises. The only way I can reach those goals and meet my obligations is to be this man. This car crash you look down on. It pays the bills."

He cupped her chin, met her eyes. "If anyone knows how hard it is to pay the bills with meaningful art, it's you, Hailey."

She tugged her chin away. "Yeah, and I'm doing fine." Fine enough. Well, she would be if she didn't have the heavy responsibility of the cottage.

"But art isn't easy, is it?" He pointed to the stacks of framed photos she was taking to Simone's. "Are those your most arty photos you're taking for your show, or are you hiding the real you?"

She crossed her arms again. "You don't know *me*, Finian. So don't try and psychoanalyze me."

"I can't just suddenly go all artsy, Hailey. Don't you understand that? I *can't*."

"So you're going to reject your past? What about *Desperate Cowboy*?"

Finian threw his hands in the air and fell into her old armchair, sending dust motes dancing as he gave a dramatic sigh. "That was a lifetime ago."

"It won awards, Finian. It was your start. Your roots."

"Don't you think I know that?" He turned his face away from her, his jaw set in a way that made shivers run up her spine.

After a moment's silence he said quietly, "That movie is incongruent with the image I'm currently cultivating. The world wants to know if I can hold an Uzi in a convincing way, not whether I can keep up a five-minute monologue without boring the audience. I'm in a world where I need to work out, not convey fifty different facial expressions without looking hokey. I can't turn around and go back to my past without losing everything. You have to understand that. I made my choice ages ago and I have to stick with it."

He turned and made eye contact. His eyes were sad, heavy.

"I'm not prepared to live on the fringe again. I have obligations, too, Hailey. I have responsibilities. I'm not a do-nothing star who has lived an easy life and goes along for the ride. There's a lot of work involved. So if you want to help me, you have to do it on my terms."

"I can't believe you're not willing to consider that there might be a different option."

"You want to know me?"

She nodded.

"Then let me paint a picture. My parents had medical bills they'd been carrying for years. Dad's not able to afford health insurance that will cover him, and every once in a while things go to hell. I've paid for all of that. I bought them a house in a decent neighborhood where they don't have to worry about someone shooting up their front yard. Then I bought it back from the bank after one of Dad's medical mishaps. I sent my brother to rehab. Then college. Started an anonymous college scholarship in the community where I grew up so other kids could get out. And I made all sorts of community development promises I'm about to renege on." He began ticking things off on his fingers. "I have an agent who depends on me. A publicist. An assistant. They all rely on me making a living, so they can pay their mortgages, feed their kids. There are producers who could lose everything if I don't bring it all to the table. I don't just sit on screen and look pretty. There's a lot of work involved. And I pay a helluva lot in taxes, too. I have commitments. And being the celebrity car-crash everyone wants to read about in the tabloids is my way of meeting them."

Hailey swallowed. "I'm sorry, I never realized."

She wanted to tell him being a bad-boy wasn't the only option and that she understood obligations, but he continued on, a storm rocking his voice.

"That's exactly it, Hailey. You have no clue about me, my life. You've only met the version of me that you want to see. The guy on vacation."

She lurched as if she'd been slapped.

"You have all these assumptions about me, but you've barely even bothered to try and learn more about me." He stood and moved closer to her. "Did it ever occur to you that this image you look down upon is something I've carefully cultivated? That it's actually part of a large, overarching, multiyear career plan? That this image is actually something planned out? That I know what I'm doing?"

She blinked. Why would he slander who he was? Finian Alexander was perfect.

"You sold yourself out?"

He nodded, his eyes sad but fierce.

"Why would anyone choose to be a disaster when they could be living their real life?" She blinked back tears, not understanding why being such a loser in the public eye seemed like the best option.

"Have you not been listening?"

Hailey hugged herself, turning away. "I just don't understand."

She'd had to take jobs that didn't fit with who she wanted to be, but she'd always kept her goals in mind and was always working toward them. But Finian seemed to be rejecting that path entirely. Everything real. And if he was rejecting everything real in his life, where did she fit in? Nowhere.

She lowered her head with a sigh.

Finian gripped her arms, ducking his head so he could see her face.

"My agent has a full-fledged plan. A plan he'll put into action if

I don't pull my head out of my you-know-what and get some publicity. He's ready to leak made-up stories that will shorten my career. Yes, it will launch me temporarily, but not for long. This is a fickle business, show biz, and I need sustainability, Hailey. I depend on the work that comes in due to my image. Others do, too. So I have to ensure everything I put out there lines up with that image in order to shut up my agent, and get the roles I want. Being a bad boy is easy to maintain, because people do half of it for me. They're always looking for the bad side and that's something that is hard to screw up." He pushed a hand through his hair. "Or at least it was before I met you." He flashed her a crooked smile. "Being this good boy you want, it's difficult, Hailey. That's going to bring criticism I can't handle. I'm not perfect, and the image you want to present to the world is one I can't maintain. I'm not that guy. I'm human."

She sagged, knowing she couldn't convince him to see her side any more than he could convince her to see his. "Finian, can you go wait in the house? I need to think."

Unable to breathe properly, she placed a hand on his chest, and despite the pain inside, pushed him out of her studio, locking the door behind him.

RIGHT. SHE'D JUST LOCKED the object of her affections out of her studio.

She sagged against the door, needing its support. She'd found the layers she'd been looking for and that had scared her. She'd had no idea he had all those obligations and commitments and was helping so many people. It made her own problems look insignificant. So what if she lost a piece of land? He was saving *people*.

But why couldn't he see that his false image wasn't doing him any favors? That it would cripple him further down the career line and that it would eat away his soul? She'd tried the whole commercial thing and it had hurt her like she'd been swimming through shards of steel.

How could anyone live like that?

How could Finian?

But more importantly, why would he *choose* to live like that when there were other options? It didn't matter what you did with your life, there was never enough money. So why not do what you loved? If he let the world see who he really was he'd go so much further. So, so much further.

Hailey didn't even know why she cared what he did. It wasn't as though they were in love and were planning to spend the rest of their lives together in Hollywood. That would be a recipe for heartache. She may as well tie her heart to a major highway and wait for a transport truck to smush it. If he wanted money and a bad reputation, then what was it to her? It wasn't her job to show the world that he was a great guy, or convince him that he could make more money by following his heart.

There was silence on the other side of the garage door. Had he given up on their argument that easily?

She blinked back tears and sat at her computer, staring at the folder of images she'd taken of him being the man she and her sisters had always dreamed of. Someone kind and caring. Sexy. She clicked through sweet images of him with Tigger, the turtles, with fans. With him dappled in sunshine. A handsome, intelligent man with more depth than he cared to show. The world needed to see this side of Finian. The world would *love* this man. She couldn't keep him to herself—and not when she knew it could help him achieve his dreams.

Determined, she selected ten photos and uploaded them to her agent, along with intriguing captions, creating a story of the Finian she knew. It wasn't enough to ruin his current persona, but it was enough to show Finian what she had in mind for an image makeover. He might never forgive her, but he also might be thanking her for the next sixty years.

Her hands shook as she moved to her worktable. She looked at the stack of framed photos for her show. Finian was right; she was a hypocrite. She was hiding behind the commercial photos, instead of selecting the more arty ones. The ones where she'd followed her heart.

She glanced at the closed door, then carefully tucked away the original stack of photos before framing the others, one by one.

If Finian only knew the risk she was taking by choosing artistic photos.

But it was her reputation. It mattered more than money, didn't it?

And if she was right about following one's heart, then everything would turn out okay.

She shook her head and smiled. She and Finian were so much alike and yet so different.

There was a knock on her door and her heart sped up. *Finian.* She glanced at her computer and draped the dust cover over it as though it would profess her guilt if he saw it exposed.

Slowly she unlocked the door and peered out into the midday sun.

Finian pressed her palm against his lips, kissing it. "I'm sorry you can't rebuild me the way you want to. It's not you, it's Hollywood."

"I know...."

"I don't want you mad at me."

She cocked her head. "But wouldn't that be good for the image and all that?"

"You know me better than that."

She drew a line down his chest with her finger. He moved closer, siphoning the air from between them as he tipped up her chin. "What do you see?"

She stared into his eyes, absorbing their intensity. "I see someone who wants to be larger than life and who will be quoted in fifty years. Someone who makes a difference. I also see a wonderful man denying his true side. You know the world would love the real Finian as much as I do."

"You love me?" He shot her one of his sexiest grins.

"You know what I mean." She slipped out of his grip, retreating as she gave him a sassy glance over her shoulder. "Women like me don't go for men like you. We like men with five-year plans."

"I have a five-year plan. It involves being bad to the bone." He grabbed her elbow, pulling her to him so he could shimmy his hips against hers. "Besides, you keep telling me I'm not bad."

"I was wrong. You're a bad, bad boy." She pushed him away, unable to stay mad at him. He was like a big balloon full of life and joy.

So damn likable.

Finian released her, his face suddenly serious as he fell into her old armchair. He heaved a sigh laced with exhaustion and frustration. "I don't know what to do, Hailey, but I can't be that Renaissance man you want. Not yet." He cleared his throat, jaw tight. "Are we still working together? Because if we are, I need to set some boundaries and I need to have the final say on my image."

She shifted her gaze away. She'd already broken that rule.

"There are some things I am willing to do with my image—a

lot, in fact—but there are some things that would destroy me within a week."

She knelt in front of the chair, clutching his face. "I want to leave a mark on your life, Finian. A marker you can go back to and say, 'That was where my life changed, and it was all because of Hailey Summer.'"

"Trust me, there will be a mark, Hails." He pulled her into his lap, kissing her temple.

"If I'm going to work with you there needs to be a certain artistic element. If not, then you have to pay me more, and I have to remain anonymous."

"Okay."

"I want to work with you, Finian. You energize me in ways I can't figure out. But I can't be selling this whole bad-boy side and shooting tabloid photos unless there is a spin to it that allows me to use my artistic, creative side."

"Fine. We'll figure that out shot by shot."

She pressed a hand against his chest. "Do you trust me?"

He gave a light laugh. "Not especially. You tend to slap me a lot."

She shook her head and smiled. "I know your audience, Finian. They are people like me and they are ready for real. They crave it."

"*Do* you crave it, Hailey?" He pushed her off his lap so he could stand. "Because it seems to me that you get enough real life. You need the lighter side. The joy and frivolity."

"I'm...I'm getting better at it."

"Because that's what Finian Alexander provides—a break from the mundane for two hours or less. Nothing more. It's all I am. And it's what people need." He clutched her chin, his voice softening. "Even you."

"You also provide hope, Finian. Hope for a better world, a

better future. Letting out your real side can only add to that. When you are real is when I like you the most, and let go of all my burdens."

His eyes softened with affection and pride.

"But, Hails, is that what you're doing with your show? Creating hope? Leaving your indelible mark on the world? Letting your artistic side out to play?"

"As a matter of fact, yes. Thanks to you, I scrapped the commercial images and I'm going to hang the more artistic ones. The ones I *feel*. I'm choosing art even if it means breaking my sisters' hearts and taking a big financial risk. You taught me that."

"I'm pretty sure I didn't."

"I have to be true to myself and I can't keep hiding behind what works. You might not be there yet, but I am." She pulled him into her arms, kissed his lips. "As much as that surprises me, we aren't that different. We're just making different choices and taking different paths. You'll see what I mean." She tugged him toward the door. "Come on. I want to share something with you."

FINN MOVED WITH AN INTENSE focus, his actions purposeful. Hailey's photos were amazing. She'd taken every one of the most stellar shots from the pile of incredible pictures in her studio and framed them. There wasn't a single commercial shot like he'd expected. He still didn't understand what she'd meant about breaking her sisters' hearts, but he understood having to make decisions that sometimes went against what family members thought was for the better good.

Here in Simone's two-story boutique, he'd ended up pushing Hailey aside, a map popping into his mind of where each photo should be hung. Getting to work with her images was a privilege, and it stirred up his creative side as he imagined himself as an artistic director as he moved around the old converted house.

This was his role, and he was getting deeper into the zone and hanging pictures faster than Hailey could prep them.

He could see the whole story laid out in her images. The conflict here in the entry hitting people as soon as they came in, the resolution finalized on the top floor. He was breathing shallowly, finding the excitement of creating with her work invigorating.

Hailey had left to find more hooks, and he could hear hurried chatter and giggling in one of the side rooms. He smiled and switched two photos. Hailey's friend Simone, the store's owner, had been staying out of the way, plying them with coffee from a small pot in her office, and running ideas by Hailey.

The energy was contagious and consuming. Fun.

Finn slipped into the entry to grab an armload of images for one of the smaller rooms, and heard Simone shush Hailey. "I can't believe you slept with him," she said in a whisper that carried through the empty building.

"More than once, I might add," Finn called. He glanced around the corner to where Hailey was flushed clear from her sandaled toes to her forehead. She smiled shyly, in a way that warmed him. He wanted more. More of everything he probably could never have.

He ducked back into the hall and leaned against the first available wall. What was this woman doing to him? He couldn't do this with her. Not now.

He lifted the framed photo in his hands. It was of him.

His breathing hitched as if he had taken a fatal blow, and he sagged to the floor. He couldn't be the man she wanted. Needed. Deserved. He wasn't this guy she'd captured in black-and-white.

Still on his butt, he leaned around the door frame, intending to call out to Hailey, but changed his mind. The two women had their backs to him, studying a photo he'd hung only moments ago.

He held the picture of himself in his hands and swallowed. This framed man was the guy he wanted to be. How had she captured him? Revealed him? Seen him? And why was his image here with her nature photos?

He hugged the picture, then, kneeling, flipped through the others waiting to be hung. The rest were all nature related, and ones he had seen earlier. Where had this shot of him come from?

Turning, he moved quietly into the room where the women were tacking tags beside each photo, with the title, artist, and price.

"When does he go home?" Simone asked quietly.

Hailey shrugged. "It doesn't matter."

"Like hell it doesn't."

"It's just a fling. It doesn't mean anything."

Simone made a derisive sound and Hailey turned with a handful of tags and sticky tack, her face pale. Finn ducked behind a rack of dresses before she could see him, listening to her move around the room, hating the fact that she thought of him as a fling.

But that's all it could ever be, right? They lived in two different worlds and he would soon return to Hollywood, leaving her behind. He had to. Besides, it wasn't as though she was going to move away from her family for some movie star who wasn't even close to her type. And it didn't matter that she saw him for who he really was, she kept thinking of him as the celebrity with the shoddy image she needed to change. And when he returned to Hollywood all she'd see was the side of him that he could safely reveal to the world.

"You seem pretty sweet on him," Simone said.

"He's a great guy. Too bad he's a movie star."

The women laughed.

"I could swear I was listening to Snap," Simone said. "Hey, speaking of Maya and your sisters, how's the cottage thing going?"

"I rented it out."

"They went for it?"

"Anything for the cottage, right? And—"

"Hey," Finn said, pretending he'd just entered the room. He placed a light kiss on Hailey's cheek and gave her shoulder a squeeze. "The show looks great."

"Thanks to you." Hailey moved to study at a row of photos to the left of the dresses he'd been hiding behind, the old floorboards creaking as she walked. "I love how you paired images. Some seem to work together based on their texture, or filter. Some even fight with their neighbor. You know, elbowing each other out of the way so they can gain more attention. But there's something else I can't quite figure out." She gave him a look that resembled admiration. *That* was what he was missing from her. *That* was what he wanted. Every day from now until the end of time. He pulled her into his arms as Simone left to answer the phone ringing in her office.

"It's a story, Hailey."

She quirked her head, her lips twisted into a puzzled shape that made him want to kiss them back into a smile.

"A love story."

She glanced at the images from the corner of her eye. "But the subject matter..."

"You'll see it. Start in the shoe room. It begins with a quiet spring, then builds to a climax before the resolution on the top floor. It's perfect."

She went to move out of his arms.

"Look later." He bent to kiss her on the lips, pulling her closer and closer until her breathing turned heavy with need. Need for him. He broke the kiss and smiled. "Thank you, Hailey. Thank you for letting me be a part of your life."

"So, there *is* more to you than fistfights and explosions?" she teased.

"Only on Fridays."

"Friday? What time is it?"

"Two."

She slipped her arms around his neck, drawing him closer. "Excellent. Lots of time." Her lips were tantalizingly close and he could smell her raspberry lip gloss, wanting to taste it. "Because I think you deserve a reward for helping me find my way with my art, as well as helping destiny."

"I think I have time for that." He slipped out of her grip after pasting a big kiss on her lips. "Let's get out of here."

FINN HUSTLED OUT OF HAILEY'S car, laughing at how she'd nicknamed him Arty. He had no idea why that made him laugh. It wasn't a great nickname and it likely meant they were going to have another fight about him following his real side, but he loved how Hailey was smiling, and how that made him smile in return.

Hanging out with her felt so right. He'd gotten to the point where he couldn't stop touching her—and didn't want to. It was becoming difficult to imagine his life back in Hollywood, especially without Hailey.

He pulled her toward his little cottage with the wooden sunflower cutouts, and she laughed, dragging her feet, all smiles. "What's the big hurry, Arty?"

He growled like a primal beast and slung her over his shoulder as she laughed and pretended she wanted to get away. "I've been promised a reward for hanging your show with artistic flair, before showing up at the opening tonight as the artist's arm candy. It's time to pay up, sugar toes." He gave her a light slap on the butt and leaped up the steps to his cottage. "I'm going to make you enjoy living."

"You always do," she giggled.

Invigorated by letting his artistic side loose over at Simone's, he banged open the cottage door, unable to believe it had only been three days since she'd slapped him for coming on to her like a big jerk. And only two days since they'd been hunkered over a rare turtle like a couple of schoolkids.

A couple.

He laughed to himself. Like that would ever work. She was getting under his skin in ways he'd never thought possible.

He dropped Hailey on her feet and slipped his hands under her shirt, his lips making their way down her bare throat. She let out a purr of contentment, her hands reaching for his belt.

Oh, things were about to get good.

He began shuffling her backward toward the bedroom when a familiar perfume, heady, overdone, and expensive—he should know, he'd bought it—froze him in place.

"Well, isn't this just too cute for words," cooed a female voice.

Hailey pulled away so fast she struck his chin with her head, making him clutch it in pain.

"Finian?" His mother joined his ex-girlfriend.

Jessica crossed her arms over her bust, which was spilling out of her tight tank top as she watched Hailey adjust her T-shirt. "We have things to discuss."

"Oh!" Finn's father just about ran over Jessica as he came hurrying in to see what the commotion was about. "Well, this is awkward."

Jessica tugged Finn's arm, her rings digging into his flesh. "I need to speak to you."

Finn's mother pulled Hailey into the kitchen, chatting softly. Finn extracted himself from Jessica and followed them.

"We need to talk about our relationship," Jessica called, dogging his steps.

"We have no relationship. I'm seeing Hailey."

Hailey grew taller, a smile lighting her face, and he stepped to her side to wrap an arm around her shoulder, planting a kiss on her forehead.

"Yeah, that's kind of a problem." Jessica slapped a tabloid on the table. "Because according to the papers you're two-timing me."

"Well, that does fit with his reputation," Hailey replied, and Finn let out a laugh, giving her a squeeze.

"That's an old photo." He glanced at the caption Kissed and Made Up.

"This is what the public wants." Jessica slapped another tabloid down. Back Together? And another old photo. She dropped another tabloid onto the growing stack. Exclusive Insider on the Girl Who Broke Up Hollywood's Favorite Couple.

He glanced at Hailey, who was reading the paper with red cheeks.

"Hailey." He reached for her, but she stepped away. She wouldn't meet his eyes. "Did you talk to someone?" He looked back to the tabloid, flipping it open.

"No."

"Of course you didn't, because there is no you and him." Jessica gave Hailey a condescending look. "Daisy, can you take this girl out for coffee or something? Finn and I need to have an emergency meeting in regards to his image, as well as this latest *development*." She bored her eyes into Hailey on the last word, gazing straight down her surgically upturned nose.

"I think I'll go for coffee, too," Finn said.

"We need to address this, Finn. Now."

Something inside him grew taut to the point of breaking. "No." He stepped closer to Jessica. "I'm tired of these games. We were never real."

She let out a throaty laugh. "What does any of that matter? This is business, Finn, not *love*."

"How did I ever think you were some sort of a reward or prize?"

"Maybe we should let them talk business," his mother whispered to Hailey.

Hailey stepped toward the door, the crease between her eyebrows deepening. "Actually, I need to meet someone, so I should get going. Thank you, anyway."

Finn caught her on the porch, ignoring the paparazzo angling for a better shot on the path between the small cottages. "I'm sorry. I didn't know she was coming. I don't want her back. I didn't ask her to come."

"Finn, it doesn't matter."

He caught Hailey's hand in his, feeling as though he was losing the one thing he'd always wished for. "It does to me."

Chapter Thirteen

Hailey stood on the dock and waited for the Walkers, her cottage renters, to return from their stay on Nymph Island. They were supposed to meet her forty minutes ago, and without her boat she couldn't run out to the cottage to check on them. Where were they? Had she got the time wrong? Had they decided to stay an extra day and she didn't get the message?

She checked her phone for messages again and tried their cell number.

Nothing. No answer.

Today didn't seem to want to go her way, and she no longer knew if she was coming or going. And why had Jessica come to Muskoka so suddenly? It was as though the woman knew Hailey was trying to change Finian, and she'd come to his rescue.

Her phone rang and she answered without checking it.

"Hailey, Cedric here. Sold your photos."

She rubbed her forehead. "What photos?"

"The ones of Finian as a good boy up in the woods. You'll have a nice slider on…which site was it…" She could hear clicking in the background.

If this was what Hailey thought was going to work for Finian, then why did she feel as though she'd just stuck a knife in his back?

"Hmm. I just lost the email. But they're sold and it was decent money. Not great, I mean, it wasn't Finian showcasing his bad-boy side or anything particularly spectacular. But I managed to convince an editor that you had something there, and another side of the Finian Alexander we all know. We'll get some speculation going about him and build it up, and you'll be there on top, right?"

"Right. Of course."

"You okay? You sound kind of funny."

She closed her eyes to stop the world from swaying. She'd betrayed Finian. Gone against her word. Sold out both of them. And for what? To prove to him that she thought she knew best? She was no better than all the righteous people telling her to take the commercial route and skip making art.

She looked up at the sky, but the moving clouds made her dizzy and she had to close her eyes again. Finian would be back in Hollywood in a flash now that Jessica had come to claim him. He couldn't ignore his career nor his image. Those things always came first.

Pushing past the tightness in her chest, she told Cedric she was fine, and ended the call.

She stood there, struggling to shut off her mind, and the image of Finian drowning in Jessica's presence, as the boat, with the Walkers in it, finally came into view—being towed by one of the Duke's Marina guys. She held the towboat off the dock, biting her lip so she wouldn't show how upset she was as the driver filled her in. "Prop fell off. Want me to bring it in and send you an estimate?"

"Fell off?"

"Yup. Looks that way. Not sure what happened, but they said they lost momentum and a quick glance tells me the propeller's gone."

Hailey sighed. "Okay, take it in."

"They've already offered to pay for the damage."

"It's an old boat, I doubt this was their fault."

In the grand scheme of things a prop wasn't so bad, and it could be fixed and paid for before her sisters even noticed. Hailey scooped up the line and shoved the towboat away from the dock. Then she hauled on the wet rope, bringing the broken Boston Whaler closer so she could help the Walkers unload.

Once she had them on shore, she pushed her boat off from the dock, letting it be towed away.

"I am so sorry, Hailey." Jenni came forward, looking immaculate in a well-fitted dress. "We'll pay to get it fixed."

Her son held up a purple shell, white on the inside. "Look what we found."

Hailey nodded to the boy, and said to Jenni, "No, *I'm* sorry. The boat's old and I doubt it was anything you did. I'm sorry you had to deal with the inconvenience."

The women watched each other for a moment, then Jenni said, "You have a real gem there. So much space. I want to run home and write a story about Muskoka. And I love how your antique wicker matched. What a find."

"It's original."

Her husband began herding his wife toward the rental car where he'd already stowed the luggage he'd hauled from the dock to the car. "Time to go, Jenni."

"Oh, let's stop for coffee on the way," she said, hurrying to catch up. She turned back to wave at Hailey as she gathered her daughters and son. "Thanks again!"

"Hope you had fun!" Hailey waved back, turning as someone behind her called, "Hailey! You're here!"

She froze as her sisters and niece came down the slope to the docks, picnic baskets in hand. Her eyes cut to the retreating family.

"We figured since the fumigation was done we could finally have our much-delayed Canada Day picnic on Nymph Island." Daphne waved a basket.

"Fumigation?" Jenni gasped as she hurried by with a forgotten bag.

Hailey turned. "No, it's okay. My sister is talking about somewhere else."

"What?" Daphne stopped a few feet away, her cotton dress flapping in the breeze, as she stared at the family climbing into the packed car.

"Never mind. I'll explain later," Hailey said.

"Where's the boat?" Melanie looked from the family to Hailey and back again.

"Can you give me a minute?" Hailey sucked a breath through her nose, dug her fingers into her hips, wishing she could run away.

Mr. Walker hurried up and handed her a check. "I can't believe I forgot to pay you! Our mailing address is on the check—please send us the bill for the boat if we broke it." He patted Hailey's hand before she could brush away the offer. "Although, since my wife doesn't fly, we'll be taking a cruise back to the U.K. If you don't hear from us immediately, it's because we're lost at sea."

"Okay. Thank you." Hailey folded the check and tucked it into the pocket of her shorts. She turned back to her sisters, who were standing agape.

Wordlessly, Hailey pointed to a nearby maple and her sisters and niece joined her under its spreading branches. Their attention flicked between the packing family and Hailey.

"I rented out the cottage. That family was there for the past few days."

Hailey's three sisters all focused on her, their blue eyes wide.

"Is that why we couldn't go out there?" Daphne asked, waving Tigger to come back from the water.

"You rented it without asking us? I thought we were in this together," Maya said, crossing her arms.

"It's in trust in my name," Hailey replied.

"For all of us, Hailey. I think renting it out is a group decision," Daphne said.

"Do we still get to have our picnic?" Tigger asked, swishing the skirt of her yellow dress.

"Yes!" Daphne replied.

"No," Hailey said.

"Did you rent it out again?" Maya asked. "I hope you're charging enough. You know…" She tapped her chin in thought. "This might be a good plan. We could fix up a few things with the income."

"No, I haven't rented it out," Hailey said, before Maya got too far off into her business world. "And the boat crapped out on them. Duke's guy just took it away to replace the prop—sounds like it fell off. So…we're not going out to the island."

"What?" Daphne stared at the empty boat slip as though it would tell her the full story.

"Did you get additional insurance before renting?" Melanie asked. "I don't think our regular home owners' policy covers this."

"The insurance was canceled years ago," Hailey replied quietly, "and I'm pretty sure the prop fell off because the boat is old, not because of anything they did."

"Why was the insurance canceled?" Melanie asked.

"It wouldn't cover the cottage's old wiring without a major increase in our premiums."

"Did you shop around? You know there are some places—"

"Maya, not now, okay? I made the decision years ago. We couldn't afford it, trust me."

"Why didn't you talk to us, though?"

"You were in school. And it was outrageously expensive, Maya. It was the same year our taxes went up by almost 30 percent."

"What?" They all stared at Hailey.

"But you haven't charged us that much more for our portion of the taxes," Melanie said slowly.

"Why did you rent the cottage out?" Daphne asked, her attention focused, again, on the empty slip.

"We need the money."

"I thought everything was fine," Maya said. "Why didn't you say something?"

"Well, it isn't fine, and it hasn't been for a really long time," Hailey snapped. The last thing she needed was her sisters telling her how she should have done things.

"Whoa!" Daphne stepped between Hailey and Maya. "You love each other. Peace and harmony."

"Shut up, Daphne," Maya said, sharing a look with Hailey.

"So, why do we need the money?" Melanie asked.

"Because if we don't pay years of back taxes the island will be seized for a tax sale on August 30."

The sisters gasped, sharing looks of disbelief.

"I'm sorry." Hailey let out a sigh, her shoulders drooping. "Mom didn't want you to know that we were behind on taxes when she passed the deed over to me, and I thought I could cover it, but I—I couldn't. She wanted you to be able to live your lives without the burden of this money pit changing the course of your destiny. She wanted you to follow your dreams and not be held back by the cottage. She didn't want it to own you."

"Why didn't you tell us?" Maya asked. Hailey lowered her gaze and her sister threw her hands in the air. "Did you ever consider asking if we could help?"

"I'm sorry." Hailey looked up. She thought of the paychecks

that would be coming in because of Finian. But even they wouldn't be enough. She couldn't pull it together in time. The cottage was going to have to go up for sale. "I'm so sorry I let you down."

Daphne, tears in her eyes, pulled her into a hug. "I'm sure you did your best."

When the two finally parted, Maya was sitting by the shore, hugging her knees to her chest.

"What did you do with our money?" Daphne asked.

"I paid the taxes, but we started out behind, and just kept falling further and further back no matter what I tried."

Tears streaked down Daphne's face and Melanie gave her a hug. Daphne said, her voice wobbling, "I guess we'd better find a way to say goodbye to Trixie Hollow."

HAILEY SNIFFED BACK THE TEARS and drove around her house twice before giving up on the paparazzi milling about in front of her house, and driving right up onto the lawn and into her backyard, as she had with Finian. Her car left pale tracks across the grass, she noted, as she dragged her tired body to her house.

All she wanted to do was sleep, but she had the opening for her show tonight. She stared at herself in the mirror of her en suite bathroom. She didn't know who she'd become. She'd kept secrets from her family, had lied to her sisters for years, then betrayed the man she'd taken to bed, and broken her promises.

Who had she become in her quest to be an artist?

Sighing, she checked her phone as she poured herself a glass of white wine. No text from Finian. Did that mean his ex was back in his bed? That the website had already posted her photos that betrayed Finian's wishes, and he was done with her? Or was he blindly getting ready to come to her opening, happy at how she'd taken his new image into her hands?

She slipped into a black wrap dress that barely grazed her knees, and pulled on her nicest sling backs. Pretty good for a local artist. She smoothed her hair into a French twist, spritzing it with hair spray, trying not to think about Finian. She swallowed against the lump of need in her throat, and braced herself against the vanity. Why hadn't she listened to him? Why had she sold those photos?

The need to be wanted, desired, kept and protected ate at her. She'd thrown any chance she'd had away. To be understood. And to be loved, however fleetingly.

Hailey smoothed the last strands of hair and mentally moved through her show, thinking of the things she would say to potential buyers. Her mind stilled, picking up the threads of the story Finian had created. It almost felt as though he'd recreated *Beauty and the Beast*. How could that be? A young woman in love. Forced to make a choice. But how had he done that with her nature photos?

Was she projecting her desires?

It's a story, Hailey. A love story.

Her mind raced through the images. Deer. Beautiful and ugly. Destroyed forests. Blooming flowers. Ladybugs after the long winter. And in the end, on the top floor, the beast turned into a beautiful prince.

Finian.

The man she hardly dared believe existed…was real.

She stared at herself in the mirror. How could she make Finian and her sisters understand that everything she'd done was for them? It was for them. Her art was her chance to change the world. Their world.

FINN NUDGED A PHOTOGRAPHER away from Jessica and ushered her into the restaurant he'd been in less than twenty-four hours ago with Hailey. It felt like a week. His phone buzzed with a text and he ignored it. He'd had so many unsolicited calls and texts in the past four hours he was going to have to change his number again.

How had Jessica unleashed the hounds so damn fast? Did the paparazzi all have private jets, so they could be there in an instant? Sea planes that could land outside his little cottage? Actually, if they were anything like that schmuck Austin, then yeah, they probably did. Finn also guessed that Jessica was likely in cahoots with at least half of them, which would explain why their "back together again" stories had spread so fast and why his little corner of Muskoka was crawling with paparazzi.

This had to be some big cook-up between Jessica and their shared agent. Finn could smell it wafting over him, cloying like the smell of garlic and butter in this place. How had he ever let them gain control of his life? His reputation? His world?

Oh yes, because he needed the money and fame.

Last night's waitress greeted them with a smile. "Finian Alexander, you bad boy. Someone new and beautiful every night." She cast an assessing look at Jessica who gave her a smile that would befit a corpse, it was so cold and lifeless.

The waitress sashayed to the same table he'd shared with Hailey.

"I've been saving it for you," she said, leaning close so Finn could ogle her cleavage while he seated himself. He made a point of looking away, of letting her know he wasn't interested. The large window to his right overlooked the sun setting on water. Beautiful.

Unfortunately, the view was instantly blocked by a flock of

buzzing paparazzi. Finn lurched back in his seat, afraid the way they were banging against the glass as they jockeyed for the best position would break the window, showering him in shards.

"Scotch on the rocks, like last night?" the waitress purred. She flicked her eyes at Jessica.

"Both of us," she answered.

The waitress turned her attention to Finn, her head cocked as if to say, *You okay with her speaking for you?*

"Yeah, sure. Whatever." Why bother wasting energy fighting over a stupid drink? They didn't care who he really was or what he really wanted.

The waitress sashayed back to the bar.

"You seem upset," Jessica said, smoothing a linen napkin over her lap. She held her back straight, the epitome of elegance with her sleek build and well-threaded outfit. Yes, she was what everyone wanted to look at across the table.

Except for Finn.

He laughed as he remembered how only a few days ago he'd thought not being attracted to Jessica had meant there was something wrong with him.

He flicked his napkin out with a snap and laid it across his lap, ignoring her. He briefly closed his eyes, willing his face to be void of any emotion. The past few days with Hailey had been like another life. A life he'd enjoyed immensely.

And he'd probably ruined any chance of keeping it by choosing a career that would make him money, but could never resemble anything close to reality. How did you mesh the fake life with a real one? A real woman?

The timing was all wrong.

"My, my. You got used to not having this." Jessica tipped an eyebrow toward the crowded window.

"Why are you here?"

"In case you haven't noticed, you're floundering. You've hit the 'just about made it' wall that holds so many back from becoming A-list. I'm here to help you through to the other side. To drive it home." She flicked a smile at the window and rested a hand over his, where it rested by his cutlery. "And to mend your poor broken heart." She flashed him a smile that had, once upon a time, turned him on.

Fighting the urge to whip his hand out from under hers, he leaned forward, smiled as if he cared, and said, "Dream on, Jessica."

He pulled his hand back as he grabbed his phone. He pretended to show her a few photos, as if bringing her up-to-date on his little vacation, buying for time as the flashes went off on the other side of the window. No more of this touchy-feely crap. They'd come here to talk business, not give the media a story. He'd been so out of it after Hailey had left that he hadn't even thought about paparazzi as Jessica hauled him away from his parents.

All he was thinking was that the sooner he heard Jessica out, the sooner she'd leave him alone. The problem was, his ex had a point. With Hailey he'd come much too close to giving in to the urge to be some amazing male version of Angelina Jolie—damn, that woman had a good PR person.

Jessica knew what he needed. Hailey knew what he wanted. And those were two very different things.

Jessica's eyes assessed him like the businesswoman she was. Monetizing him. And while he thought this should bring him relief, in fact, right now it made him want to punch the air and fight her ideas to the death. When Hailey had looked at him, even when she was behind her camera, he'd felt safe, understood, *seen*.

But this wasn't about who he was. It was about money. Fame.

Nothing real.

Nothing like Hailey.

The waitress placed their drinks on the table. "Tonight we have a really lovely—"

"That's fine, thank you." Jessica waved her away.

Finn fought the urge to apologize to the server, who looked hurt. Canada was getting to him.

"Do you have it in you to make the A-list push?"

Finn gave a slight nod, leaning back to sip his awful drink. "Not just a visit, Jessica, but a long-term stay."

"You've had a taste of the good and bad now, and maybe you want to change your mind?"

"You know what I want."

The waitress, who was walking by with a tray of drinks, met his eye, and he gave her a wink. She just about dumped its contents on him as she wobbled. "I'm sorry," she mumbled, blushing like crazy as she carried on.

His game was still on, but all he could think of was the hurt look in Hailey's eyes when she'd left him at his cottage hours ago. He checked his phone for a text from her and got tired of wading through the incessant stream of texts from people he'd never get around to blocking. Definitely time to ditch the number.

"Do you have a burn phone?" he asked Jessica. He waved his hand. "Never mind. You're probably the one who gave out this number, anyway."

"You were ignoring my calls."

Carefully, he unclenched his hand from around the glass of scotch.

"So?" Jessica asked. "What do you want? Other than to have that waitress come by and rape you with her eyes again."

"Jessica..."

"She was undressing you. Why do you think she came undone? You're such a *bad boy.*" Jessica's voice had turned to a low, promiscuous growl full of promise that would make most men run to the washroom in search of condoms. "So, what do you want?" She waggled her eyebrows suggestively.

Finn angled a shoulder to block the sight of the cameras to his right. "I want to be like Julia Roberts."

Jessica tossed her head back, her perfect hair bouncing as she let out a loud trill of laughter, her fingers lightly touching her throat. She leaned forward, the smile still on her face. "Hon," she said, her voice serious, "I hate to break it to you, but you're no Julia Roberts. That girl put in her time. She stayed focused on her goal and worked her fingers off while protecting her girl-next-door image. That woman knew who she was at all times—cute and fun with a giant laugh. Easy to love. Whereas you are a bad boy. One who is suddenly a Boy Scout with a degree in art who saves turtles that are uglier than Christopher Walken."

"It's not a degree." Finn forced himself to lay his hands flat on the table. "It's a minor in film studies."

"You're not big enough, Finn. Not solid enough to be *yourself*. Or for that matter, to shun big stars from being in your life. There's no room for a real life."

"Julia married the grip, had a family, lives a quiet life. Her life is real *and* she's A-list. That's what I'm talking about."

"You are not marrying the grip." Jessica grabbed his hand, her nails digging into his skin. "You haven't put in the time. Your audience isn't going to follow this sudden move. This is a departure from who you've been, and they're going to be confused. It would be like Coca-Cola suddenly going on an antisugar campaign."

"It's hardly the same."

"You can't marry the paparazzo. She's a nothing. A nobody."

"Why not? You sleep with them."

Jessica sucked in a breath, her eyes flashing. "Being in bed with someone from a business perspective is a lot different than setting up house."

"Since when does the world get to decide how I live my life?"

"Since the moment you stepped into the limelight and other people's income began to depend upon what you do there."

Finn closed his eyes and let the scotch burn a path down his throat, before waving for a second drink.

The waitress brought him another, shooting a worried glance at Jessica. Yeah, she had a right to be worried. Jessica chewed up the world and regurgitated it for lunch.

A new round of flashes snapped off beside him as he started his second drink. The goddamn paparazzi. He was ready to throw a table through the window to make them go the hell away.

"Live your real life in the background," Jessica said. She stroked the top of his free hand, which clenched under her grip. "Once you are solidly A-list."

"And when will that be?"

"Right around the time you ask me back," she said with a sly smile.

"That would be rather awkward. You and me and Hailey all living together in my little house. You following us around, trying to interfere and make room for yourself."

Jessica laughed. "You really think she's following you back to Hollywood?"

"You and I don't belong together, Jessica."

"Oh, I think we do."

"Give me one solid reason."

"Demi Moore and Ashton Kutcher."

"That's not a reason."

"Why do you think they brought Tom Selleck in to date Monica on *Friends*? The same reason Derek set us up together. We're infusing classic star and new man on the block. It boosts us both. You know, place the known with the lesser known. Cross-pollinate audiences." She cooed and patted his hand. "Sorry, baby. Am I hurting your pride?"

"No," he said, his voice hard. "Please continue."

"I breathe legitimacy into your stardom by being with you. And you breathe new energy into mine." She stood, ditching her napkin as she swiftly grabbed his face and planted a long, soulful kiss on his lips.

Hailey was going to be really, really mad when she saw this in the papers.

"And you and that girl?" Jessica said, his face in her grip. "It'll never last. You don't live in the same world, let alone the same country."

FINN SHOVED JESSICA through the throng of paparazzi and into a waiting limo, and was struck again by how different his world was when she was in it.

The way she arranged limos and paparazzi. Jessica was always working. Always building the image. Whereas he'd come here to hide out and try being human. Because really, when it came right down to it, that was the big difference between them, and why he couldn't live a true Hollywood life.

"I'm never going to be A-list, am I?"

The flashes from the paparazzi died off as the car pulled away from the restaurant, and he blinked away the white spots in his vision.

Jessica continued looking out the window, adjusting her neckline. "Lot of rocks here, aren't there? And not a palm tree in sight."

Finn pushed into the seat cushions. "Maybe I need to make it public that I'm the benefactor behind my community charities."

"Why would you do that?"

"Why not?"

"This is because of that girl, isn't it?"

"Who? Hailey?"

"She's going to destroy you and all you've worked for."

Finn thought of all the things Hailey had changed within him over the past few days. He'd come here hoping to fix himself, and she'd taken one look at him, slapped him, and in the process somehow started to turn him around. Got his head put on straight, and pointed him in the right direction. Helluva good slap to be able to do that.

"Maybe I need to tear down this bad-boy image so I can rise again. Stronger. Better. Brighter. New."

"You sound like a sentimental, lovesick fool purring like a friggin' pussycat."

"I'm serious, Jessica. Why can't I change my image? Why can't I somehow leverage my good deeds? Why does it have to remain a secret?"

"Because it will destroy the image that Derek and I have built."

"Exactly."

"What are you getting at, Finn? You signed up for this. You know this has always been a good deal for all of us."

"You've never cared about the real me, Jessica. You don't know me, love me."

"And does *she* love you?"

"It's all about fame and the bottom line with you. I want more."

She squared off. "Are you really doing this sentimental shit? Why can't you be happy with what you have in Hollywood? Why do you think you deserve love on top of it all?"

"I'm getting real, Jessica. Real with myself. My life. With what I want." He called to the driver, "You can let me off here."

"We're in the middle of the woods!" Jessica exclaimed.

"I'd rather ride with the paparazzi. I can be anyone with them."

"They'll have forgotten you by tomorrow if you change tactics!"

"Have a nice life, Jessica."

"Don't ruin your career! I read that you are saving turtles and that is not acceptable! Get back in this car this instant!"

"Jessica, let's face it. You don't really care, and there are about a thousand young men out there who are ready to take my place. Go find one of them to be your new puppy. I'm done." He checked his watch. "In fact, I'm very late for a date with a woman who accepts me for who I am."

Chapter Fourteen

The early morning sun shone brightly as Hailey dropped the tabloid onto Simone's coffee table as though it had burned her. She couldn't breathe. She couldn't think.

That…that *bastard*.

And the worst part was that she deserved it for betraying him. But this wasn't even a tit-for-tat move. It couldn't be. There hadn't been enough time for him to have seen her photos in *Celeb Dirt!* and retaliated by kissing Jessica at *their* restaurant in Port Carling.

"Where did this come from?" Hailey pointed to the front page photo of Jessica and Finian.

"Austin dropped it off. He said the paparazzi are still all over your lawn, too."

Hailey sagged onto the couch and Simone joined her.

"You can hide out here as long as you'd like."

She nodded, her stupidity burning through her. Hadn't she known he'd do this to her? Hadn't she known she was only a sideline distraction as his summer fling? A way to pass the time until Hollywood wanted him back?

It had felt real because he was an actor. No other reason.

At least she'd also managed to pull a punch with her own photos.

"Is this why he didn't show last night?" Simone asked.

Hailey shrugged, blinking back tears. "I guess so."

"You okay?"

"No."

"What are you going to do?"

Hailey rubbed her eyes and shook her head. "I don't know. List the cottage with a Realtor?"

"No, I meant with Finian."

"Roll over and play dead?" She gave her friend a pitiful look and moaned. "I feel like a complete loser, Simone. I promised myself I'd never fall for a summer man and his games again."

"I know. But he was a movie star." Simone shot her a wicked grin. "You slept with Finian Alexander."

Hailey let out a laugh and shook her head, her eyes tearing up.

"Oh, girlie." Simone gave her a half hug. They sat in silence for a moment. "I don't think you should list the cottage."

"What?" Hailey turned to face her.

"I know. You owe money and could lose everything, but don't you think…don't you feel…?" Simone raised her hands in question.

"Feel what?"

"That something's going to happen?"

"Could you be a little more specific?"

Simone shrugged, her cheeks flushing. "I don't know. It just seems like with you Summer sisters some miracle appears in the final hour, that's all. Or maybe I'm sentimental and don't want to see the cottage go." She brushed off her jeans as she stood, yawning. "I'm probably just being a romantic. I'm going to go make coffee. Want one?"

Hailey nodded.

A few moments later someone knocked at the front door and

Hailey glanced toward the kitchen before getting off the couch to answer it, hoping the paparazzi hadn't found her.

"I'll get it," she called, as the banging became more insistent. "Wow, don't break down the door!" Hailey wrenched it open to see a wall of paparazzi lurch forward from their spot on the sidewalk, a flurry of shutter clicks blocking out the sound of the tree frogs singing in the adjacent woods. She shielded her face and slammed the door.

The knocking started up again and Hailey peeked through the eyehole, her heart beating furiously. "Um, Simone?" she said, raising her voice to be heard across the main floor.

"Yeah?"

"Are you expecting Jessica Cartmill?"

"I'm guessing she would be here for you."

"Great," Hailey muttered. She opened the door, shielding her face in advance. Reaching out, she pulled in Jessica, who was wearing a typical celebrity-hiding-out getup—large sunglasses and a floppy hat. "What the hell did you bring to my friend's door?"

"A hail storm. That's what they've dubbed it." Jessica lowered her glasses, taking Hailey in from her bare feet, up past her borrowed nightie, to her messy French twist left over from last night.

"Why are you here? How did you find me?" And why wasn't it Finian at the door? "And thanks, by the way, for bringing the paparazzi." She opened the door and yelled, "Get off the begonias!"

Jessica moved into the living room as if she owned it. "We need to talk about Finn."

"No, we don't."

"He thinks he loves you, and he's about to self-destruct because of that small little fact." Jessica sounded begrudging.

Hailey opened her mouth, but so many things came to mind she couldn't figure out which one to choose, so she shut it again.

"Why do you think he loves me?" she asked finally.

"He's trying to sacrifice years of hard work."

Hailey sat on the couch, trying to sort things out. Did that mean Finian saw her point of view in regards to his image? And if so, then had everything she'd felt with him actually been real? She raised a hand to her mouth. Had she just messed it all up by releasing nice-guy photos of him without permission?

No. He'd kissed Jessica last night and hadn't come to her opening as promised.

He was still a schmuck.

"You've seen the side of Finian that his agent and I have been trying to hide for years. And that's a problem."

"It's *his* career," Hailey said, still trying to puzzle things out. "*His* life."

Jessica gave a hard laugh. "Yeah, but it isn't. Okay? Things are getting out of control with the pictures you released to *Celeb Dirt!* —oh, yes, I know it was you. It's pretty obvious, Hailey Summer. And you're destroying him with this. You understand?"

"What do you mean?" She needed to sit down. No, she already was sitting. She needed to lie down.

"It's going viral," Jessica continued. "Everyone is already yammering on about this supposed soft side to Finn."

Hailey wrapped her arms around herself. She'd sold out the one thing that had been great about her summer. And for what? An old building on an island that she was going to lose, anyway.

She closed her eyes. She needed to talk to her sisters, sit on the dock on Nymph Island, figure everything out, and get grounded again.

Standing, she led Jessica to the door, warring with her emotions.

"What do you think is going to happen to Finn's career as an action hero now that everyone is thinking he's out here playing house in Canada?" Jessica asked, her voice resentful.

Hailey's cheeks burned and her hands shook. "If it truly mattered to Finian, he'd be here. Not you."

"You don't get it, do you? You don't *get* what it's like to be a celebrity."

"And you don't get what it's like to be real." Hailey turned the doorknob.

Jessica laid a hand on Hailey's and she fought to keep herself from flinging it off.

"You hurt him, Hailey. He needs someone like me to protect him. He's a lost man trying to become a big star, and he's going to be eaten alive. And you know why? Because of you. If he falls, it will be because of you. Because you used him and you broke his trust."

"Don't play me." Hailey yanked her hand out from under Jessica's.

"You don't even know what game we're playing."

"Actually, I do. But it's a game for two and you're the third wheel." She opened the door, the crowd of photographers moving closer like a wall. "Have a nice life, Jessica."

"YOU WHAT?" FINN HELD his aching head. His ride with the paparazzi the night before had evolved into a long bender. They'd gone searching for Hailey at the opening, but finding everyone had left, they'd moved on to her house, where the lights were out. Then they'd started checking out the local bars, hoping to spot her. Eager to help local businesses, they'd purchased drinks in each establishment and before long, the night had involved him and a few others waterskiing in the dark as they, unsuccessfully, tried to find Nymph Island. It had been a fun way to blow off steam about Jessica, and would probably result in getting his mug back in the tabloids as a temporary measure while he tried to figure out his life.

However, now Jessica was standing beside his bed, insisting he come and deal with some sort of crisis that sounded a lot like her having chewed out Hailey to no effect.

She thrust a tablet full of "good boy" images at him.

"Aspirin," he said, trying to focus.

"Taken by your *girlfriend*. She posted them on *Celeb Dirt!* along with some chirpy 'family man' captions. Happy?"

He glanced at the images. Definitely taken by Hailey. He groaned and rolled over, tugging the blanket over his head.

What the hell did he miss while he'd been passed out?

"What time is it?" he groaned. It felt as if he'd just dragged his ass to bed.

"Two. In the afternoon."

He *had* just gotten to bed. An hour and a half ago. He needed sleep. Caffeine. Hailey.

"Go away unless you're Hails," he said.

"She's done with you, Finian. Don't you understand?" Jessica's voice was close, as though she was hissing at him through the covers. "She got what she wanted and she's done. Washed her hands of you and your crap."

"Am I in the tabloids? For bad-boy stuff?" He hated the way his voice rose in hope, betraying his emotions. His vulnerability.

"Yeah, online. A hazy shot that does you no justice." Jessica whipped the blankets off him and he groaned as the bright light stabbed his eyes. She thrust the tablet at him again.

He took another glance at the photos. Definitely Hailey. He read the captions and suppressed the urge to hurl.

"I thought this was what you wanted," Jessica said.

He glanced at the tablet again. The unexpected betrayal hit him again like a punch to the gut. The one person he'd thought he could trust, and she'd taken the version she wanted of him—the one he'd told her to keep quiet—and sold it to the public. She was no different from everyone else.

What a fool he'd been. And he'd even been warned by her old friend Polly at the party in Windermere. *Honey, you just have to watch Hailey. She'll tell you one thing, then do the other.*

"Doesn't anyone want me for me?" he moaned.

"Oh, stop feeling sorry for yourself, and get up so we can fix this."

"There's nothing to fix, and didn't I already break up with you today?"

"That was yesterday, and it's gone viral, Finn."

He pulled a pillow over his face, the soft cotton comforting. Of course it had gone viral.

Wasn't there anyone in the world he could trust, and who would want the best for him and not themselves?

He tugged the tablet over and took a closer assessment of the damage. His stomach churned as he flipped through the images. He looked beautiful. Happy. Real. Content. Successful and confident. Like someone he'd like to be. Someone to be envious of.

But that was his private side—a side he'd shared only because he'd trusted her.

He stood and threw his shoes against the wall, making Jessica jump.

"Why did I even leave the 'hood?"

"Do you want to see a bender photo from last night?"

He glanced at an image Jessica brought up on the tablet. He paused for a better look, his anger still pumping through his veins. "Is that me pretending to eat a spotted turtle?" He swore and swung at the air before collapsing on the bed, diving his head under a pillow that smelled of Hailey.

Hailey had been right to sell him out. He was a big, fat jerk.

"The good news is that with all this controversy around you, you should be able to help those charities of yours. The bad news is that this could be the burst of light before your stardom implodes."

"I don't want to think about it."

"I told that woman to back off."

Finn lifted his head, wishing Jessica was a cup of coffee and not his needling ex. "You what?"

"She needed to be warned. She's just some small-town chick who doesn't understand the consequences of messing with your image…"

Finn couldn't hear the rest of what Jessica said over the rage of blood roaring through his ears.

He leaped out of bed. "Quit interfering."

"Um…helping?" She gave him a valley girl look.

"You're making things worse. Stay away from her and quit meddling in my life. Didn't I already tell you to leave me alone?"

"You're confused, Finian."

"I know, and you're only making it worse. I need to see Hailey."

"You aren't going to have a life if you let her near you. Did you hear they are stopping the development of a very lovely resort and spa because of those old things—and because of you." Jessica folded her arms, eyes narrowed. "Just remember Finian, if you go down, so do I."

"Go home."

Jessica turned on her heel, and with a glare, left the room.

Finn sagged, trying not to think. Trying not to feel.

Being a celebrity sucked.

He tugged the tablet closer and, unable to resist, flicked

through the photos again. Ten images of him happy and relaxed. Looking like a family man, with Tigger in one of her fluffy party dresses resting on his hip. One of him smiling at Hailey over a cup of coffee, his hair bed-head messy. One of Hailey smiling over her shoulder at him while he was strapped to her back for parasailing. The amazing shot of him with the turtle in the reeds. One she'd taken in her studio, where she'd caught him just before a laugh. His eyes were lit up with what looked an awful lot like love.

Was he really this man? Could he be this person *and* fulfill his obligations? Could he make a difference with something as innocent as an endangered species? What would happen if he said "amen" to these photos and began a life worth living? A life full of meaning?

He ran his hands through his hair, wishing he had a crystal ball so he could look down the paths presented to him, so he could see where they would take him. And which path would lead him to Hailey. The one where they ended up happy together.

Finn reached for his vibrating phone. *Derek.* He flipped it on its face, wishing he'd lost it in the lake last night.

A few moments later the cottage phone rang, then his mother entered his room.

"Derek is on the phone for you."

"Tell him I'm sleeping."

"He said he needs to talk to you even if you're, uh, indisposed."

"Thanks." Finn took the phone and turned it off.

His mother raised a brow, the *Toronto Sun* dangling from her hand. A familiar face was smiling out from the pages.

"What's that?" he asked, pulling the visual arts section from her grip.

"Hailey." His mother gave him a questioning look. "You missed her opening last night."

"Yeah, I'm an asshole, Mom."

"Language, please, Finian."

"Sorry."

One last look from Daisy and she closed the door, leaving him alone with the article.

Finn read the story about Hailey. New York galleries were already abuzz about her show at Simone's. And critics loved how she'd hung a story and not just photographs. It was an unexpected surprise, they said. But the worst was that she'd given him due credit for hanging the show. Him. Finian Alexander. Linked to her artistic statement.

He lowered the paper and pushed the heels of his palms into his eyes. His cell began vibrating again and he knocked it off the bedside table, smashing it underfoot until it cracked and its screen went black.

Swallowing hard, he slowly tugged on a pair of jeans. He was a fake bad boy who was hiding his artistic side, and she was winning awards and getting big paychecks for revealing that fact to the public.

Never trust a noncelebrity especially when she had a camera. Rule number three. And he'd broken it along with all the rest.

And for what? A girl who didn't love him back.

FINN PAID THE MAN in the cherry-red boat handsomely not only for figuring out where Hailey's Nymph Island was, but also for transporting him there. It had taken him a while to figure out where to find her, but luckily, Muskoka was a helpful place. He cast a glance behind them as they sped across the water, watching the trail of paparazzi following them.

The loud boat tore across the lake, throwing waves as it spun around a sharp, rocky point on a horseshoe-shaped island in order to slip between the two islands. The driver chose the smaller island, protected by the horseshoe, and cut the engine as he cranked the wheel, swamping an old dock that supported a leaning boathouse.

Hailey. She was basking in the late afternoon sun, drink in hand, along with her three sisters, Tigger, Simone. They all had their mouths bent in various expressions of distaste due to his arrival. But it was Daphne who flew to her feet, fist raised, as she shouted to the driver. "You harbinger of death! Where did you get your boating license? Canadian Tire?"

"He probably did," the woman beside her quipped. Finn guessed she had to be the sister he hadn't met yet, Melanie. "That's where we took the test."

"There's a law about speed limits, and you are well within thirty meters of shore—sensitive shoreline, in fact!"

"Maybe he needs a measuring tape. Men do tend to have a poor sense of length." Melanie rocked back on her heels, arms crossed.

"Loons nest on this shore, as well as mergansers." Daphne stormed toward them and Finn paused, one foot on the wet dock, one foot still in the boat. "How many nests did you just swamp? How many babies did you just drown in your reckless display of testosterone? How many family lines just came to an end because of your need to show off?" Her eyes filled with tears, and Hailey drew her back into the fold of women.

The driver asked Finn, "You sure you want off here? That one's crazy. I'd say she'd eat you for supper, but I'm pretty sure she's vegan."

"Nah, she's cool." Finn climbed onto the dock and pushed the boat off, hoping he'd be able to get a water taxi to take him back—and quickly, if things didn't go well. He was losing the indignant Hailey-you-used-me speech he'd created in his mind, and was starting to feel as though maybe the women would go after him instead of the other way around.

The boat roared away, swamping the dock with water again. Finn cringed as the women threw the driver icy glares before turning back to him.

Oh, hell.

Maybe next time he should ask an older gentleman in one of those long, 1920s wooden boats to take him for a ride. That way maybe he'd arrive without his foot rammed down his throat.

"Finian!" Tigger came bounding toward him, leaping into his arms.

He held her up, squinting as if unable to recognize her. "Is that Tigger?" He looked at the lifejacket clipped over her bathing suit, then up at her. "Where's your big dress?"

She giggled and said, "I have a ruffle on my suit. See?"

He placed her back on the dock. "It's a very nice ruffle. Very Tiggeresque." Finn ran a hand through his hair and gave the women a sheepish half smile. "Uh, sorry for my poor arrival."

He looked at the cluster of them, iced drinks in hand. He was crashing a celebration without a ride back. A few boats holding paparazzi drifted past the dock and he felt more uncertain than ever. When he was on shore it had seemed like the thing to do—come out here to shake Hailey's hand and congratulate her on one-upping him. Basically, get a leg up with a passive-aggressive dig designed to make her feel guilty for outing him to the world as someone who was faking being a badass. And for intentionally ruining him and going against their deal.

"How are you going to get home?" Maya asked, stepping forward.

"Um..." He glanced at the sisters. There was something was off...as if he was the one in the wrong, and not only for the way he'd arrived.

He took a step back, almost falling into the water. He caught himself and quickly threw on a role. Confident man in charge, who was supposed to be here.

And action!

"Could I talk to you, Hailey?" He reached through the group of women, pulling her out by the elbow.

Hailey's chest heaved, and her sisters and friend dropped back, eyes narrowed at Finn. He drew Hailey around to the other side of the boathouse and into the cool shade. The dock was worn, soggy in parts, and the walkway was narrow compared to the sunny side. Hailey leaned a shoulder into the green-stained siding and crossed her arms, probably trying to block out the boat filled with paparazzi drifting in the water behind her.

"So?" she asked, her voice low so her words wouldn't carry over the water.

"I think you're officially fired." He had a brief image of him adding, *Fired because I love you.* Then sweeping her into his arms. He shook off the daydream. "I'll have my assistant send you payment. I keep all the photos and retain their copyright."

Hailey bristled. "No."

"They're photos of me."

"I'm the photographer. You didn't ask for copyright. I didn't sign it away."

"I want them."

"You can't have them."

"Wow." He shook his head and let out a huff of air. "You know, I came here to offer you congratulations."

"For what? Surviving being stood up at my show opening? For being stupid enough to not foresee you getting back together with your ex as soon as she arrived?"

"Wait. What?"

"I saw the pictures in the tabloids of you kissing, Finian. Everyone did."

He ran a hand down the stubble on his chin. Oh, hell. He'd forgotten about Jessica and her unwanted kiss.

"I can explain."

Hailey slapped him hard across the mouth, making his lips sting.

"Son of a bitch, Hailey!"

"You and your two-timing ways aren't wanted here. I don't appreciate being jerked around. Got it?" She crossed her arms again, glaring at him with contempt. "I thought you were real. I thought you were *different*."

She whirled, glaring at the paparazzi shooting images as if they'd never seen something so juicy. "You guys get all that?" She pointed at Finn. "He's a jerk, all right. I was mistaken. You can ignore all that good-boy, family man, environmentalist stuff I leaked, because it's not true. He's asswipe."

She turned, hands thrust out to push him into the lake. He snatched her by the wrists, and spun, lessening the momentum of her attack.

"Damn it, Hailey." He pulled her close, making eye contact. "We were good together."

Hailey's head tipped down, her lower lip trembling as she yanked her wrists out of his grip, pushing past him.

He jogged to catch up, snagging her hand, forcing her to turn around. "I'm sorry, Hailey."

"Well, I'm not. I'm glad I know who you are now. Before I fell in love." Her voice choked on the word *love* and his heart tore.

She fled up the dirt path that led to the looming structure on the hill above.

"We're celebrating the cottage!" Tigger said, bouncing in front of him. She tugged his hand, trying to gain his attention. "We had a picnic. Mom says I waited long enough to go swimming again. You can't swim right after you eat or you die. Did you bring your bathing suit? We have a beach!"

"A beach is nice," he said, his attention on Hailey's retreating form. He placed a hand on Tigger's shoulder, anxious to follow the girls' aunt. "I've gotta catch up with Hails, okay? Hopefully we can talk more later. I bet you're an awesome swimmer."

Tigger gave a reluctant nod and he took that as permission to tear after Hailey. The cottage path rose between towering white pines and stunted maples, arriving at a large green cottage with a white wraparound veranda. He climbed the steps to the veranda, careful where he placed his feet on the sagging boards. This place was ancient and he could almost imagine late-Victorian ladies traipsing along the gray-stained floorboards, parasols over their shoulders, as they vacationed in their summer house, away from the pressing heat of the city.

Hailey, swinging in a hammock in a corner, stopped moving when she noticed him.

"I thought it was real, Hailey. That we were real. How out of touch am I?" He let out a huff that bordered on a bitter laugh. "You played me. Used me for your own reward."

"I did not *play* you." She stood, indignant. She raised the hand that had slapped him, and he touched his still-stinging, swollen lips in response.

"No, you did. When I met you, I thought it would be great if you posted photos of me online—bad-boy stuff." He took a step closer, lowering his voice. "But I trusted you and let you see the real me. I felt as though I could change my life when I was with you, and I couldn't be anyone but my real self. I let down my guard and all the while you were one step ahead." He clapped briefly. "Well played, Hailey, well played."

She stared at her feet, shoulders slumped. "I'm sorry, Finian."

"I hope you enjoy your career, because you just ended mine."

Chapter Fifteen

Hailey watched the boat take Finian away as it disappeared around the island as she sank into her Muskoka chair.

She was supposed to be happy today. Her sisters had forgiven her. Her show was doing amazingly well, with almost a third of the inventory already sold. The weight was supposed to be easing off, but instead she felt as though it was getting worse.

A tear trailed into her margarita. She'd been wrong to sell the photos of Finian. How had she ever thought she was in the right and that it would turn out okay? Why had she tried to change him? Didn't she like him for all his flaws and the way he was a contradiction?

The celebration on the dock had turned quiet, and Tigger, fed up with the lack of party atmosphere, had gone to check on her fairy houses.

"So? What was that all about?" Daphne asked.

Hailey shook her head, unable to speak over the lump in her throat.

"Oh, hell." Daphne leaned over and gave her a half hug. "You fell in love."

She blinked hard, wishing the tears would stop falling. "No, I didn't."

"That's going to sting for a while," Maya said, topping up Hailey's margarita.

They sat in silence as squirrels scolded each other in the trees overhanging the dock.

"So, let me get this straight." Maya held out her hands as she did when she was trying to sort things through. "You went paparazzi? On your *boyfriend*?"

Daphne made a shushing sound and Simone patted Hailey's hand.

"He was just…just a…"

"You thought he was going to summer fling you," Daphne said, her mouth in a serious line.

Hailey nodded.

"But he was more than that?" Maya asked. She leaned back in her chair, downing half her frozen drink. She gasped and clutched her head as brain freeze set in. "Was this for the cottage?"

She nodded again.

"Hailey!" Maya sat upright, her chin dropped in horror.

"It wasn't just the cottage, though. I thought…I thought…"

"She thought," Simone said, "if he saw how he could be a nice guy in the tabloids instead of being the messed up celeb, she could help him rebuild his image and further his career. You know, help him be real."

"But he's totally a jerk?" Daphne asked.

Hailey tipped her head back, watching the stringy clouds drift by overhead. "He's not, though. He's really nice." She let out a sigh. "And I messed up."

"Oh. My. God." Maya scooted to the edge of her chair, angling toward Hailey. "That viral stuff about him being a good guy and an artist was you?"

She nodded.

Her sister fell back into her chair. "Wow. Remind me to never piss you off."

Mallards drifted by, heads tilted sideways, probably wondering if the women would be good for tossing out a snack.

"Someone must be feeding them. I hope it's not bread. It'll muck up their gizzards," Daphne stated.

"No wonder he's upset," Maya said. "You just redirected his image. Hugely." She shook her head, beaming with pride. "My big sister."

"Except…" Hailey let out another massive sigh, longing for Finian and the fun times they'd had together.

"Oh, honey." Maya slipped out of her chair so she could lean over her big sister and give her a hug.

Daphne's attention focused across the water to the next island. "What are they doing over there?"

Melanie leaned forward. "They're knocking down Salty Dog!"

"But it's over a hundred years old," Daphne protested, her face falling as a bulldozer went at the west end of the old cottage across the strait. The women watched in silence as the building caved in with a loud crash and a cloud of dust.

"Good. That place was about to fall over," Maya said, returning to her seat.

"Maya!"

"It's true. The one side was buckling."

"But the heritage," Daphne moaned. "It's gone. They could have fixed it."

"I heard there've been a lot of private sales over there this summer," Melanie said. "Thank goodness the camp for teens is still there, though."

Hailey counted the cottages along the shoreline. As far as she knew, only one was still in the founding family's possession.

Daphne stood. "We have to save it."

"I think it's a little late for that," Maya said, finishing her margarita. "I've got to get back to the mainland soon. Late shift at the Bar 'n Grill and the dealership in the AM." She let out a sigh.

Daphne turned to look up the path to their cottage. "We need to claim this as a heritage site."

"Daph." Maya ran a thumb and index finger over her eyes. "There is nothing culturally significant about our cottage."

"Actually," Melanie said, her eyes lighting up, "if we could prove it held cultural value or interest we could ensure the property stayed as is and reap some tax benefits."

"Does that mean you're keeping it?" Simone squealed in delight.

Maya stood up and clapped her hands. "What do you think the odds are that we can save this place in time?"

Hailey shook her head, sagging into her seat. "Not great."

She'd just sold herself—and her boyfriend—out while trying. She was done.

The only thing she could do was try and appease her guilt by finding Finian and apologizing until he forgave her.

HAILEY PUSHED THE BORROWED boat faster across the lake, ignoring Melanie's continuing questions about what the rush was. Where would Finian have boated to? Bala? That would be a hell of a long ride. Had he rented a car to take him to Port Carling or Windermere before hiring the boat to bring him to the island? Windermere was on the wrong side of the water, making Port Carling the obvious choice. But where would he go once he hit shore? Where could she catch up with him and beg him to forgive her?

She should have listened to him. Should have tried to understand. It was his life, his career, his image. Just because he'd slept with her, it didn't give her the right to interfere. She liked him for who he was, and that should have been enough.

Right now his life dictated that he needed to be a Hollywood star, with all the attitude and ego that entailed. It was like when she used to do portraits and "pretty" photos to pay the bills—before she could shift to full-time art. That's where he was, and she hadn't respected it. She'd been that annoying know-it-all who'd stormed in with her own plan. Her own vision. And ruined everything for him.

After docking the boat, she said goodbye to the others and headed to her car, driving straight to the Sunflower Cottage. Laughing to herself, she pulled over and partway there and picked up her phone, dialing Finian's number. How had she forgotten about phones?

Voicemail. She left a quick message, then for good measure, sent him a text that said *I'm sorry. Can we talk?*

She could see a lamp on inside the cottage when she arrived, casting a warm light. The door opened when she knocked, and someone she didn't know frowned out at her. Was she too late? Had Finian checked out already? She turned to scope out the two paparazzi who'd stopped spitting sunflower seeds to focus on her when she'd driven up. They took a few more leisurely photos of her from their spots and she smoothed her unruly hair with a sigh. She needed to start wearing a hat.

At least the good news was that Finian had to still be around.

"Are you Hailey?" asked the man.

"Do you know where Finian is?" Hailey countered, trying not to inhale his spicy aftershave.

"Come inside."

The television flickered in the corner, some celebrity show dishing out gossip, with Finian on screen. Her photos. She stopped and stared. Those were her pictures on screen. The overexcited show host began spouting information she'd given *Celeb Dirt!* about his vacation. And then there were photos of her that must have been taken by Austin. Her and Finian kissing at The Kee. Holding hands out by the marsh. Looking so in love she had to sit on the first available chair.

The clip ended and the man standing beside her asked, "Happy?"

She looked up to see him glaring at her, arms crossed.

"You've destroyed three years of hard work. My hard work. In three days."

Hailey stood. "I'm sorry, you are...?"

"I'm his agent, Derek Penn. You've thrown a carefully detailed plan out the window. His career is over. He just lost a role, thanks to you. Now there's a nice little hole in the action world that he used to fill."

Guilt rolled over Hailey in waves. No, wait a second...

"You know what? You've obviously done a very poor job." She watched in amusement as his face turn purple. "Because if a girl like me can waltz in with a couple of photos and ruin the image you built up, then I guess...well, I guess he needs someone a little better suited to making a brand or image."

"You don't understand the damage you've done."

"Neither do you." She resisted the urge to shove him hard, angry at the way he'd used Finian. *Her* Finian. "You've been stuck up Hollywood's a-hole so long you don't even understand the public! Didn't you just watch that?" She pointed to the television. "People *love* the contradiction I've shown them. They love that Finian is showing maturity and has another side. A side that is *real*. And that he has depth. That he's more than some car crash for them to laugh at. He's a good man and you're destroying him for your own benefit. This is about more than money. This is his life! Look at actors like Harrison Ford and Leonardo DiCaprio.

They're no train wreck. They have depth, are well loved *and* they are well-paid stars. If you truly cared about Finian, you'd want to give him a real life, too."

Finian's father appeared in the doorway. "I'm going to have to agree with the little lady on this one. Goodbye, Derek." He turned to Hailey. "I think we need to go find my boy, don't you?"

FINN ACCEPTED ANOTHER DRINK from Austin and knocked it back. The man was staying at the far end of the bar, but seemed to sense Finn needed something. Something like firewater, and space. Lots of space.

He called down the bar to Austin, "I'm not a family man."

"I know."

"I'm not back together with Jessica, either."

"I know. But that's not what she or your agent are saying."

Finn shut his eyes. How had his life gotten so far out of his control that he'd let other people—people who saw him as nothing more than a commodity—take over? And how had he read Hailey so wrong? Was this mess because she thought he and Jessica were back together? That he'd been using her?

If so, it meant she cared. A lot. Deeply, even.

He wiped a hand down his face, caressing the stubble on his chin.

What did it matter? He'd lost the role he'd been angling for. He'd lost roles before, but he had felt like a shoe-in before this mess with Hailey. Derek had been right. The world was not ready for the real Finian Alexander.

"Are you in love with Hailey?" the photographer asked.

Finn pursed his lips and held in his breath. Without meaning to, he nodded. Son of a bitch.

"She's a great gal."

He gave a half nod.

"Heart of gold."

Finn let out an anguished snort.

"Anything she does, she has a damn good reason to do it. You had this coming, you realize that, right? She expected you at the opening. She was waiting."

"She ruined my reputation. In less than a week." Finn ordered another drink. He could prove tonight that his badass side was real. Damn real. He would let his demons out and propel his image back to where it was supposed to be. He'd make that producer regret not hiring him.

"Don't you ever hurt her."

Finn frowned, turning to face Austin. "Honor among paparazzi? Well, that's refreshing."

"Something pushed her to do this."

"Money? Fame? A need to pull the first punch?" So many reasons. But none of them felt like the Hailey he knew.

Austin paused. "The cottage. It's been in the family for generations. I heard it was up for tax sale."

"Thanks to my arty, environmentalist side it probably isn't any longer," Finn said bitterly. "I bet she got well paid for those images."

Austin laughed. "It's about time you gave back to the community." He sent Finn a challenging glance. "What? You think your reputation can't handle having a hidden side? Give me a break."

"I lost a role because of this."

"Are you sure that's why?" Austin shot him a look that got in under Finn's confidence and gave it a ding.

Before he could retaliate, a hand landed hard on his shoulder. "There you are." For a moment he was expecting it to be Hailey.

It was Derek looking like the cat that ate the canary. Anger flashed through Finn, lighting up every dark corner within him.

"Excellent, you've been talking to Austin. I've rented a small cottage a few miles down the road and hired a decoy for later. But right now, you and Jessica are to go to the cottage and get down and dirty. Austin, I'll hire you to take a few photos, and kaboom. Back in the press as a—"

Finn landed a punch on the man's jaw, his knuckles cracking.

"You asshole. Don't you get it?" Finn shouted. "You're messing with real people. Real lives. I don't love Jessica. I never have. She's as fake as a Louis Vuitton handbag in a Chinese market. I can't believe I thought it was normal to pretend to be in love with her." He glanced up from where Derek was stretched out on the floor, and saw Jessica backing out of the room, tears in her eyes.

Austin had disappeared. Finn had finally done something badass and it wasn't even going to be news.

FINN WAS DRUNK.

He was going to hurt in the morning, but it would be worth it. Judging by the peeved looks the polite Canadians were giving him, he was becoming loud and obnoxious. Right on schedule. If he was in the U.S. he'd be in a brawl by now. He'd be proving he was tough shit. But Canada was a hard act. He eyed a mean-looking guy in the back. Maybe he could hit on his girl and…

Finn sighed and hung his head. Hailey was right.

Even Austin was right about him losing the role. It wasn't because of her. It was because people were getting tired of his schtick. He needed to get real, and Hailey's betrayal was the very thing he needed to push him into the life he'd come here to contemplate turning to in the first place.

Shaking his head, and doubting his next move, he asked to

borrow the bar's phone, then made a collect call to his agent's cell.

"Derek! Buddy ol' pal."

"Finn, you changed your mind. I was worried."

Finn laughed at the relief in Derek's voice.

"Man, I only forgot to tell you to go outside and play a nice little game of hide and go fuck yourself." He went to lower the phone in its cradle, ignoring the raised eyebrows of the bartender, then lifted it back to his ear. "Oh, yeah. And I'll be taking care of my image from now on. Any plans you have in the works? Put 'em on hold. Better yet, shred them. We don't work together anymore."

He hung up the phone and dialed his old film buddy, hoping he still used the same phone number he had back in his college days.

Turned out he did.

"Bruce?" Finn tried to keep the slur out of his words.

"Yeah."

"Finian Alexander. I heard you have a role for me?"

"Finn! Man, good to hear from you. You know your agent already turned me down?"

"Well, lucky for you I just fired him. You fill the role yet?"

"I haven't."

"Great, because I say yes to your film deal. Arty is my new nickname, you know."

"Finn, are you drunk?"

"Yup."

"Maybe we should talk in the morning."

"Nope. Count me in. I want to do this." He paused and let his head loll to the side. "This is what I want. For myself." Despair washed over him. He was ending his career, which would lead to broken promises. But he just couldn't hold his head up any longer. He kept thinking the next movie would help him reach his goals, but it never did. He just dug in deeper. And deeper. And further from who he really was.

"Oh, man. This is so great. I'm going to rewrite the script for you. Your new life has gone viral, man. You're brilliant. You just shot your star into orbit."

"Yeah, something like that."

"You're all everyone is talking about."

"Really?"

"For real. I'm stoked. I can't believe you're going to do this. We'll reshape parts of the film and help build you up as a Renaissance man. Like a stepping stone into a new world. A new you. Dynamic. Revitalized. Refreshing."

Finn clutched his head. "Okay, you're going to talk me out of it if you keeping spewing all that bullshit."

His friend laughed as they hung up.

Finn supposed if his life was going to go to south he might as well create a masterpiece to be proud of before the final flush.

He pushed his hand into his face, supporting himself on the bar. He didn't want to live a fake life anymore, and his head hurt. His heart hurt. Everything hurt from years of holding it all back. Letting out a laugh, he finished his drink. Oh, how sweet, innocent Hailey had played him. She'd worked him right into something that might turn out to be the best move of his life.

Everyone loved the real Finn? Was that true? He turned to ask someone, but found the stools beside him were empty.

He got another beer from the bar, took a long pull as he exited onto the street, then smashed the bottle on the pavement. No more drinking tonight. He needed to think about how he would manage the pressure of sustaining his new, soon-to-be image.

"Is this who you want to be?" a woman called from the

shadows as he swept a foot through the beer and broken glass, dispersing it.

He leaned over and braced himself as he spotted a figure that reminded him of Hailey.

His mind had to be playing tricks on him.

"Hailey." He staggered toward her as flashbulbs blinded him.

"Is it?" she asked again.

"Hailey!" Paparazzi surrounded him and he suppressed the urge to flee. They crowded forward, breaking into his space. He was drunk and they were too close. It was all too raw.

They were shouting questions at him. At her.

He had to protect her. But where was she?

Someone jostled Finn, elbowing him in the gut.

"Hailey!"

"Are you two in love?" called a reporter.

"Is she carrying your love child?"

"Why is your agent here?"

"I saw your parents. Did you have a secret wedding?"

The paparazzi were mobbing Hailey and she cowered, arms raised protectively. They were going to tear her apart. Finn lunged through the swarm and reached for her. He yanked her toward him and he heard her slap someone nearby.

"Let go of me!" she hollered.

"Hailey, it's me!"

She dived through the bodies between them, landing against his chest. She gripped him hard, pressing so close to him he could feel her heart beating against his chest.

The crowd continued to shout questions, egging them on.

"Are you two in love?"

"Where's Jessica?"

Finn shoved people out of the way, not caring if he was breaking cameras. He held Hailey tight in his arms, trying to protect her. "Back the hell off!" he yelled.

He couldn't move without stepping on someone. There was no car in sight. Nowhere to run to. Nowhere to hide.

He wrapped himself tighter around Hailey and began forcing people away by backing into them. He needed Security. Fast.

"Why'd you kill your brother?"

Hailey stiffened in his arms as he jerked in surprise.

"What gang did you belong to?" another photographer called, setting off a new chain of questions.

"Do you still wear its colors?"

"How much money do you owe?"

"Is your father dying?"

"Is your charity going bankrupt?"

"Will the medical aid run out?"

Finn held Hailey so tight he was afraid he was going to suffocate her. He needed out of here. Now.

He was failing.

Breaking promises, and he'd been living his real life for only five minutes.

He couldn't even keep Hailey safe.

A large man with a square face and a limp pushed between them and the crowd as though he were a hot knife gliding through butter.

"Got your back, Mr. Alexander. Follow my lead."

Finn tailed the man as he created a path to the street, where an idling car waited. Finn carefully kept Hailey's shaking body between himself and the brick wall of muscle leading them. At the car, the guy opened a door, shoved a paparazzo away and urged them to climb in.

Finn froze. How much did he trust this stranger?

Austin turned from the driver's seat with a grin. "Thought you two might need a ride."

Having him at the wheel made Finn even more nervous than riding with a stranger.

"What?" Austin asked. "Didn't you hear what I said, Finn? Hailey and I go way back. I owe her one for breaking her heart." He shot Hailey a wink and she dived into the car, Finn hot on her heels.

"Evander de la Fosse," said the brick wall as he wedged himself between Finn and the door. He offered his hand. "Private security. Ex-marine."

Finn shook it. "Finian Alexander. And this is Hailey Summer. Thanks for your help. Both of you."

"Hi," Hailey said to Evander, her body still pressed against Finn. He loosened his grip on her and kissed the top of her head.

"You okay?" he asked.

She nodded.

He wondered what she thought of the questions. Particularly the ones about his brother. Finn rubbed the familiar ache in his chest and wished he'd told her everything earlier.

"That was intense out there, man." Austin grinned back at them as he drove away from the mob. "Welcome to the big time."

"Yeah, maybe."

"No, that was insane. You hit something good."

Finn peered out the back window at the fading flashes, the headlights tailing them. Was all this because of Hailey? He kissed her head again, keeping her close.

"I'm sorry," she whispered.

"For what?"

"For selling you out."

"Was all of that you? The questions?"

"No." She shifted away. "What was that about, anyway?"

He smoothed her wild hair, unable to refrain from kissing the top of her head yet again. "I'll tell you later."

They made eye contact and he wondered if this was it. If once she knew the real man—the one final layer he hadn't shown anyone—she would never want anything to do with him again. She'd see what a failure he'd been and continued to be. How he'd made grand promises he couldn't possibly keep, and how thin he'd stretched himself in order to hold his demons at bay.

Austin pulled up at some docks and everyone bailed from the car. The photographer stopped near a small boat.

"This yours, Hailey?" Austin asked. "It looks different."

"It's borrowed. We can take it."

"Okay, in." Austin shuffled them into the boat and cast off under the flash of frustrated paparazzi who were without the means to follow them out onto the lake. They scattered, phones to their ears, swarming a nearby teen who had an outboard.

"Don't do it!" Hailey called out to the youth, hands cupped around her mouth.

He looked at her, uncertain.

Austin tore across the lake, cutting the engine as Evander reached for the edge of the listing dock on Nymph Island.

"Still have that wood boat out here—Big Bertha?" Austin asked.

Hailey shook her head. "Sold it years ago."

"Well, we'll take this boat back to the marina. Let us know if you need anything. Distraction. Security. A ride back tomorrow. In the meantime, Evander will escort you to the cottage and I'll stand guard down here."

"Thanks, Austin."

Evander passed Finn his business card as they made their way up the dark path. "I'm in the area and it's easy for me to get to you fast. My direct line is on there."

"Can I get you on retainer?"

The big man nodded. "Consider it done."

A boat roared between the small islands and Evander immediately dropped behind Finn, protecting him as Finn pulled Hailey closer.

"Want me to stay outside your door tonight?" the bodyguard asked.

"I think we'll be okay, thanks." Having some guy standing outside the cottage all night, being eaten by mosquitoes, didn't seem fair even if he was being paid. "But I could use your services tomorrow, I'm sure."

They made their way up the steps, the boards protesting under Evander's weight.

"What headline do you think they'll tack onto this?" Hailey asked Finn as she unlocked the cottage.

"I'm sure something about you and Jessica." He regretted the comment even before she turned away, her brows pressed in a tight line under the solar lantern by the door. "Don't let it bother you, our relationship was just a front—a publicity stunt."

"Ours or Jessica's?"

"Jessica's. And it's over. Was before I even stepped foot in Canada."

"Want me to check the place out for you?" Evander asked Hailey.

She let out a laugh. "I'm sure it's fine, but thanks just the same."

Finn thanked the man, who promised to be by in the morning, and Hailey shut the old wood door behind them. For a second Finn wondered what he'd walked into. Stuck on an island with a woman who held his heart, but had sold him out.

"Do cell phones work out here?" He laughed as he patted his pockets, searching for his absent phone. "Or do you have a land line? This is starting to feel pretty remote."

Hailey was a breath away, staring at him.

"When do you go back to Hollywood?"

"I haven't decided." He ran a hand through his hair and took a step back.

"Why not?"

Her hope was like a cutaway from a dark scene to a bright one.

"Because," he said, as he stepped closer, his feet making the kitchen floor creak. "I think you were right."

Her eyebrows shot up.

"I wasn't being myself. And while this could all come crashing down around me, at least it will be more likely to happen on my own terms. Not like being a bad boy. Those days were numbered."

"It won't come crashing down."

"I promised charities things I might not be able to deliver."

She moved into the large living room, turning on a small lantern set on the table. She cocked her head. "What *was* all that back there, Finian?"

"The truth."

She waited, face pale in the dim light.

"Schools. Medical care for families in need." His chest tightened and he had to force himself to keep breathing regularly. "I have a charity where I try to keep families from falling into the world I did. The public persona you have come to know is an easy role for me to play because that's who I used to be. I used to steal as a kid. I had to. Bread on the table and all that."

She angled her body away, her bottom lip drawn between her teeth.

"We look like a great family now, but the truth is my two brothers and I used to run with a rough crowd. Julian was shot in a gang war."

Hailey grabbed Finn's arm as though he needed steadying.

"I didn't kill him," he whispered. "Not like they said out there." His voice shook as his throat contracted. "I was there, but I didn't kill him. I couldn't stop the blood."

He bent over, his head too light to keep him standing, the image of his red hands haunting him.

She was reaching for him, and before he knew it Finn was in her arms, tears streaming down his face. She stroked his hair, and without realizing what he was doing, he had her shirt off, her body pressed against the throw rug on the floor. He ran his hands through her hair, his fingers and eyes racing over her skin as if blindness was coming and he had to memorize every physical feature or he'd perish.

Promises he'd made were about to be broken. She'd opened wounds and uncovered secrets, and yet he couldn't step away from her. He needed Hailey and her forgiveness. He needed her to make it all better. Drag him through hell so he could find heaven. Not only in her arms, but in the world. His life.

Starved for her to save him, he ravished her with kisses. He craved her like a balm for all his open wounds.

"Heal me, Hailey."

"I can't." Her voice was breathy with need as he skimmed his lips over her warm body.

"Please."

"You have to do it yourself."

"Help me."

She pulled his face to hers, kissing him soulfully. "Always," she breathed. "Always."

"Forgive me."

"Nothing to forgive." Her lips were moist on his bare shoulder. "*I'm* sorry. I crossed a line."

"Cross another one with me now." His mouth moved down her chest, flicking the clasp of her bra and baring her breasts. "I trust you, Hailey."

"Ohmigod, that feels good."

He tugged off the rest of her clothing, and she pulled him into a room with a patchwork-quilt-covered bed.

"I wanted you to reveal me, Hailey." Finn watched her face as he lay wrapped in her arms, softly stroking her cheek. "I just didn't realize you'd *see* me. I was like an invisible soul no one had noticed for years. And then there you were. Seeing me. And it all became love and rumors. Somewhere along the line I started to believe I could be me. With you. With the world."

She let out a shaky breath and he knew she'd heard him, just like she saw him when nobody else did.

"I love you," he said.

"That's the rumor," she laughed. "But is it the truth?"

"No, really, Hailey. I love you with all my heart."

She pulled his body to hers. "I love you, too, Finian Alexander."

Chapter Sixteen

Finn smiled at Hailey and held her loosely in his arms. "Sure this will work?" he whispered, eyeing the reporters gathered for his outdoor press conference.

"Of course. It's my plan, and as you are aware, my plans always work when we're talking about your career and image. Look what I've done for you so far."

He laughed and kissed her hair. She'd definitely turned him from a bad-boy disaster with a sagging B-List career into a multilayered man in the week and a half he'd known her. He couldn't wait to see what the future had in store. He might just be a lucky son of a bitch and get it all.

He hugged her closer, pressing himself against her warm body. "Let's see. Since I've known you, you chased off my ex-girlfriend, led me to fire my agent of five years, convinced the world I'm an endangered-turtle-eating environmentalist—"

"Hey, that wasn't me. You did that one on your own, but thanks by the way. The government is suddenly very interested in all the things she's been telling them for years and she's well underway in terms of saving their habitat."

"That's wonderful." He gave her a light squeeze. "But I need to clarify that you drove me to that bender, Miss Hailey Summer, by not waiting around for me to finally show up after your opening."

She gave him a pouty frown and he continued, "Let's see... where was I? Oh, yes. A family man, a bad boy with a gangster past, a charity creator...oh, and how could I forget? Totally in love with an award-winning photographer who is now on New York's hot list."

Hailey spun out of his arms, laughing, sunshine dancing on her face.

He tugged her back, never wanting to let her go. Not until he knew absolutely everything about her and more. He loved Hailey, from the way her hair smelled to the way she curled her toes in her sandals every time he gave her a kiss.

Hailey's reporter friend, Rick, waved Finn over to the microphone. Evander, brick wall that he was, was stationed behind and to the right, arms crossed, shades on, and looking every bit the professional bodyguard.

"As you may have heard," Finn said to the crowd, "I've turned over a new leaf."

A group of women in the front row screamed their approval, and he flashed a grin at Hailey, who was waiting off to the side. She gave him a thumbs-up as he turned his attention back to the gathered fans and reporters.

"It does not mean I've become a vegetarian. It doesn't mean I am going to rehab. It simply means that I have been living two lives, and thanks to Hailey Summer, my hot new photographer girlfriend, I have discovered that it isn't authentic, genuine, nor fair to you.

"So I have decided that the two lives I've been living are going to merge. I'm still going to enjoy myself at parties." A group in the back let out a whoop. "However, that does not mean I'm going to indulge in wild shenanigans that get me into trouble, as well as the limelight." The group let out a low groan. "Yeah, sorry, guys."

Finn ran a hand through his hair, doubting where he was

going with this, and whether he could sustain his new identity. Could he be Mr. Artistic Movie Guy? He trusted Hailey, but this was a wild leap into the unknown. He glanced over his shoulder and made eye contact with her. She gave him a small smile, her arms wrapped around herself. He took a deep breath and turned back to the microphone.

"There are many actors I deeply respect. Actors who have made a difference in this world. I have been working, secretly, on becoming one of those men. Someone who can make a difference in this world instead of creating a little diversion from real life and real life problems."

"What's wrong with that?" someone called, and the crowd chuckled appreciatively.

"For the past few years I have been donating everything I can afford to the charities and scholarships I set up in my old neighborhood. Meaning some months I almost had to go to the food bank myself—"

"Finian!" someone hollered. "Tell us about your brother."

Finn swallowed and tried to ignore the rush of adrenaline that pumped through him as the reporters surged forward, sensing this tidbit would be bonus-worthy come payday.

"I wasn't always famous, living in a nice house. There wasn't always food on the table. It's a familiar story for kids growing up in poverty and in inner cities. Gangs were common. Deaths just as much so. I didn't break that stereotype. I come by my image somewhat honestly."

He paused and took a sip of water, hating the way his hands were shaking, his heart pounding. Slowly, he unraveled his past to the crowd, explaining how his brother Julian was shot in front of him and his other brother, Adrian. At that moment he had vowed to transform his neighborhood into a safe place to live.

The sun was hot on his face when he finished his tale of how he'd promised his inner city neighborhood the moon—everything from ridding shop owners of gang-related problems, to after-school programs, to scholarships, and free health clinics. He'd promised everything his family hadn't had. And every dime he hadn't required for clothing and food in Hollywood had gone straight back to his old neighborhood. Yet he wasn't sure he'd made a difference.

The crowd was so quiet he could hear the highway running beyond a grove of trees. He looked out into the sea of faces, wondering how much this Canadian crowd would understand about poverty, gangs, and medical bills ruining lives. Probably not a whole lot.

"I thought I could change my community, and I believed I could do it on my own. I've been trying to live up to my promises, scrambling from movie to movie in hopes that somehow, if I could just get famous enough, get paid enough, I could solve the problem."

A murmur went through the crowd.

"But I can't. Not all at once and not on my own."

Rick held up a tin can. "I'm taking donations to Finian's charities! Pass it around."

"Thanks, Rick." Finn gripped the microphone and pushed away the emotions he was feeling. He cleared his throat. "As for my career…I'm off to film *Man versus War II* as scheduled. I was not fired from that film, despite the rumors." He smiled. "*Hangman's Destiny* is coming out in…I've lost track of the days. Somebody help me out."

The crowd laughed and someone shouted out a date that felt entirely too soon.

"Thank you. There will be plenty more movie surprises in the coming months, as well. Stay tuned."

He turned, facing Hailey, the love of his life. The woman who had not only given him a chance, but had given him the chance to really live. A chance to start over. To be humble and honest. And real.

Most of all, to be real.

"Thank you for being by my side and seeing the real me."

He stepped to her, letting Rick wrap things up. Finn slipped his arms around Hailey, breathing her in. "Thank you for fixing my brokenness, Hailey."

She tipped her head back to gaze into his eyes. "Anytime, sugar buns." She lifted herself onto her toes and placed a kiss on his lips that made the crowd go wild. Breaking it off, she flushed, her eyes full of love.

He could get used to this.

"Will you come to my movie premiere with me?" he asked, nuzzling her ear.

"I thought you'd never ask."

"I want to be everywhere you are, Hailey." His lips made their way across her cheek to her waiting lips. "All the time."

"*All* the time?"

"Every single second."

"How are we going to manage this?" she asked.

"One project at a time."

"I can work just about anywhere there is nature. And I've always wanted to go to Europe. Any movies planned out there, Finian Alexander?"

"I'll see what strings I can pull for you. Oh, and I meant to tell you that Julia Roberts was asking who took my new head shots. Maybe you could make it in Hollywood, too."

Hailey gave Finn a playful shove. "Yeah, right."

"It's true."

Her eyes sparkled in the sunlight and he fell a little more in love with her.

"Don't you have reporters waiting for a one-on-one with you?" she asked.

"I hope they're not the only ones." He gave her butt a pinch and turned to the line of waiting journalists, knowing his life would never be the same, now that Hailey was in it.

HAILEY TRIED NOT TO SMILE as her sisters and mother looked from her to Finian and back again, puzzling everything out.

"You guys forgave each other?" Maya smiled. "Nice!"

"Days ago. We wanted the same things, just…differently." Hailey gave Finian's hand a squeeze and he wrapped his arm around her shoulders, pulling her close in the wicker love seat on the cottage veranda.

Melanie poured a margarita from the pitcher and handed it to Maya, who took a grateful slurp.

"Love conquers all," Daphne said in a wistful tone.

"So, what are we going to do about the cottage?" Maya asked. "Are we selling it?"

Hailey blew out a deep breath and leaned forward. "I almost have enough money, but…" She shook her head, looking to her sisters.

"It's up to Hailey," their mother said. "She's carried the burden long enough, so she makes this decision."

"What if destiny makes it for me?" Hailey teased.

"That would be fine, too." Her mother smiled, and Daphne clapped her hands together.

Tigger, who was just off the veranda, trying to tame

chipmunks by bribing them with sunflower seeds, said, "I got one! Ohhh, he ran away."

"Don't move, Tigger," Daphne called over the railing. "You're scaring them. Be very still. And quiet."

"Oh. Right."

"Maybe we *should* sell the place," Maya said. Her eyes roved over the veranda as though checking the structure and estimating its real estate value. "We could take the proceeds and rent something each year. Maybe in Florida one winter?"

Daphne gave her a wistful smile, but Hailey could already see the look of loss in everyone's eyes. She'd continued the Nymph Island tradition and fallen in love with Finian here—or at least it was where she first really realized she was in love with him and said "I love you." She wanted to give her sisters the opportunity to follow that tradition, as well. Even if it was going to be difficult.

Finian, as if sensing her thoughts, gave her a gentle squeeze.

How was she going to do that while she and Finian trotted around the globe, covering her photography shows and his movie filming and premieres?

She shook her head, knowing that it was meant to be, it would happen.

Her mother tugged at the blanket draped over her lap as the leaves on the maples and oaks whispered to each other on a breeze.

"Are you cold, Mom?" Daphne came over and tucked the blanket around her.

"Okay, how's this for an idea?" Maya took a sip of her drink. "I'll sell a few business articles to get us closer to our tax goal, and we'll rent this place out as an executive retreat for a week or two. Hailey got, like, eight hundred dollars for a couple of days, so maybe I could charge—"

Hailey sat forward, eager to jump in with suggestions.

"Hailey," Maya warned. "This is my idea, my plan, my way of trying to help, and it's going to be different from your ideas, so let me continue."

Finian's hand slipped to Hailey's knee and she eased back in her seat. "Sorry, go ahead."

"Anyway, we can get more if we offer it as a rustic retreat for businesses and corporations. I can work as an assistant, which will be great for me—I really need more experience on my résumé for when I move to Toronto in the fall. I can do up an ad and put it on Kijiji later today."

"What about your jobs, though?" Daphne asked.

"They both suck. I need to rub elbows with real muckymucks."

"But we can't use the cottage if you rent it out." Daphne frowned, hugging herself.

"Use it and lose it. Besides, it'll only be for a week or two. We'll survive." Maya took a gulp of her drink and winced. "Why are we always having cold drinks? They give me brain freeze."

"Because we love you, and are trying to prevent you from getting drunk faster than the rest of us." Daphne smiled at Maya, who gave her a playful shove. "I'll ask for honorariums where I volunteer. Maybe they can help, or I can have some sort of sale. I have all those paintings I've made. Maybe I can sell some at the farmers' market or Simone's."

The sisters nodded.

"Did you send in the tax appeal?" Melanie asked Hailey.

"I did. I haven't heard back, but Betsy said she'd try and expedite it for us."

"I think it's time we were all responsible for our fair share of the tax bill," Melanie said. "Full cost."

"And upkeep and maintenance," Maya added.

"And I think we owe Hailey a lot for how much she's covered

over the years." Melanie flipped a page in the notebook where she'd been tallying and writing all afternoon.

"No, it's fine."

"It's not fine," Maya said. "We need to help you, Hailey."

"Help is fine, but there's no need to try and cover me retroactively." Hailey turned to Daphne, who was the poorest of the sisters. "Don't worry, Daph. We can arrange something."

"You can work off your portion of the bill," Maya suggested.

Melanie tapped her notebook. "Where have you been getting all this money, anyway, Hailey?"

"I do have a job, you know."

Melanie gazed at her, eyes serious, quiet, probing. "Did you remortgage your house? Or leverage it or something? Win a lottery, perhaps?"

Hailey tucked herself closer to Finian, who tipped her chin upward to read the truth in her eyes. Damn, they were tag-teaming her.

"Hailey!" the women cried together.

"You could lose your house?" Melanie said. "Oh, my God, Hailey!"

Hailey looked at her feet.

"Somebody, pour me another margarita," Maya said, waving her glass. "We have to sell this place."

Daphne poured a new round for everyone.

"Can we give destiny a little more time?" Hailey asked.

The sisters shared a look.

"Destiny? Why?" Finian asked.

"Because we all love this place and it's a part of us," Maya said. "Hailey's our big sister who loves us, as well as a big idiot who thinks she has to take care of us." She got up to give her big sister a hug.

Melanie cracked up, joining in the hug. "Sometimes, Maya, no filter between your mental gas pedal and your mouth is an okay thing."

Hailey released her sisters and snuggled closer to Finian. She gave Maya a knowing look. "This is a year of destinies. Destinies and dreams. Let's hang in there a little longer and see what the universe brings us, shall we?"

Chapter Seventeen

Hailey rolled her eyes at Maya and gave Finian a quick peck on the cheek. He'd been in Canada for two weeks and was starting to talk about leaving some clothes at her place when he had to go back to Hollywood in a few days. She liked it. She liked it a lot. Especially since she was going to his movie premiere as his official girlfriend.

Cinderella, shove over, Hailey was in the house.

"Move that table there," Maya commanded, as Hailey grabbed one end of the large table in the cottage's large attic. "Connor MacKenzie is going to be here in less than two hours and I want to be early to meet him at the airport. It's essential we get off on the right foot."

"You'd think he was the king or something," Hailey laughed, giving Finian a bump with her butt as he walked by with some power cords for the WiFi hub Maya was trying to set up. Hailey only hoped the cottage's ancient solar panels could keep the old battery charged well enough to power everything Maya needed. If she had to run the generator to charge the battery it would cost her a fortune in gas.

"Hailey, you don't understand. Connor is one of Toronto's biggest businessmen. He *is* royalty in the business world. Everything he touches turns to—"

"Gold?" Hailey interjected, dusting off the table with the sleeve of her sweater.

"Sold?" Finian added.

"Spending two weeks with him could alter my entire future."

"No pressure." Hailey lined the table up in the alcove and breathed in the attic's warm, old-wood smell. Would Maya's spending two weeks on Nymph Island with a man continue the island's legacy of matchmaking? If Hailey didn't have to go to New York to accept an award, or down to L.A. to set up a last-minute show she'd snagged, or to Finian's premiere, she'd stay parked here, watching and waiting. "I still can't imagine you taking orders from some business dude."

"I'm his assistant, not his maid."

"Aren't those essentially the same thing, when he's not bringing any of his own staff and you offered maid service with the rental, Miss Assistant?" Hailey shot her sister a mischievous grin.

"I know what happens on this island," Finian said with an eyebrow waggle.

Hailey blew him a kiss and smiled. "Good things."

"Yeah, yeah, whatever. This could be my big break." Maya let out a breath and rolled her shoulder before giving a clap. "We need to straighten the cords from the surge protector. And do you have the WiFi thing set up Finian?"

He shrugged. "I think so."

"Well, I need you to know so." With shaking hands, she connected her phone to the WiFi network to test it. "Everything has to be perfect. My whole career depends upon this. He could shoot me up the corporate ladder. Plus, he's renting this place for enough that we might be able to fix the chimney."

"Actually, girls..." Finian gathered the two sisters together with a hand on their shoulders. "I took the liberty of hiring someone to fix the chimney." He drew them onto the small deck and had them look up to where the chimney stood, repaired and restored. "I figured half the charm of the living room was a working fireplace, and that your renter would like a fire now and then."

"Finian!" Hailey paused, staring at the perfect chimney. No more missing bricks or crumbling mortar. "This money should have gone to one of your charities!" His neighborhood needed his support more than the Summers needed a working chimney.

"Your mother gave me her blessing."

Hailey gazed at him. There was a mischievous twinkle in his eyes. Almost as if...almost as if he was trying to help Nymph Island along in matchmaking Maya and Connor.

He pulled Hailey into an embrace. "And I do happen to find fireplaces romantic."

She blushed, thinking of the first time she and Finian had made love, and how the firelight in the Sunflower Cottage had added to the moment.

"Wow. Thank you." Maya turned to them, then hesitantly gave them both a big squeeze.

"Finian, you know you didn't need to—" Hailey began.

He raised a brow.

"Fine. Thank you." She gave him a squeeze in turn. Sometimes it was okay to let others help carry the load.

Hailey and Finian followed Maya down to the boathouse. They were all going to ride into town, in the newly fixed boat, so she could go pick up their new tenant. As they walked, Maya kept letting out loud, gusty sighs.

"Nervous?" Hailey asked, hitching her new camera backpack over her shoulder. Finian had been right; it was dang handy. And really not that expensive, if someone else was buying it as a gift.

"I'm so nervous I feel like I have to pee every five minutes."

"It'll work out." Hailey bit her lips together so she wouldn't offer advice, and Maya could own this task without an interfering big sister.

"Fire in the hole!" crackled a voice from across the narrow channel.

Hailey ducked as a loud boom rocketed toward them, shuddering through her ear canals.

Finian threw himself over her, tugging Maya down onto the dock as small rocks rained around them.

"What the hell?" Hailey yelled.

Maya popped her head up from under her arms. "They're blasting on Baby Horseshoe."

Finian leaped up and cupped his hands around his mouth. "Hey!"

Maya stood beside him and added, "Ever hear of a blast mat?" She turned to Hailey. "They can't be blasting right now. This is supposed to be a quiet business retreat, not a construction zone."

A man in a suit stood on the dock across the narrow strait, waving.

"I'd like to give him the one-finger salute," Hailey grumbled, dusting herself off.

"He's coming over," Maya said.

They watched the man row across the water, looking awkward and out of place in his suit.

"Bring a broom?" Maya asked, kicking rocks off their dock. "Maybe a first aid kit?"

The man stepped out of his rowboat, looking uncertain as he stood on their turf. "My apologies. The name is Aaron Bloomfield."

"Harold, pleasure to meet you," Maya said.

Hailey shot her a "be nice" look.

"It's Aaron," he corrected.

"So sorry." Maya looked anything but. "We're in a bit of a rush to meet someone. I expect you will have cleaned off our dock—and not onto our sand beach, please—by the time we return. And that you won't have damaged our property any further." She strode into the boathouse and climbed aboard their boat.

Finian, arms crossed, glowered at Aaron who stood watching, before following the sisters into the boat.

"I'm representing Rubicore Developments and the work we're doing over on Baby Horseshoe Island," Aaron said, standing beside the boat and pointing through the open door to where the sharp, rocky point on the island had been leveled by the blast.

The sisters shared a look. He was ruining it. Ruining the island, their view. Everything. This wasn't what you did when you found a beautiful place.

"We're planning to spiff up the cottages over there, and were wondering if your island was for sale."

"No," Hailey said, just as Maya replied, "Make us an offer and we'll see."

"Are one of you the owners?" The sisters nodded and Aaron presented them with a sealed envelope. "At your leisure. Offer expires in August."

"You come prepared. I like that." Maya started the engine, tucking the envelope in the pocket behind the driver's seat. "Finian, cast us off, please."

He obliged, then sat beside Hailey who gripped his hand, knowing the summer's adventures were only just beginning, and that there would be something in store for all her sisters before destiny was done with them.

Hello Summer Sisters Readers!

Do you enjoy reading romance?
&

Would you like to be the first to hear about new releases from Jean Oram?
&

Do you love saving money on ebooks?
&

Do you want to get in on exclusive giveaways and FREEBIES?
&

If you answered yes to any of these questions you're going to love my author newsletter.

For fast & easy online sign up go to:
www.jeanoram.com/FREEBOOK

Book Club Discussion Starters

1) In real life do you believe fans of movie star Finian Alexander would support his sudden image change from bad boy to nice guy? Or do you believe there would be backlash and skepticism over his change in behavior? How do you believe this change in image will impact his career?

2) Why do you believe Hailey never told her sisters about the taxation issues with Nymph Island until it was almost too late? If she had told her sisters sooner, what do you believe would have happened? In what ways do you believe it would have impacted everyone's lives?

3) The author researched birth order personality types when developing the Summer sisters. Do you feel she did a good job of characterizing the four sisters in terms of their roles in the family and the way they interact and behave with each other? Why or why not?

4) How is the setting of Muskoka important to this book? Why do you think the author chose that location over somewhere more well-known such as Hollywood? How would the story have differed if it had been set in Hollywood or New York?

5) Have you ever met a movie star? Do you feel you would be as 'cool' about the fame as Hailey was with Finian? What do you think would be difficult for you?

6) Why do you believe Finian is so determined to help his old neighborhood? And why do you believe he tried to keep his past and promises a secret?

7) How has Hailey changed Finian's life and vice versa?

8) What did you think of the supporting characters such as Jessica, Finian's parents, Hailey's mother, and her friend Simone? Do you have a favorite or least favorite?

9) What do you think will happen in the rest of the series? Will the sisters sell the cottage, lose it, or save it? Will the rest of the Summers have a chance to fall in love on Nymph Island before the summer ends or will something else happen?

10) What did you think of Austin Smith the paparazzi friend? Do you feel he redeemed himself in the end? If so, how? If not, why not?

The Summer Sisters Tame the Billionaires

One cottage. Four sisters. And four billionaires who will sweep them off their feet.

Love and Rumors ~ Love and Dreams
Love and Trust ~ Love and Danger

The Blueberry Springs Collection

Book 1: Champagne and Lemon Drops—ALSO AVAILABLE IN AUDIO
Book 2: Whiskey and Gumdrops
Book 3: Rum and Raindrops
Book 4: Eggnog and Candy Canes
Book 5: Sweet Treats
Book 6: Vodka and Chocolate Drops (Coming Summer 2015)
Book 7: Tequila and Candy Drops (Coming Winter 2015)

Do you have questions, feedback, or just want to say hi? Connect with me! I love chatting with readers.

Youtube: www.youtube.com/user/AuthorJeanOram
Facebook: www.facebook.com/JeanOramAuthor
Twitter: www.twitter.com/jeanoram
Website & Lovebug Blog: www.jeanoram.com
Email: jeanorambooks@gmail.com (I personally reply to all emails!)
Up-to-date book list: www.jeanoram.com

I'd love to hear from you.

Thanks for reading,
Jean

Jean Oram grew up in an old schoolhouse on the Canadian prairie, and spent many summers visiting family in her grandmother's 110-year-old cottage in Ontario's Muskoka region. She still loves to swim, walk to the store, and go tubing—just like she did as a kid—and hopes her own kids will love Muskoka just as she did when she was young(er).

You can discover more about Jean and her hobbies—besides writing, reading, hiking, camping, and chasing her two kids and several pets around the house and the great outdoors—on her website: www.jeanoram.com.

Made in the USA
Charleston, SC
16 May 2015